Praise

"L. LAMONT"

Praise & Worship
Published by The Late Bloom, LLC
Copyright © 2021 by L. Lamont

Please send your comments to the address below.
Thank you in advance.

L. Lamont c/o
www.thelatebloom.com
info@thelatebloom.com

This book is available at quantity discounts for bulk purchases.

Printed in the United States of America.

ISBN: 978-0-9966569-1-7

Requests for information should be addressed
to the above address.

*This is dedicated to all the faithful men in the world,
and the women who love them*

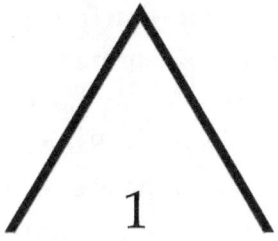

1

Faith Without Work is Dead

In 2007, at a bougie Halloween themed charity ball for breast cancer awareness, Renee and her band were the entertainment for the evening, and I happened to be in the audience, fanning out. What's crazy is, nearly a decade ago, when I was fresh out of grad school, living in Chicago, I went to her concert, on a date, mouthing the words to her hit song *"Love is real."*

The night of the ball, my intentions were crazy; I simply wanted a selfie with her. My confidence was secured by the fact that I, Gavin Adams, was a newly published author, a budding sociology professor at Rice, and the owner of a used 2005 *B.M.W. 330i.* I inched towards a colleague who sat at a table closer to the stage, hoping for a seat, but the crowd's reaction to Renee overshadowed my play. Everyone stood on one accord like a congregation under the spirit. And after her thirty-minute set, she thanked the crowd, exited stage left, never to be seen again.

But a week later, on a humdrum Sunday afternoon, while walking the aisles of *Whole Foods* for kale chips and shit, I was uncertain but familiar with a face down the way. Her disciplined perusal of cantaloupe was quirky and cold, *is that fucking Renee?* I regrouped, casually gawking, but looking left to right, for discretion. Getting within a few feet, she looked up at me, and our eyes glanced momentarily; *that's fucking her.*

I played relaxed and stopped in front of the strawberries, with a resolution; *it's now or never.* Clearing my throat, refashioning my tan linen blazer, I turned around confident and poised. "Excuse me. I couldn't help but notice, are you Renee?" She stood there, fruit in hand, seeming shocked that she was recognized, and hopefully, attracted to my 6'2, 225 build, and style. She cracked a smile behind her black *Ray-Ban* wayfarer frames and a form-fitting, burgundy *Baby Phat* velour sweatsuit.

"Hi," she answered.

"Crazy, I just saw you at a charity event last week."

"Oh cool, for breast cancer awareness."

"Yeah, you were good. You playing any clubs around town?"

"I'm doing *Great Day Houston* next week."

"Cool, how do I get a ticket?"

"Ah…call the show, I think?"

She was respectfully dismissive of a dumb ass question.

"Sure, yeah, I could do that, okay."

"Nice meeting you," she offered, with a cue.

We walked in separate directions, and now there was no reason for me to be in *Whole Foods.*

Geeked, I drove home with an incomplete shopping list, ready to brag to a friend about meeting my '90s celebrity girl crush.

"Adams…" Miguel answered.

Miguel Franz, my friend, and a colleague, had ties to the local media scene, from his days as a producer at KPRC.

"Miguel, brother, need a favor. Can you get me a ticket to *Great Day Houston*?"

"Yeah." He answered curiously. "Since when did you…"

"I know, but guess who I met in *Whole Foods*?"

"Who?"

"Renee, can you believe that shit? She lives here."

I waited for Miguel to fan out with me, only to hear, "Doesn't ring a bell…"

"Seriously? You don't remember *"Love is real"*? That was her biggest hit in '98."

To be honest, it was her only hit.

"Doesn't register, but I'll make a call."

"Cool, thanks."

Sure enough, a week later, standing in a line of 100 outside the studio, in 55-degree weather, scarf and pea coat sharp, I was gassed to see her again. When I entered KHOU's television studio, imagining the situation, I realized the level of creepiness I'd reached and considered leaving; *I'm officially stalking her ass…this is stupid.*

In the studio, I took a seat next to an elderly Asian woman, maybe late sixties, who looked like a regular audience member. I didn't give a fuck how lame it seemed. I was anxious for Renee to see me and possibly reward my "follow through" with a date. However, when taping began, the first guest of the show was a guy from Baytown, who carved out a niche for himself designing dog hoodies. Next was an actress I'd never heard of, from a daytime soap that had been off the air for ten years. In between taping breaks, my agitation grew, coupled with a small talk from my sixty-plus-year-old neighbor.

"I could sure use a damn doughnut right now, does that sound greedy?"

"You only live once."

Finally, the stage crew arranged instruments and microphones for her set. Shortly after, the host introduced her, and the crowd erupted in applause, cheering, with some standing. Even I stood, somewhat out of character.

"Today we have a real treat, one of Houston's very own R&B stars who came to fame in the late nineties with her smash hit, *"Love is real,"* and did we mention she's a graduate of Jack Yates High? Everybody, let's welcome our home-grown sister, friend, and songstress, Renee."

Everyone continued to clap, and cheer as before, while I focused on her line of sight; I needed her to spot me.

The band began playing, and Renee waved to the audience with a million-dollar smile. The crowd swayed to the rhythm, while my eyes remained locked on her vision. *Look my way, look my way.*

The studio lighting was dimmed, which fucked up my plan. After finishing the first song, the beginnings of a medley, I was salty. Being 6'2 and positioned at an aisle seat, I was going unnoticed. My patience was classically thin. Nevertheless, as she transitioned song to song, I continued hoping, *look this way, babe, …c'mon.*

For a moment, I was delusional. When Renee eventually looked my way, I took it as a stare. So, after the show, I called Miguel to share the news.

"Dude…."

"Yo…"

"Thanks, man."

"Oh yeah, *Great Day Houston*, yeah, how was it?"

As a Gemini man, it was second nature to embellish and elaborate a more colorful narrative.

"Low key, she's singing and shit, notices me in the audience, and hits me with a stare."

Miguel, being of sound mind and rational thought, hadn't processed a 'stare' as a love connection, but more an acknowledgment of the guy she met in *Whole Foods*.

"Wow…"

"C'mon, in the middle of a song?"

"What? I'm just saying."

"All right, fuck it, I'm in love, motherfucker."

For the first time in a while, I was charmed by someone other than myself. For weeks, I went back to that same *Whole Foods* off Buffalo Speedway, every Monday, Wednesday, and Friday, after class, hoping to run into her. Occasionally, I'd go on a Sunday, to the point that clerks began recognizing me and my awkward purchases; two cans of clam chowder and a bar of soap, or a package of ground beef and toothpaste. My desire had become a dark eagerness on the verge of obsession.

But finally, on a Wednesday evening, January 9, 2008, at 7:14 to be exact, we'd see each other again, in *Whole Foods*, on the same aisle. I was the one checking the melons this time, as she turned the corner. Unconsciously, I looked up to discover her walking my way, with those familiar black Ray-Ban wayfarers.

For nothing more than recognition, her eyes danced in shock, and I replied, "Hey there." Off put by coincidence, she offered a warm smile.

"You were at the taping…"

"You saw me? Wow, you remembered too, you're good."

"Yeah…"

"Gavin," I answered with my hand outreached. We shook hands and waited. "So, this is weird now; twice in the same aisle, I think it's a sign."

"I know, right?" She followed, with an awkward silence.

"Maybe it means we should have dinner?"

"That was good."

"Oh, I understand. You're Renee."

"See, no, don't do that."

"What?"

"I'm barely home…"

"And most guys can't handle that, right?" I interrupted.

"That's correct."

"No, seriously I understand, it's cool." Being agreeable was a tried and true icebreaker.

"May I formally introduce myself for the next time we meet?" She crossed her arms and smirked.

"Dude, okay."

"I'm not a stalker, and I don't live with my mother." She laughed. *Great, she laughed.*

"I'm single for real, for real, no kids, I'm a professor at Rice, I love Mexican food, especially *Pappasito's*, the one on Richmond."

It was thirsty, for sure. My lips quivered, and my heart raced, but it was now or never.

"Cool, I appreciate that."

"Was that too much?"

"I mean, c'mon, you're a handsome guy; you're busy too, I bet."

"I'm not in the streets like that. Give me some wine and a movie. I'm good."

"Okay."

Unbeknownst to her, our dialogue became an analysis, in search of the truth; hers.

"You know, it may be hard to believe, but I can relate to being a celebrity."

"Oh?"

"Seriously, I'm also an author."

"You write, that's cool."

"I just came out with my first book."

Being an author seemed like the sort of eclectic thing a woman like her could appreciate. She could assume I'd understand the frustration of writer's block.

"What's your book about?"

"Without boring you, I researched for my Ph.D. in sociology. The effects of divorce on African-American males under thirteen in major urban cities."

"Interesting…"

"I could give you a signed copy, over dinner."

"Your persistence is charming, Mr. Gavin."

Being the consummate gentleman, I looked down and blushed.

"Can't fault me for trying."

"Give me your number, I'll call you for lunch next week, and you can pay."

We shared a laugh, but the prospect of a lunch date made my year.

"I'm going to hold you to it."

"You do that," she replied.

We stood in silence, in that classic moment when something new is born. I put my number in her phone and held my hand out to seal the deal.

"Take care," she continued.

"You too."

I went my way, and she went hers, but this time I completed my grocery list without regard for the awkward possibility of bumping into her again.

The following week, she never called. My pride was touched, even bruised. This feeling of thirst was killing me. Never had I wanted a woman so badly as I wanted her. Never did I put such effort into the hunt, having to wait for an answer.

But for the uneasiness I experienced, I was learning patience. I was learning that pedigree meant nothing to a woman like "Renee." My good looks, physique, and social standing only meant shit to me in my world.

The week after, I stayed poised for a call, hoping to hear something like, *"Hey Gavin, sorry for taking so long, I've been busy, let's have dinner instead."* Or, *"Hey Gavin, let's just skip lunch, come over to my place, and I'll cook for you, how 'bout that?"* But by Sunday, it was evident; Renee had other shit to do.

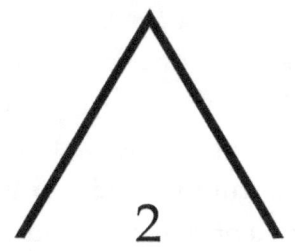

2

Redemption

Renee maintained a busy life of ease. Two weeks prior, she scheduled a *Well Woman* exam for the following Monday afternoon. Afterward, there was her weekly Yoga class, something she rarely missed unless on the road.

Then, there was a maintenance appointment for her 2004 Lexus SC 300, her last extravagant buy, for the bullshit she'd gone through in L.A. Tuesday was no different; she had a meeting with financial planners about her current savings of $873,560, a high amount thanks to the sale of her L.A. condo, but far from the millions she'd had at her peak. It was crunch time for this thirty-three-year-old R&B has been.

By Wednesday, yet another appointment awaited with a leasing agent about a mid-rise apartment in Upper Kirby. Later that evening, she had a rehearsal with the band, followed by post-rehearsal libations of *Appleton* rum and tightly rolled primos.

Thursday morning, she slept in 'til nearly noon, hungover by the excesses of a night with the boys. Being the only female in the band, her competitiveness always led to overindulgence, the very thing that stripped her of motherhood.

By the weekend, it was girls' time with her *BFF*, Denise Beasley, a friend since their days at Yates High School. Denise, a dentist and divorced mother of twin teenage boys, had acted as Renee's refuge many times. When it got to be *too much*, she'd hit I-45 north for a bit of fresh air from her favorite boo.

She drove out, 10:48 that Saturday morning, to De Soto, a sleepy suburb outside Dallas. She made it a habit to bring gifts for the boys, something cultural and worldly from their favorite auntie. This time, she kept it simple and brought copies of *The Autobiography of Malcolm X*, requiring a completed two-page book report upon her next visit.

She loved being "Auntie Risa" in place of motherhood. The pain of remembering the custody battle and the moment Judge Rivera ordered parental rights to Jacob, still hurt. She bared her soul in tears, broken beyond repair, but Denise remained a strong shoulder. She'd taken time off to be with Renee during her severe bout with depression. But these were better times between girlfriends who'd seen each other's lowest point, like the time Denise called about her unexpected college pregnancy and subsequent abortion, or the moment Renee was pulled over on Sunset Boulevard for swerving, eventually getting a D.U.I. *'Girl...I think I'm going to jail.'*

Renee confided in Denise, about everything, especially her relationship with Charlotte, and all the sacred details of their affair. But this newest thing, this blip on the radar, didn't seem worthy of discussion, at least not in-depth. Gavin was cute in passing, but she had no real intention to commit to a lunch date. Besides, Gavin was nothing more than a 'guy' in a long line of guys, genuine or not.

The following week, after their second *Whole Foods* encounter, Gavin was back to life, his professorship, department meetings, and nights alone in his mid-rise apartment off Waugh Dr., just to the west of downtown Houston. With views of the city, he could mull over his next book, with vivid imagery captured in a daydream, and still, he thought of Renee.

I was sprung, and my ego, bruised: *what's this dumb ass shit she pulling?* I took walks along Buffalo Bayou, which only led to more overthinking. Surely, she misunderstood me. Yes, I was crushing, but not like a fan. I could be a real situation. On the other hand, the waiting seemed desperate and made me angry. *She had one fucking hit song and she acting like this? I'm good.* Embarrassed with the idea of giving Miguel my usual play by play, I avoided the topic.

"So, how's the Renee thing going?"

I focused on my cup of coffee in the faculty lounge. My body language was dismissive, with my back turned to him. *Fuck you!*

"What Renee thing?"

"No way…you practically came on yourself weeks ago. Weren't you guys going on a lunch date?"

"Oh, that…nah, she had a scheduling conflict."

"Scheduling conflict, huh."

"Is that impossible?"

"It's nothing, just joshing ya."

"And what the fuck is *'joshing you'* anyway?"

Over time, the burn went away; I went on dates, fawned over by available women, in search of salvation. Still, the good-looking, author, and professor from the *'Nati,'* my ego was back. Renee's diss ignited a creative streak to my latest novel. My frustrations were replaced with descriptive prose between fictional characters, seething with every stroke of the keyboard:

Her eyes read the intricacies of my secret place, vulnerable to touch. But could she see me? Could she see the love the way I saw it, pure and full, void of shape, but beaming with all the colors of life? Her eyes were bright and focused on my lips. I wanted to caress her hair and face, take her hand in mine and walk away from formalities, and small talk reserved for the unsure. But she chose to be cautious.

Almost a month to the day of our second *Whole Foods* encounter, I received an unexpected text from her that read, *'hey stranger, you still down for lunch?'* I stared at it with a smirk; *finally, closure.* Rather than replying immediately, I waited five minutes.

'Is this my imagination?'

'How's tomorrow? 4PM at Straits in City Center, your treat', she replied.

I was slightly fucked up and wrote, *'I still have to pay after being stood up for a month?'* Then I deleted it.

'Cool, see you then.'

I sat there and smiled in redemption. The next day, Thursday afternoon, driving I-10 west was paced with lukewarm heat blowing to the sounds of *Sade's Lovers Rock*. Fresh cut and shave, embellished by a few spritzes of *Issey Miyake*, I was outfitted in my charcoal plaid wool blazer and a purple V-neck cashmere sweater of choice, business casual with tapered indigo jeans and chocolate suede ankle boots.

For the time that it took me to reach the restaurant, my well-versed script ran a million times. *Hey, looking good, glad we could finally meet, is this your spot, it's beautiful.* My main objective was not to be a fan, but rather, the audible in the history of other guys.

When I arrived, I sat in the car with jitters and a running engine. I flipped down the visor for a peek in the mirror, assessed my eyebrows, my nose, and goatee. Afterward, I popped a mint, shut down the engine, and proceeded out the car. When I entered the restaurant, I looked around, hoping she'd be there first.

"Welcome to Straits, table for one?" The hostess asked.

"Two, please."

As I walked to the table, the place was nearly empty, but for a few patrons. When I was seated, the anticipation was crazy. Preoccupied with body language, my strategizing began. I sat straight, looking forward with both hands on the table, but then I felt anxious. Then I pulled my phone out and surfed, but then I looked like an introvert. So, I sat leisurely, legs crossed, enjoying the window view of passersby, waiting.

"Good afternoon, sir, could I start you off with a drink?"

"I'd like a Long Island, please."

"My pleasure."

As the gentleman waiter walked off, I tugged at my blazer, assured that she'd walk in at any moment. I wanted to send a text, but it looked overbearing; *she'll see me.*

However, ten minutes had passed with no sign of Renee. My fear of rejection, a second time, bubbled. With another sip, the sweet and sour taste of patience met with the bitter rumblings of irritation. I looked at the menu, allowing for five minutes more before checking out.

"Can I start you off with an appetizer, or would you like to order?"

"I'm okay for now, thank you," I graciously snapped.

The designated countdown began at that moment. I'd never contact her ass again, nor entertain any, out-of-the-blue bullshit; I had self-respect. Looking at my watch and then towards the courtyard, thoughts of Pilar, my last relationship, came to mind. Assessing the reasons things ended, the blame was all me. In retrospect, I was always the late one. Pilar called my constant tardiness for planned affairs, conceit, and in this regard, I finally understood.

By 4:13, looking at the second hand of time, steadily moving towards an exit, I motioned for the waiter to close the tab. But no sooner than I could get his attention, in my peripheral view, she walked in. Focusing on the entrance, Renee had that classic, fashionably late swag that made me sigh in relief. She immediately spotted me as I waved her way. The Belle saved me.

Her 5'5 frame floated, and I enjoyed every bit of it; hair pulled back, aviator sunglasses, large hoop earrings, cream-colored silk tank-top with a dangling knotted pearl necklace. Her jeans were fitted, distressed with bleach spots for effect. She carried a small black quilted clutch, wore orange patent leather, platform high heels. Considering the weather, I thought she was a little underdressed. But she was charm and allure, wrapped in a smile. I stood to greet her, conscious and submissive, *should I shake her hand or hug?*

"Hey there," she spoke as she reached out her hand.

"Hi, looking good."

"Likewise…"

"You been here before?"

"Funny, I was going to ask the same thing, but you have," I rambled.

Damn, shut the fuck up.

Renee was late because she'd overslept during her occasional afternoon naps. When she woke, the clock read 2:38, for which she lay five minutes more, before pleasuring herself. It was time-consuming but necessary.

"This is my little get-a-way, nothing special, just good food and drinks," she answered.

"Would you like a glass of wine?"

"Uh, let me see…oh, hey Spencer," she said when our waiter returned.

"It's been a hot minute, girl," he answered.

"I know, baby, just busy. It's good seeing you."

"Girl, I was about to cut somebody behind you."

"For real, who?"

I sat there, enjoying Spencer's colorful version of a Black woman.

"Tracy gone say, '*Clarissa doesn't fuck with…*excuse me sir, *don't mess with Straits no more 'cause we stopped serving them blue cheese potato chips.*'" They shared a hardy laugh, infectious enough for me to join. "Sorry, sir, we haven't seen Ms. Thing in a while. We just catching up."

"Don't mind me. It's cool."

"Spencer, this is Gavin, Gavin, Spencer."

"Nice to meet you again," Spencer responded with his professional voice.

"Likewise."

"So, will it be the usual? Cranberry tonic with a Mediterranean salad?"

"Did you order already?" Renee asked.

"No, it's okay, go ahead."

"That's fine, Spence, and for you, sir?" she continued.

"I haven't decided, give me a second, Spencer."

Spencer gave the nod and walked away.

"So..."

"So..." Renee replied.

"Who's Clarissa," I asked curiously.

She laughed, holding her head down.

"Well...Clarissa's my real name, Clarissa Renee Gentry. Renee is for the world."

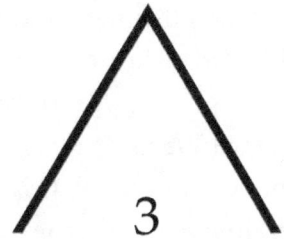

3

Trial & Tribulation

Gavin was conscious of overtalking, while Clarissa was merely polite. She decided this would serve as their first and last date if he did.

"So…a professor?"

"Dr. Adams, at your service."

I was impressed, a little. I couldn't remember the last time a professor shot at me. Most guys I dated were in the business. Dating a civilian was foreign.

"So, no kids, huh?"

"No baby mamas," he joked.

His bougie ass tone stung. I was pissed; *he's not a fan, he'd remember when Bobby was born.* The tabloids even gave Bobby a nickname, "Mystery Bundle." From the time I was three months pregnant, until his birth, my management team found creative ways to quiet the rumors of a love child. In public, an assistant would hold Bobby, or if my ex and I were together, Bobby would stay behind.

"Baby mama."

Sensing a fuck up, he walked it back.

"My bad, that came out wrong."

I gave the nod, accepting his apology — *this motherfucking bougie ass frat boy…just what I need.* An awkward silence followed until I decided to give a second chance.

"So, where you from, any brothers and sisters?"

"I'm an only child. I'm originally from Cincinnati, but I bounced around after college. Are you from Houston?"

"Born and raised, Third Ward, to be exact."

I thought back to my childhood at 1420 Hadley, living in the shadows of downtown Houston, with the ease and feel of country living. Life was beautiful in that 1,300-square foot, beige wood-framed, three-bedroom, one-bathroom house. My father Ezra and I would sit on the porch at night, especially in the Spring, and he'd sing old Doo-Wop tunes in his rich falsetto range.

"I had an older brother; he died before I was born."

"I'm sorry to hear that."

"Sometimes, I wonder how different my life would be with him around."

Gavin's attention made me talk more. I spoke of my working-class background, which kept me sane. When I wasn't singing in the choir at *Wheeler Avenue Baptist Church*, I harmonized to classic *Janet* or *Whitney* ballads with Denise, and Monique, the third member of "Down South Dames," a group we formed our sophomore year.

"May I ask a question if you don't mind," he asked.

"Sure."

"What made you have lunch with me?"

Stunned and pleasantly surprised, he was impressive.

"Good question. No reason."

"What kind of guys usually hit on you?"

"Cornballs who think they know me."

"Did I come off that way?"

"Honestly, I don't remember much about the first time we met."

His face crumbled; he was respectful, though, I didn't forget that. It was creepy when he showed up at the studio that day, but he was showing me something.

"Low key, I was nervous as hell. I almost talked myself out of approaching you."

"I guess it paid off."

He remembered everything, what I wore, how I looked, my hairstyle and the scent of my perfume.

"And then I waited like a year to hear back from you."

"All right, that's my bad. I am busy for real, though."

"Maybe we could plan a dinner date now for next month."

"Okay, you doing too much."

We continued, with his university talk, and me with a vague description of life as a has-been, at home with her folks.

Throughout lunch, Gavin listened to the details and quirks of my life. When we finished, he asked if I'd walk with him to his car for the book he promised.

"So how should I sign this, 'To Renee,' or your real name?"

"However you'd like."

"How do you spell your real name?"

He chose wisely.

"C-l-a-r-i-s-s-a...Clarissa."

Gavin signed the book, *'To Clarissa, thank you for a wonderful afternoon that I'll never forget, may this book bring you the same pleasure and delight that you brought me.'* I smiled, even though it read like a sugary sack of bullshit.

"Thank you; I'm looking forward to reading this."

Not sure of an exit plan, Gavin initiated a respectful and appropriate hug, the kind meant to establish a boundary between his and my chest. I obliged his effort and copped a feel. When he slightly bent his 6'2 frame to accommodate my 5'5 stature, I caught a whiff of his cologne. I placed my right hand on his lower back, and my left on his upper arm. He peeped my inspection and flexed.

"Clarissa, the pleasure was mine."

"Likewise, Gavin."

"Not to be pushy or anything, but I'd like to take you to dinner someday." It was refreshing to hear a grown man's plea. Today was the daydream I longed for, after maintaining a desire to be loved, for so long.

"We'll see."

"Okay, I'll take that."

"Thanks for the book and lunch."

"No problem. Can I walk you to your car?"

"I'm good, thank you."

When I walked away, he stood at the front of his B.M.W., studying the rhythm of my bounce. Suddenly, I felt "girlie" with inexplicable butterflies. When I arrived at my car, I sat in the driver's seat, entertaining thoughts of the dude from *Whole Foods*. It'd been years since breaking down the walls. My last fling was right after leaving Charlotte and California. Within six months of being back in Houston, I reconnected with an old high school boyfriend, Antonio "Tony" Blaise.

Back in the day, our senior year, Tony was the All-American track and football star with a full ride to Texas Tech. I was the shapely brown skin chick with a pretty voice who liked skipping class. Nonetheless, love was supposed to keep us together after Yates, but fate separated us. Tony and I stayed in contact through letters and phone calls until we no longer did. I immediately began going on the road, deep in the life of a background singer.

And yet, in a moment of desperation, I reached out to him in the summer of 2005, after learning he was still in Houston and working for the Houston Police Department. Our rekindling was slow. Tony hadn't been entirely clear about his situation, alluding to the possibility of a divorce that never came. Things reached a climax when his estranged wife discovered a hickey on his chest; he put a stop to everything in solidarity to a lie. It was nothing worthy of heartbreak, but our little fling was special.

Weeks had gone by since the day date with Gavin. The ins and outs of a daily grind carried on, with Clarissa's hopes and hustle, and Gavin with his course work and re-writes. And yet, they thought of each other. Gavin sent just one text to keep his memory alive; *'Hey Clarissa, just saying hi…hope all is well.'* Clarissa smiled at the text during the madness of moving into her new *Galleria* midrise. Appreciative that he'd thought of her, she replied, *"Doing well. Got a gig at Scott Gertner's next Friday, come check us out."* Not expecting such a quick response, he replied, *"For sure."*

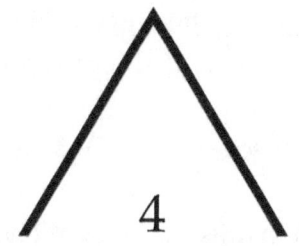

4

Supplication

Moonlight and a Friday night drizzle set the tone for a manifested destiny. *Scott Gertner's Sky Bar* was the setting for the evening. I chose to wear my trusty charcoal grey pea coat and houndstooth scarf, with a black velour blazer, grey cashmere turtleneck sweater, matching grey wool slacks, and black monk strap loafers. For the drive, I played a re-mastered *Best of Nina Simone* CD, one of my favorites thanks to my mother, Faye.

When I arrived at the lobby, I stepped into the anxious energy of a weekend crowd. Sporadic lights danced in the dimly lit room, against the heavy bass beat of *Guy's* "Groove Me." The backdrop of Houston's cityscape view from the 20th floor made for the kind of night reserved for those in love with '80s R&B. I was nodding my head to the soundtrack of my freshman year at Carver High while scoping the room for "bodies."

Over the past few years, Clarissa made it a point to gig here, even as her fame declined. It was the Sky Bar that launched her start, paying her dues as a background singer and eventually a solo artist. Since moving back and forming her band, *Risqué*, Clarissa, and the guys played the joint once a month.

I looked at my watch, noticing five minutes before her start. Again, here I was strategizing my place in the room, managing to snag a spot just left of the band's set up, under the shadows of an overhanging light. As the DJ continued with *Marvin Gaye's* "Sexual Healing," Clarissa and the group made their way onto the parquet flooring.

"Y'all ready to get risqué?" The DJ asked, with the pulse of a good vibe.

The crowd replied in unison, "Yeah!" The vibe was right as the band tweaked instruments and mics. Clarissa stood with a teacup, peering back at the audience, ready to slay her congregation in the spirit.

The bass player struck a note; the drummer clicked his sticks, and Clarissa voiced the count, "One, two, three, four..." On the downbeat, the beautiful chaos of harmony filled the space, as Risqué went into a cover of *Earth, Wind, and Fire's*, "Lover's Holiday." Clarissa's command was evident from the start; her posture, eye contact, and vocal mastery were spellbinding. Members of the audience stood, raising their hands in praise, mouthing the words on one accord, the entirety of the first verse, *'love, has found a way, in my heart tonight...'* I looked around, magnetized, as she transformed the room, and for a glimpse, I knew why I could fall in love.

For the next thirty-five minutes, they took us down memory lane, from covers of *Chaka Khan's* "I Feel for You" to *Cameo's* "Word Up," straight into a reggae version of *Phyllis Hyman's* "When You Get Right Down to It." Song after song, they finessed nostalgia like a rollercoaster ride, until finally taking a fifteen-minute break. Approaching her would seem the ultimate thirsty move, so I stayed at the bar.

"*Hendricks's Gin,* please."

"Sure thing."

Just as I settled in, scoping the room, I noticed a familiar face, followed by an uneasiness that made me want to disappear.

Pilar Francis, the corporate baddie I thought I'd marry, had been out of my life for a year now. I looked away, opting to be indifferent, but it was childish. She glanced my way, and being cordial, decided to speak to an old friend.

"Gavin?"

"Hey."

"Gavin," she repeated, like a taunt.

"You good?"

"I'm well…how's life? Still at Rice?"

"Rice is Rice, how's Shell?"

"Shell was Shell; I just started my firm four months ago."

"Oh, congratulations, that's good."

"Thanks, it was crazy at first, but now, I realize it was God's plan."

"Cool."

For an awkward five seconds, I continued a phony look of interest, waiting to be pardoned, until she asked another question.

"So, what's up, how's life? It's been a year, dude."

"I know, that's crazy, time flies."

It was the anguish of resurrected old feelings; *you ended things, what the fuck do you care?* My delusional, bruised ego, ended things, growing tired of what I considered a *'mother-son'* relationship. Pilar, being mature and intuitive, asked, "Do you want out?" for which I replied, "It's for the best."

"Just working on another book, staying out of trouble."

"A second book, Gavin, that's amazing."

Her spirited reply took the edge off, but nothing was forgotten.

"What's it about?"

"Learning to forgive."

The read was loud and clear, but she was game. Pilar, being used to my slick mouth, usually countered with reason.

"Ah, that sounds thought-provoking, great concept. Well, good seeing you, let's have a drink sometime?"

"Right."

Pilar walked off, but not without appreciation for her unwavering dedication to the gym. Her physique was the antidote to misunderstandings and wandering eyes, and perhaps I stayed too long because of it, but tonight was about Clarissa. Clarissa, on the other hand, refreshed and ready to perform, spent most of her break speaking with Bobby.

"You had a good day, boo-boo?"

"Mom, stop calling me boo-boo."

Bobby Finch, a.k.a. "Bobby Bird," a.k.a. "Boo Boo," was becoming a most inquisitive young man for his age. Cognizant of the situation, he often wondered about mommy's living arrangement.

"Sarah doesn't call me boo-boo."

"Well, Sarah, can't. She didn't carry you for nine months."

"Mom."

"Yes, Bobby Bird."

"I wanna see you."

I pulled away from the phone, with my head bent by reality. Jacob didn't deserve this power for the nine months I submitted to being human, nor for the mistake of being human and driving drunk.

"Oh baby, you know I love you, right?"

"Yes," he answered in a pitch capable of breaking any heart.

"You have to ask daddy; if he says it's okay, it's okay."

Not the best rationale to offer a seven-year-old, it was the frustration of being an absentee mother at the ruling of the California judicial system.

"Okay, baby, mommy has to go. Let's sing our song right quick."

"You go first."

"We always start together, Boo…Bobby Bird."

"Okay," he responded, in a typical reluctant seven-year-old tone.

"You're the biggest part of me, part of me, part of me, you're the biggest part of me, and you plus me make one."

I was immediately emotional but caught myself.

"I love you, baby."

"I love you, mommy."

"Okay, bye Bobby Bird, I'll call you tomorrow okay?"

"Okay, bye, mommy."

Bobby gave me life, but hanging up killed me.

The show goes on; I stood, gathered myself, wiped my face, and took a deep pull from the joint.

"What's up with Bobby?" Trigger, our bass player, asked.

"That's my boy," I answered with a smile. "All right, y'all, let's go."

We walked out into the glory of *Roger & Zapp's* "Computer Love," and it made me feel good, looking at grown folk dance in the spirit.

Meanwhile, Gavin nursed his drink, vibing, and patiently waiting, but the thought of leaving crossed his mind. Logic and infatuation didn't mix; *is she feeling me?* Suddenly, he saw her and the band, and he was back in his happy place.

"Are y'all ready to get back with the groove," the DJ shouted.

The crowd responded, "Yes!" while the band stood in position, ready to take hold of the rest of the night.

"Without further ado, Risqué!"

This next set was songs from her albums, songs she'd written for others, along with more covers. Then they played her number one hit, "Love is real," and the crowd swayed, with hands outstretched, pleading to believe. Gavin was arrested by her everything, with the harmonies of the band, and perhaps his libation of choice.

"Boss, another one?" the bartender asked.

"Yeah."

I kept my eyes on Clarissa, while in a daydream; *tonight, we kiss.* Her voodoo wooed me. *I need to push up…yeah. I'm gone walk her to the car, say some fly shit, and kiss her. I bet she been waiting on me anyway.*

My vision was so clear that I got hard, with Gin in hand. What started as a simple kiss became the imaginings of a robust PDA session, with her pressed up against the car in liberation, a million miles from the Sky Bar. No audience, no band members or music, just us all alone in the parking garage, uninhibited by life or status.

I collected myself, went to the restroom for a splash of water, but not before taking another glance at Clarissa. She flashed a smile to the audience while singing the words to the latest song. I imagined it was to me and returned the favor with a wave likened to a bashful, Idaho farm boy; I was buzzing.

When I reached the restroom, I pumped myself up for what was to come; "C'mon motherfucker." After the splash, I wiped the excess water from my eyes, examining my face and inebriation. The hours that turned into days, weeks that turned into months, all culminated for this beautiful and pretentious unfolding. I returned to the bar, full of moxie. "Close me out."

When Clarissa would casually glance in Gavin's direction, with the space of noise and funk between them, she did wonder; *maybe he's different.* For his time and effort, perhaps it wasn't about her celebrity. Admittedly, the benefit of a relationship meant consistent dick, but possibly, getting Bobby back. As shady the notion, it was for a good cause.

When the second half of the band's set concluded, Clarissa made one last pronouncement; "We love y'all so much." The band played softly to the benediction, "Every time we come here, y'all show us so much love, thank you. We dedicate this song, for everything, throughout my career, the ups and downs, the good, the bad, and the ugly." The audience shared a laugh, being the one's front and center, watching her life play out in tabloids and magazine shows.

"If you know nothing else, know this," she stated. The band immediately went into a rendition of *Patti LaBelle's* "Somebody Loves You Baby," one of her signature closers for their performances. "I love my city...you guys gave me my start, and I'll forever be indebted...I love you."

Charmed by her showmanship, I applauded and took one last sip from my cup, with thoughts of what was to come. When Risqué concluded their set, they walked off to the back for more red cups of *Hennessey.* I waited five minutes or so, deciding to send Clarissa a text that read, *'Good show!'* About three minutes more went by before she responded, *'Thanks for coming, hope you had a good time.'* Excited, I wrote, *'I wish I could say goodnight before I go.'* Against her usual judgment and perhaps coming off the euphoria of excellent performance, my plea tickled her fancy; *'5 minutes.'*

As promised, Clarissa walked up behind me, with a gentle tap to my shoulder. I turned around and played chill.

"Renee."

"Professor."

"You don't mind if I call you that, do you?"

"That's how you met me, right?"

"Touché."

We held that familiar gaze, the kind reserved for something sure and awkward.

"When will I get a chance to meet the band."

"Go ahead and introduce yourself, they cool."

I wanted a special introduction, a distinction of my place in her world, however insignificant. I brushed her reply off and answered, "Maybe next time." Honestly, I hadn't earned the right of any introduction to any person or group, much less the band.

"Well, I hope you enjoyed the show cause I's tired."

"Of course. I wanted more."

"Awe, sweet."

The careless bang of *50 Cent* playing in the club, made time standstill. Our vibe seemed stronger, enough so, that I walked her to the car this time. When we reached the elevator, amongst a small crowd of folk waiting, I asked, "Are you hungry?"

"Not really; had an early dinner before I got here, but thanks."

"Okay."

The return to silence sucked. I was hoping for light-hearted chit-chat for the lead-in to my play for a kiss.

When we arrived at the second-floor level of the garage, the brisk winter chill burned a little, providing the perfect excuse for a quick goodbye. I stood in front of Clarissa, as she stood, with hands tucked away in her red leather motorcycle jacket, at the door of her car.

"It was good seeing you, professor."

"As always."

Graciously, I leaned in for a hug, obliging our preset boundaries. Our ears braised each other's, with a faint mix of cologne and perfume. It was a generous five-second hug, that gave me enough time to rethink my next move. *Just kiss her forehead.* I leaned in for a swift and passive-aggressive show of affection, but Clarissa looked at me like it was corny.

"Do I get a bedtime story?"

"Jokes…"

We laughed, all while wondering if I'd made an ass of myself.

"I could do better."

"Oh?"

I mustered the nerve, stepping closer, and putting my arms around her. I leaned in, eyes closing just before a retake, but not before Clarissa burst out laughing.

"What?"

"Your face…"

"I'm trying to be romantic in this cold ass weather."

"Okay, okay."

"No laughing,"

"I promise, no laughing."

But again, with my second approach, we laughed and for a longer time. Nevertheless, with the innocence of a goodbye hug, Clarissa positioned her head in preparation. A goodnight smooch turned to red hot chemistry. Clarissa found herself yielding to a distinct vibe. I, on the other hand, lost my damn mind. Being present, I kissed her intently, partly aroused that it was *Renee*, but mostly falling.

I was accommodating, with sway and swagger intended to convince her of everything. The interlocking freeform of tongues expressed an unknown language, with disregard for onlookers and gawkers. We were transfixed to another plane, vibing in 55°

weather. When the orchestration had come to an end, we opened our eyes, shocked, embarrassed, but committed.

"Damn."

"You crazy," she replied with a smile.

"You all right?"

"I'm good."

"Was that too much?"

"Maybe."

I laughed, slightly nervous.

"What you 'bout to do now," I continued, hoping for more.

"I'm 'bout to get my ass in this car, out this cold, and into my bed."

"All right, well, be safe; text me when you get in."

"Okay…"

I watched her drive off, waving goodbye. I walked one level down to my car, with a full-on erection, pissed, but grateful. *I kissed her.* When I got home, my mind stayed in that moment, full of idle, sexual energy. I got in my king-sized bed, with moonlight bouncing off the walls, fantasizing of what could've been. Clarissa's skin was up against mine, made for the warmth of bodies swaddled in a comforter, in sync to a daydream.

Minutes later, I reached for the box of tissue on the nightstand and cleaned up. I turned on my side, gazing at the brilliance of the sky before falling to the ease of night.

During Clarissa's drive, she thought about the kiss and how it made her feel, the thrill of PDA, and being out of character. She'd never been so blatant, not even with Jacob, much less with Charlotte. But tonight, life was unusual, igniting a freshness that was once bottled by circumstance and disappointment. That kiss gave life to her aspirations, with a conscious fear of being played.

When she got home, she immediately went to start a hot bath, plugged her iPod into the speaker box, and began to unwind to the sounds of *Sarah Vaughn*, with a glass of sweet red dessert wine in hand. She seemed to float from room to room, confused by a feeling, doing her best to be distracted by undressing and checking the water line in the bathtub every so often. Finally, she got in, slowly sinking, bearing the heat and steam, gradually becoming released. And still, the thought remained; *this feels like something new.*

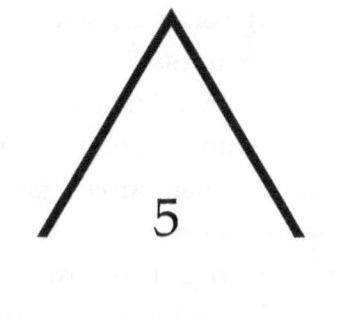

Wholly Spirit

Half past 7 in the morning, worlds away from the kiss, Gavin and Clarissa laid in separate beds, mutually in awe of an unscripted flash in time. The mystery of it all made no sense, but who would be the first to break the silence?

I woke to beams of sunlight through my bedroom blinds, thinking of Clarissa. I got up and made scrambled eggs with cheese, turkey sausage patties that simmered in my fancy stainless-steel pan, accented by a jumbo cup of orange juice with pulp. I sat amongst the cluttered aftermath of splotched grease, broken eggshells, and speckles of cheese across the grayish granite countertops, imagining her sitting there or standing across from me, complaining about the mess, laughing, eating, but there.

I promised myself to chill, unlike the way I was with Pilar. She was the manipulative mind-fucker, who could immerse me into these emotional black holes, the kind that tore at my ego. She made it easy to feel like her teenage son, a spoiled brat who needed introducing to the real world, hers. Even in the bedroom, our dance was orchestrated by her will. I couldn't remember a time throughout the length of our relationship when I went a week without *eating*.

Life never felt so invisible, so unnecessary. Bad blood aside, there were good memories of Pilar. She upgraded my fashion sensibilities. Her knowledge of labels, color schemes, and delicate fabrics was appreciated. I'm not saying I had no fashion sense, but she gave me a vision. She'd often ridicule my look with tough love; "You're wearing that?" My unwavering commitment to pain was justifiable by all the right dinner parties, galas, and public places with her. The looks and stares were generous, and it tickled us.

Pilar, the ambitious corporate lawyer and daughter of Riverside's upper crust fit the bill of a worthy mate. She made perfect sense for a woman who was dead set on marriage and children by 35. Conceivably, if we ever married, divorce was imminent. And still, she crossed my mind, remembering the genuine quality of her tone when she'd say, "I love you."

Honestly, I feared to be alone for the rest of my life. I feared my father's DNA, with a guilty ability to shit on a good woman. Being with Clarissa made commitment doable. But I wondered if a girl like her could see the light of day with a guy like me.

By 10:45, Clarissa was prepping for a scheduled visit from the maintenance guy. But she immediately thought of Gavin, the kiss and all, while tending to the routines of a lazy Saturday morning and afternoon. Washing and folding clothes, a marathon of *Good Times* played four hours straight, but she found time to call Denise about last night.

"Girl," Denise answered in that familiar way.

"Boo love."

It was a few days since the last cackle fest when Denise talked of cussing a patient out for pinching her ass. We hadn't gone a week without gossip for over twenty years. Any and everything was open season, especially matters of the heart and bedroom.

"Girl, I walked in on one of your nephews being nasty."

"No girl, did he finish?"

"You are so fucking gross, Risa. I cannot stand you."

I loved the normalcy of our friendship. For all the years of chaos disguised as Renee, her support got me through the summer of '98 when I was on tour, nearly twenty-five pounds underweight from an intestinal virus, just for the tabloids to accuse me of being on drugs. She was also there for me the night I got pulled over on Sunset Blvd. in my black, 2000 Mercedes SL 600 convertible, and arrested for a DUI.

I remembered everything so vividly. The top was down, and in the distance, the sky had shades of orange and purple. Lil' Bobby was seventeen months and sitting in the passenger seat, well underweight. I was fresh off an emotionally charged shouting match with Brent Laramie, Vice President of A&R for the label. I tried to drown the hurt of being 'let go' from my contract, with a bottle of *Crown Royal*, just like Daddy. The sting after only two albums in four years, the embarrassment, the separation from Jacob, and the confusion of Charlotte all hit at once. I needed to breathe. So, after balling my eyes out thirty minutes straight, with Bobby crying along with me, I looked at his freckled babyface, into the twinkle of his brown eyes and spoke, "Mommy is sad."

The energy in my condo suffocated me. I called down to the concierge to have the Benz pulled up. I strapped Bobby into the car seat while the valet looked sheepish with concern. Walking to the driver's side, I reached for my cell to call Denise.

"Risa."

"I hate these motherfuckers, I swear to God!"

Bobby and I swerved into traffic from the circular condo drive. The unknowing of the night and uncertainty of tomorrow weighed on my soul.

"What girl…"

"They cut me."

Tears flowed uncontrollably, while the chilly night breeze made them ice cold.

"The record company?"

"Yeah."

Bobby was confused, observing the pattern of tears on the right side of my face.

"Where y'all driving?"

"I need air; they got me fucked up, I'm tired…"

Swerving through traffic, the acceleration of the car matched my mood.

"You got Bobby with you?"

"He right here, looking crazy."

"Where y'all going, just go back home and calm down."

"I needed to get out that house girl, I'm …I need to breathe."

I continued weaving through lanes, right hand gripping the steering wheel, left hand holding the cell, and my demeanor in shambles.

"You know you're the only one I can talk to; all mama gone do is judge me, and Jacob the bitch, all he wants is custody, with that fucking new TV show money."

"What about Charlotte, you ain't told her?"

I couldn't imagine talking to Charlotte. We were at odds at the time. Earlier in the week, after a significant fallout, with irredeemable words, we split. Charlotte, being sure of her love for me, forced a random and premature conversation I wasn't ready to have. An entire year was spent in the shadows, a year filled with secret kisses behind closed limousine doors, and sexual romps at *The Beverly Hills Hotel*. Charlotte wanted more; she wanted to be above ground.

"We on bad terms, I don't wanna talk about that bitch…talk to your nephew so you can see he's all right." I handed Bobby the phone, but in the awkwardness of the handoff, coupled with my buzzed driving, it caused Bobby to drop it to the floor. In a momentary fit of anxiety, I reacted, swerving into the right lane. A police officer driving two cars behind saw the ordeal and hit the lights. When I noticed the ricocheted vibrance of red and blue through the rear-view mirror, my heart sank. I was consciously driving drunk with a minor.

But for the present day, I triumphed through the storm with one last fight. Those urges for a man hadn't gone away. Today's conversation was a revelation.

"I think Imma start talking to this dude."

"For real?"

"He might be something. I don't know yet."

"No shit, a hundred years later, somebody got a shot?"

We laughed, but I agreed with Denise, this was outside my norm. Being suspicious of men and their intentions caused me to grow numb. Jacob and Charlotte shaped me; I could be cold on demand.

"It's not that bad; you know why I do what I do."

"C'mon, you shut guys down so fast. Tell me a dude you've dated in the last year?"

I went quiet, slightly giggling to a confirmed read. It was a practice.

"Ah, where's your dick in a glass?"

"Bae Bae, you ain't never got to worry 'bout me and Dallas, Texas."

"Oh, it's like that?"

"Bitch, I don't tell you everything."

We enjoyed the carelessness of singlehood in our thirties, with enough experience in heartache, that love had become laughable.

"I'm only telling you about this guy in case I come up missing."

"Okay, so what's his name, what he do, is he fine?"

"His name is Gavin, he's a professor at Rice, and he looks good enough."

"A professor at Rice? He Black?"

"Yes, from Cincinnati."

"Cincinnati…Mid-West nigga…different."

"Why?"

"You usually date industry dudes, this is amazing."

"I ain't in love, bitch, we just gone see."

"I didn't say you in love, hoe. Did y'all fuck?"

"Niecey, you know they gotta wait."

"It got cobwebs, though."

It was funny and sad, but most of all, real. I couldn't remember my last sexual encounter. But secretly, neither could Denise.

"So, when am I meeting the mystery new dick?"

"There's some vetting to do. I'll decide soon enough."

"Whatever you do, don't run him off."

"I never run them off, I may send them on their way, but I never run them off."

"Girl, bye."

"Bye."

With somewhat of approval by Denise, the prospect of this new thing wouldn't be suffered alone.

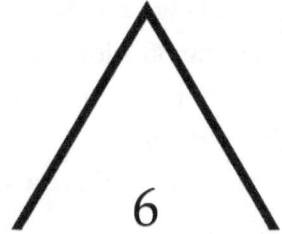

6

Faith of a Mustard Seed

Clarissa was iffy about calling him. The itch felt thirsty, and spreading her wings too early could mean getting played. But after hours of rehearsal with the band, followed by a customary nightcap, the edge had worn off. With the ease and privacy of a drive home, she called anyway at 11:11PM.

"Hey, what's up," he answered groggily.

"You sleep? My bad, we can talk tomorrow."

"No, it's cool..."

"No, really, call me tomorrow."

"Okay, cool, good night."

I was upset for being so random, but he called back.

"Didn't we just agree tomorrow?"

"I wanted to talk," he answered.

"About..."

"You know what about."

Doing my best not to take the bait, I was gasping for air. His way was uncomfortable and correct.

"You tell me."

"Okay. The kiss..."

"It was nice. I mean, what?"

"Nothing..."

"You're a good kisser, Gavin."

He enjoyed the game. We were vulnerable, but the chemistry was there. Plus, I was buzzing off a joint and a glass of *Knob Creek*, fucking up all reason, but then I thought of Bobby.

"So, you date single mothers?"

"Baby ma…women with children don't scare me, but it depends."

"Depends on what?"

"Crazy ass fathers with old feelings."

"A good chick wouldn't let that happen."

"True."

I could stand my ground with Jacob, but could Gavin stand his ground with me?

"Well, look, I'm almost home…"

"No problem, you good."

"That's sweet, but get some sleep; we can catch up tomorrow."

"Okay, be safe, goodnight."

"Goodnight."

A refreshing play of cat and mouse, Gavin sent a text at 9 o'clock sharp; 'Good morning, hope you slept well. Let's have dinner, your choice, my treat.'

Appreciative of his 21st century approach, the effort got a *'B+,'* to say the least. An intentional fifteen minutes later, I responded, 'I'll let you know.' He shot back with a reply that read, 'Cool, see you in a month.' The sarcasm was cute and annoying. I replied an hour later, as punishment, 'Whatever.'

The thrill of a new thing boosted my creativity. I wrote new love songs, something I hadn't done for almost a year.

'Could it be, the simple things are not enough for you, so hard to find a peace of mind, you couldn't see it through…'

The sweet taste of curiosity brought back memories of my devotion to Jacob, Charlotte, and Tony, but was there anything left to give?

Cautious with love was my safe place. Looking for signs, I needed God on this. Gavin needed to understand all things,

Clarissa Renee Gentry. His patience would have to suffer my lifestyle, shows on the road, late-night rehearsals, and the unsettled desire to be a full-time mother again. My biggest fear was his inability to hold me in those times of crisis.

On faith, I suggested a date, place, and time; 'let's do seafood this Wednesday, La Griglia on Gray, 8PM?' I waited thirty seconds to send the text, letting go and letting God.

Staring at the message afterward, I put my phone down and stepped away into the ease of my balcony, glass of Merlot in one hand and his book in the other. With the backdrop of Richmond Ave., I strummed through the pages. I started with his bio; *'A brash new voice in the literary world, Gavin Adams's, The Consequence of Chance, delves into the world of...'* My cell phone rang; it was Denise.

"What's up, girlie!"

"Did y'all fuck yet?"

I laughed so hard, but Denise pressed for details.

"Girl, we just talked about him, leave me alone."

"I'm only looking out, sis."

"That's your best advice, have sex?"

"It's not time?"

"Maybe I could fall in love first?"

"This is 2008, the rules done changed, we 'bout to have a black president..."

"That has absolutely nothing to do with my sex life."

"What you waiting on, damn it!"

"Love and patience, that's not too much to ask."

"O' Hallmark card ass..."

"We might have dinner Wednesday, we'll see."

A vulnerability was throughout my tone. Partly embarrassed at what I said, I saved face.

"Then again, I may have to cancel."

"Cancel for what, don't play hard to get, Risa!"

"Who's playing hard to get? You know my situation."

"Okay, priorities, girl. Understandable, but you been alone long enough. Yes, some choices didn't pan out, that's life. Make mistakes. Live like a human."

Denise was more than a friend, she was a sister, and the only one capable of telling me about my shit. Being patient enough for the truth; all I had to do was allow life to happen.

"Three heartbreaks in a row would make anyone skeptical."

"And a two-year hiatus should be enough time to lick your wounds, Risa."

"Bitch…"

"I love you too."

Denise could sympathize with the course of my love life. She was there for the late-night phone calls filled with despair. Together, we'd gone through countless boxes of tissue and bottles of Riesling, soul searching for the remedy. Nevertheless, I willfully changed my thinking for no other reason than his persistence.

Just minutes after Denise and I ended our call, he replied with a text that read, 'It would be my pleasure.' Low key, my secret celebration was a breakthrough. Yes, I would be a trophy, but not like that. He seemed to want to know me like he wanted to take the time to fall for me.

'Almost forgot, what's your address, I'll pick you up around 8?'

I waited on the offer, concerned with revealing where I stayed.

'I can meet you there, coming from a prior engagement.'

'That's cool; see you then.'

7

Oh Taste and See

An overcast Wednesday morning felt doubtful. Although Gavin loved the rain, he wasn't sure she could stand it. Lying in bed five minutes more, he daydreamed off into the bland of the sky outside. Then he got up, at the edge, thanked God for another breath, and proceeded to piss, shower, and shave. Mulling over his plans for the day, he was pleased with reaching the 100th page of his latest book. Partly inspired, he had her to thank. For the last few months, he'd been on a rollercoaster ride of emotions, anxious and irrational. Coming alive again, his vision of a thing with her was coming true.

When I walked into the faculty lounge, I was chill with a cup of Starbucks in hand, poised for 5 hours of lecturing. Even Miguel's interrogation of things, wouldn't annoy me.

"Adams," Miguel offered.

"Franz."

I had a class in thirty minutes, a comfortable stretch in time to call La Griglia for reservations. *Maybe she made reservations, why wouldn't she make reservations, she picked the place and time.* I continued reading the arts section of the Houston Chronicle.

"What's up for tonight?"

"Little date."

"Cool…hey, whatever happened with the singer chick?"

"It's her."

"Oh, it's her."

I smiled triumphantly.

"It is."

"Sticking it out, buddy? Good shit," Miguel mocked.

"Whatever."

"So, when can I meet her."

"Oh, you wanna meet her?"

"What…you're my friend. She's your friend; we're friends."

"Like a double date?"

"No, just us three for happy hour, something like that."

"No, Paula?"

"Must you speak that name."

"Really…"

"Wait till you get married. Anyway, I gotta skedaddle, good luck with tonight."

"Thanks."

Looking at the time, it was 10:37AM, twenty-three minutes before class, and enough space for me to quench my thirst with a text; 'just checking, everything cool for tonight.' My pride kept me from asking, 'did you make reservations?' Surprisingly, she answered back in real-time, 'see you at 8.' A settled matter, I continued my leisure reading.

Throughout the day, with a few spells of rain, three lectures and a small spat of a disagreement with a student over a grade, I packed my tan leather messenger bag, hopped in my car, and stopped by The Black Walnut Café in the village, for my favorite 'Boston burger.'

After reaching my apartment, scoffing down said burger, and checking emails, I watched MSNBC for updates on Barrack Obama's presidential campaign. Never imagining the possibility of an African American president in my lifetime, the campaign had gradually become an integral part of my daily life. With lively barbershop debates and faculty lounges tirades, I wondered if Clarissa found politics interesting.

Later on, by 6:30, I began my process of getting fresh, straight to the closet for the proper attire; "I could put this with this, get the pink handkerchief, tan belt and shoes." Satisfied and prepped, I laid it out like an Easter Sunday outfit. Then I showered for a meticulous scrub from the sole of my feet to the shampooing of my hair. Afterward, I dried off, still with droplets of water making a trail to the kitchen, for my customary, pre-game *Metropolitan*. A few sips, the burn and sweet of it, crisp and refreshing, got my mind right. Then I returned to the bedroom to get dressed.

First, the iPod; I needed the right flow, that adequate bounce to rock too. "Let me play...no let's play this." *"Kiss"* by Prince, a suitable jam for the evening echoed off the walls. Standing in front of the mirror, I mouthed the words, applying deodorant, followed by cocoa butter over my hands, arms, and face. And finally, my ritualistic nine-shot spritz, choosing from any of the eight bottles of cologne on the sink, I settled for the *Cool Water*. Two spritzes to the left wrist, rubbing both wrists together — two spritz behind each ear, and then three to the chest.

Following a thorough brushing of teeth and hair, I was ready to close the deal. My weapon of choice was a linen and cotton blend, two-piece, two-button, heather grey *Ralph Lauren* suit, with a white Oxford dress shirt, and pink handkerchief for color. Completing the look with matching tan belt and shoes, silver cuff links, and Movado watch, I was out the door.

'I'm on the way, see you there.'

Confident with my chosen look, and grateful that it hadn't rained, the anticipation of us had me on 100. For all the waiting, rescheduling, and that benchmark kiss, tonight was the evidence of things not seen.

My relaxed drive, complemented by the sounds of a *Joe Sample* CD, was smooth as the speed I drove. Along the way, a text came through; 'Be there soon.' I looked back at the road, more determined. But instantly, I was disturbed by a few thoughts; *will she kiss me like last time, maybe she was drunk, she gone play me if I try it again*. Immediately, I shook it off with a new, positive affirmation; *whatever will be, will be.*

Thirteen minutes later, I pulled into the strip center parking area of the restaurant. Sitting a few minutes more, I went to the armrest for a breath mint, checked my nostrils in the rearview mirror, turned off the car, and proceeded in. To my surprise, she was already there, standing behind another couple speaking with the host.

"Excuse me, ma'am?"

I tapped her on the back, and she turned with a smile.

"Hey," she answered, followed by a hug.

"You been here long?"

"I just walked in."

"Cool."

Standing side by side silently, small talk avoided, we seemed equally nervous. When the couple ahead of us was escorted off, I approached the reception desk, waiting for Clarissa to acknowledge the reservation. Instead, she stood beside me, waiting for me to speak. I looked at the host, who offered a friendly smile and said, "Welcome to La Griglia, do you have a reservation?" I looked at Clarissa, who looked back at me.

"I thought you made the reservation."

"I suggested the place and reservation time."

"Oh...okay, so obviously we didn't make a reservation, do you have available seating?" The embarrassment was cute but unnecessary. The host looked at his reservation book.

"I'm sorry, there won't be available seating until 9:30." I shot a silent slug at Clarissa, with a hunched brow that read, *'see?'* "Would you like to take that time slot?" Looking at each other, neither of us had an interest in waiting that long but hoped the other would say it first.

"We're gonna pass, but thanks," I answered.

We turned to walk out and immediately entered the beginnings of evening rain.

"I know a place if you're down," I offered.

"All right, I'll follow."

The drudge of a wet Wednesday drive, with Houston's infamous potholes, sucked immensely. Offering her a ride was the better choice that slipped my mind. Purely off instinct, I drove towards a favorite new Tex-Mex restaurant in the Heights, Tommy Tio's, for their Margaritas. Notwithstanding the #15 combo: flour tortilla tacos, stuffed with grilled shrimp, grilled onions, peppers, topped with Monterey Jack cheese, complemented by refried beans and rice, with the refreshing contrast of avocado slices and sour cream.

Under fifteen minutes, we arrived at Tommy Tio's gravel laid parking lot, with heavy rain pouring down. We parked side by side, with very low visibility, barely enough to signal to each other to get out of our cars. I braved the elements first, walking over to her driver's side door, holding my suit jacket over my head, "I got you."

With zero enthusiasm for the direction of the evening, she reluctantly got out to the covering of my already dampened jacket; "Thanks." We scurried to the refuge of a dry place, walking through the doors to the sights and sounds of regulars.

The welcoming aromas seemed to calm Clarissa's nerves and adjust her attitude. "I hope you're in the mood for the best margarita in town."

She looked at me, face and clothes still wet, and replied, "It better be." Less than a few minutes after being seated, following the customary presentation of tortilla chips, salsa, and two cups of water, the real conversation began.

"So, explain if you will, how…" Immediately I laughed. Bracing myself for the slugs, this would be an entertaining few minutes of back and forth. "I mean, tradition calls for the gentleman suitor… you, to take a cue from the lady…me."

"Duly noted, and for the record, I think you're even more attractive when you're wet."

Clarissa looked unamused.

"Really."

"What?"

Easing into the moment, a waiter approached the table, taking our drink order. However, I hadn't a clue that I was dealing with a heavyweight, capable of drinking me under the table.

"Be easy with these," I suggested.

"Gotcha," she answered with a wink.

She laughed, thinking of her heyday when the money flowed, and the cocaine lines were long, she partied till the break of dawn. A 1.75 liter of dark Jamaican rum was like a soda can. On numerous occasions, she'd blackout in private, shielded from the looming paparazzi hungry for another celebrity debacle. Even still, after years of excess, now and then, she'd submit to the cooling burn of a glass of *Wild Turkey*, neat, with the sounds of Sarah Vaughn caressing her soul.

"Thanks for sticking it out, it's crazy tonight," I offered. To me, small talk reeked of desperation. In her presence, in the lowly Tommy Tio's, she was still Renee in my eyes. The honor of another free gathering, with margaritas on the rocks, no salt, a basket of chips and salsa, seemed surreal. The best thing about a stormy night, loud and unrelenting, was the pleasurable sight of her sitting across from me, along with the smells of Tex-Mex.

"This must be the go-to spot, all these people in here," she spoke.

"Oh yeah, it's salsa night."

"You can dance?"

"I'd like to think so, especially after a few of these."

Clarissa gave the nod, nonchalantly. Moments later, the waiter returned, ready to take our dinner request. Clarissa settled on a chicken enchilada platter, while I went for my regular. I also requested another round of margaritas.

"A second one?"

"Don't worry about me, I'm good...you, on the other hand, should be worried."

"Yeah," she answered curiously.

"Just remember, I told you so."

"No competition over here, I promise."

We shared another gaze, something more than words. It was sexual energy ignited by good tequila and crazy rain. I grazed her hand on the way to another chip, while Clarissa accidentally kicked my right foot. The night belonged to ambiguity and a high-calorie count. Clarissa found herself engaged in someone other than herself. And for the next twenty-two minutes, my vulnerability had become attractive.

"Food looks good," she offered.

"Want some?"

"Sure, just a shrimp."

I reached for my fork, picked the biggest shrimp I could find, and just as I was putting it on her plate, she tapped her lips, *here*. I smiled and complied. When she took the shrimp from my fork to her mouth, she chewed, with her eyes locked on mine, slow grinding my emotions.

"It's good?" I asked, while she continued her burlesque show.

"Pretty good."

I enjoyed the tease and the second margarita. Not sure of where the night would go, I hoped for a chance for one dance, and maybe another kiss by the end of the night.

"We gotta get some Salsa in before we leave," I proposed.

"I don't know. I'm a little afraid," she answered.

"Of what?"

"Of you embarrassing me."

The ice broke.

"I promise it'll be something you'll never forget."

"Now I'm worried," she answered.

We enjoyed the nuance of adult conversation. I reached for my glass and raised it. "I'd like to make a toast to you, Ms. Clarissa Gentry, for having the best comebacks I've ever heard."

She raised her glass as well, with a smirk. "Whatever man, you still paying for dinner."

Drink after drink, laugh after silly laugh, the vibe flowed with discussions of personal hopes and dreams, and the happenstances of life. Under the influence, I was comfortably transparent about my family, particularly the former rift and repentance between Mama and I. Clarissa, no longer guarded, was compelled to mention Bobby.

"Yeah, we all have our crosses to bear. Mine is the love of my life."

"Ex?"

"My son Bobby."

Startled, low key, I hadn't remembered ever hearing of a son, but I played it cool.

"How old is your son?"

"Seven going on seventeen."

"Wow, that's awesome."

"Yeah, it would be if I could tuck him in every night."

Awkwardness prompted me to break the tension.

"He's with his father?"

"In beautiful Malibu, California."

I could hear the anguish that resonated in her words.

"But that's neither here nor there. For now, these margaritas are hitting very nicely, and I'm ready to dance, so…let's see what you got," she offered.

The cadence of salsa music had filled the place. As we walked towards the small crowd of other couples, already in motion, we found an open spot, and Clarissa stood in front of me, at the ready. I put my left hand up, prepared, and in position.

"Show me what you got," she declared.

I smiled and led off with my left foot, confident in my capacity to bullshit my way through the song. Clarissa smiled the entire time, thoroughly amused.

"I see you," I praised for her ability to keep up with my bullshit. She was still a former R&B star with years of impeccable timing; she made me look good.

"I see you too."

Our bodies ebbed and flowed, complemented by the occasional misstep. Clarissa pardoned my skill level a thousand times, but I stayed committed, willing to adjust to her.

"You all right?"

"I was just about to ask you."

Beads of sweat formed at our brows, something was brewing. But after a few songs of dancing and twirling to the staccato of a cha-cha, we called it a night. Later after paying the bill, we walked out to the calm of a passed-over storm.

"Had a good time?"

"Pretty good, thank you."

"Cool…I hope we can do this again."

"Whenever," she answered.

"Whenever huh, what's up right now?"

"It's a school night; you need your sleep, sir."

"Stop playing, you not down for a nightcap?"

"What bar we going to now?"

"Mine, my place, if that's cool."

Clarissa laughed; she knew what it was.

"Your place, huh? I got a bar too."

"Same difference…"

"How far are you?"

I reached in my pocket for my keys and answered, "follow me."

Under the spell of lust and moonlight, we drove down White Oak Dr., while Clarissa had second thoughts about her hoe-like judgment. Every intersection she passed was an opportunity to bail, but she held it together. After parking at my building, we rode the elevator up to my third-floor apartment, still intoxicated and unsure of the moments ahead. I opened the door, letting Clarissa in.

"Nice décor…balcony view of the city." Luckily, I washed the dishes and picked up around the place earlier in the day.

"Thank you." I turned on the lights that hung over the counter space of my kitchen.

"Make yourself at home. What would you like?"

"Surprise me."

I appreciated her vote of confidence. With the green light she'd granted, I decided on a drink I mastered during my frat boy, Columbia days.

"The Pickle Tickle," one-part *Jameson* whiskey, one-part pickle juice, and two green olives with the pit still inside, was an asshole party drink meant to pay homage to the after taste of fellatio. I sat beside her, handed her the glass, and offered cheers. She took one sip, looked at me, and said, "What the fuck is this?"

"You don't like it?"

"It's gross."

"I can make something else."

"Yeah…what do you call this?"

"It's called a Pickle Tickle."

Clarissa immediately laughed.

"Oh my God, did you make that up?"

"It's just an old college drink I'm good at making."

"Pickle tickle, huh, because of the pickle juice? What's the tickle part?"

I smiled and dropped my head.

"It's a stupid drink we always made at our frat parties."

"Oh, so the pickle was like the dick?"

I laughed at the truth.

"Something like that, but more like the taste of it."

"You and your frat brothers made up a drink based on the taste of dick?"

"No, it was just meant to be a joke that stuck, no gay shit."

"So, I was drinking a drink based on oral sex?"

"That's the joke, yeah."

"Do you have any vodka?"

"Yeah, you want something else?"

Clarissa put her glass on the end table to her left, hiked up her skirt, and began pulling her thong panties down.

"Let's make a new drink tonight, my treat." Her brash delivery was offensive and sexy as fuck. Not being one to back down, I raised the ante when I put my glass down, walked over, got on my knees between her legs, and met her match. Clarissa was pleased by my moxie and asked, "What shall we call this?" I looked up and responded, "Gimme ten minutes."

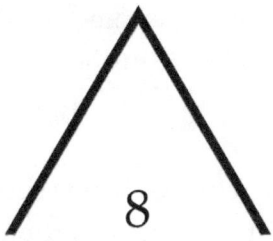

8

In The Beginning

After rising from the toil of creating a new drink, "pink blossom," one-part vodka, and one-part pink lemonade frozen concentrate, we decided to date. Without labels, life carried on through random calls and rendezvous to match. We found ourselves on board for a relationship.

Miguel had become acquaintances with her on a first-name basis. However, six months in, she raised the question of what to call ourselves, to the world.

I went over for dinner many times before, but for this one particular night, it was for clarity. When I arrived, I removed my shoes, a rule since day one. I sat in my spot on the sofa with a cocktail half gone. The array of herbs, possibly basting over chicken, baked in the oven.

"Smells good, Risa." Clarissa could burn.

"Should be done in ten minutes," she answered.

"You want me to check it?"

"Sit yo ass down, ten minutes."

She wore this form-fitting, salmon-colored sundress, meant for something.

"What do you think?"

"Nice."

"Thanks."

I looked back at my iPhone, checking e-mails, and the *'gram,* while "Living Single" played in the background. But she had intentions. Her play of food and flesh entirely distracted an overdue conversation.

After changing, she returned in boy shorts and a tank top, still in character. She went to the stove and pulled out the glass pan of a chicken casserole. "Dinner's up, set the table, sir." Both of us had an appreciation for ceramic plates, metal forks, and glasses for dinner.

"What do you wanna drink?"

"Water's fine."

A few minutes later, the table was set, and we sat, prepared to enjoy it.

"Dear God, thank you for this food that we're about to eat, please bless it to our bodies, and bless the hands that prepared it in your name we pray, Amen."

One of the things she liked about my A.M.E. way, was that it reminded her of those old days around the dinner table when her father would say the blessing. To her, a man who could pray, even over his food, was patient.

"Good day today?"

"Good."

My mundane life was refreshing to her. It eliminated industry talk and the underbelly of competition. My second book was finally complete, and she was finally getting real work from L.A., besides the four jingles she sold to advertising companies. Her biggest comeback was the placement of a song she'd written for a debut artist on one of the major labels. As we were experiencing moderate success, the atmosphere seemed ripe for a firm understanding.

"You ever thought about writing full time? You have a following."

"Yeah, but honestly, life as a college professor ain't so bad."

"So, you're not settling?"

"No."

"So, if you sold a million books, you wouldn't stop teaching?"

"Now, that's different."

She was cunning, but I was familiar.

"That's interesting," she offered.

"How so?"

"You make a major move, based on an outcome...what if it never happens?"

"What's wrong with planning? Yes, I believe I'm talented, but I gotta maintain my lifestyle without it being a burden to anyone, especially you."

"Why would it be a burden to me?"

And there it was, the setup.

"Aren't we partners now...six months?"

"How so?"

"We've been dating for six months."

"Yes?"

"That's a thing."

"How would you define a thing?"

"Well, I'm not dating anyone else, are you?"

"I'm not," she replied.

"So, are you, my girlfriend?"

She paused with a look of hesitation.

"Are you prepared to be exclusive?"

"I've been prepared."

"Which means?"

"I've learned the difference between Clarissa and Renee."

A crafty one-liner didn't sway her. She wanted more.

"What have you learned?"

"While Renee enjoys the spotlight, the adrenaline rush of the stage, the adoration from fans and whatever, Clarissa wants love and respect, and to be understood."

"Okay...appreciate that."

"Could you appreciate us officially being something?"

"Yes, I could," she answered, allowing me the honor of closing.

"So, will you be my ride or die, my homie-lover-friend?"

"If you'll be my baby daddy."

"We doing this, for real?"

"Are you for sure, Gavin?"

Her question disrupted the flow.

"Didn't I just ask?"

"Since I've been dating you, what defines our relationship?"

The conversation was unexpected, dripped in third-degree bullshit. It was more mind fuckery, like the beginning, only this time, it went beyond necessity.

"To be honest, the struggle was real, and you were testing me and shit."

"I was testing you?" She interrupted.

On the defense, her shock was theatrics.

"Be honest. You didn't put me through it?"

Clarissa looked away with a guilty grin, confirming a read.

"If you feel that way, but as I told you, I needed to see your intent."

"You had fun, though."

"I'll be your girlfriend, exclusively, if you'll be my boyfriend, exclusively."

I leaned in for a kiss and an agreement, and from that moment, it was the birth of something new, not entirely understood. Clarissa hadn't been a girlfriend since Charlotte, a guarded situation. Neither one of us were sure of monogamy, other than the months already in the books.

The days ahead were terrifying for me. Having weathered Clarissa's hazing, there was no blueprint, no frame of reference for how to love her. Pilar and the other women before hadn't captivated me.

The more I learned of her desire to be a full-time mother again, to reclaim her career, and to trust someone fully, made her real. To remain objective, I secretly decided to follow her lead, avoiding any assumptions that would run her off.

Friends and family were made aware, first with a visit to Clarissa's parents out in Sugar Creek. The ride was a little nerving for me; one of my cardinal rules was never to meet mothers. However, I wanted to meet her people, to digest the folks in her life, understanding that they'd possibly be a part of mine one day.

When we arrived, I was a cliché with sweaty hands that slightly shook, so much so, that Clarissa noticed. "You okay?" Briefly paralyzed from some deep-seated fear of meeting her parents, this was a new level of commitment.

"I'm good, you ready?"

"Yeah, and you don't have to eat anything, just saying."

We walked side by side, with our hands occasionally brushing each other. The proclivity to grab her hand, some official act, irked me. A million thoughts rushed through my head, mainly the judgment that would come. Having changed my ways, particularly for Clarissa, mothers could usually sniff bullshit. There was no recourse for a good read.

"Risa…" Clarissa's mother answered while opening the door. I imagined her being Clarissa's height, color, and weight. But she was the total opposite; somewhat taller than Clarissa, her skin tone was rich mahogany, complemented by her short-cropped, grayish-white hair. Her thin frame teetered frail. The corners of her eyes and lips were replete with the creases of time. She wore her age well, as the saying goes, *'black don't crack.'* "Hello, handsome sir, nice to meet you. I'm Hazel," she offered with her hand extended.

"Nice to meet you too. I'm Gavin."

"Oh, I know," she answered with a smile.

It was good to know.

"I hope you've heard good things."

"Mama where's daddy?"

"Ezra! Ezra, come down, your daughter and her friend are here!"

Instantly, the nerves came back. I expected some big, brute of an older gentleman, with a scowling brow, maybe 6'2 or 6'3. Instead, Ezra was about an inch or two shorter than Hazel, looking like

Smokey Robinson. His jet-black hair and pearly white dentures convinced me that at some point in his life, Mr. Gentry was a ladies man.

"Hey doc, call me Ezra," he offered, with his hand extended.

"Nice to meet you, Mr. Ezra."

"Come on in, have a seat. You wanna beer, young man?"

"Sure, thank you, sir."

The setting of this traditional two-story home, with sporadic knick-knacks detailing the years of their lives, included family pictures with Clarissa as a pubescent starlet, with a *'Salt – N – Pepa'* bob cut, a green silk blouse, a cheap gold-plated necklace, and gold bamboo earrings with her name in the middle. Off in the distance, I spotted her gold plaque. "Oh, wow, is that for…" Ezra beamed with pride while I walked closer to read the inscription.

"Yeah, that's the album that bought this house."

I continued scoping the den area, with more family pictures, more of Clarissa with barrettes, pigtails, and missing teeth.

This visit was a milestone, as the glittery shine of her celebrity had officially worn off. At the crux of it all, she was an African American woman blessed with making it to the upper echelon of society.

Had she'd never become Renee, she'd be off my radar. My usual taste came from a pool of women associated with the circles I ran. The Jack & Jill, debutant ball, cotillion, ivy leaguers who thought of entertainers as "lucky."

"Youngblood, here you go," Ezra spoke, flashing those pearly whites.

He handed me a cold bottle of *Heineken,* a beer I despised but accepted with a smile, "Thank you." I looked over at Clarissa, who was looking down at her phone. Ironically, the *Texans* vs. *Bengals* game was on.

"Who you going for young blood," Ezra asked.

"I'm from Cincinnati."

"Oh yeah? I was in Cincinnati, back in eighty…eighty-eight."

"Awesome," I replied. Clarissa cut her eyes at me. *'What?'*

"Y'all hungry? Mama finished a pot of mustard greens; you eat greens?"

The last time I'd eaten greens was at a family reunion in Greensboro, South Carolina, in 1995.

"Hazel, get young blood a bowl of greens! You want hot sauce?"

"Oh, I'm good, Mr. Ezra; thank you."

"You don't eat greens, professor," Clarissa mocked.

"Risa can eat a whole pot by herself."

"Risa, you want some greens?!" Hazel yelled from the kitchen.

"Okay, mama!"

"What you teach young blood?"

"I teach sociology."

"Sociology, …like dealing with people's problems and thangs?"

Clarissa looked over with a smirk, waiting for my response.

"In a way, but more with society. A sociologist may study the effects of poor living conditions, to determine if those conditions have hindered the progress of the members of a community, their well-being, and things of that nature."

"Oh, okay, I get it now. So y'all the type to work with the government, politicians, business folk…"

"Exactly, we may be hired to research certain groups of people, or whole cities, to see the inner-workings of it. That information is beneficial and valuable."

"I see, well, can you do some research on these youngsters walking 'round with their pants sagging, showing they ass, all that type of shit," Ezra fired back.

"I wrote a book that talks about that; I'll give you one if you promise to read it."

"Jack, I'm retired with all this free time, I ain't gone lie to you, if it ain't *Sports Center* or *ESPN*, I'm in that backyard in my little garden with a Heineken."

"I understand, Mr. Ezra." Just then, Hazel came into the room, holding a tray with two bowls of steaming hot mustard greens, with a pie cut slice of cornbread. "Risa, get them TV trays for you and Calvin," Hazel commanded.

I smiled, but Clarissa was quick to correct her; "Gavin mama, Gavin."

I got up to help her, and then took over, helping to set up her tray. Hazel took note and smiled, while Ezra gave Clarissa an approving nod.

Twenty or so minutes of eating greens, watching the game, and random questions from Ezra, the '*itis*' had come, but I didn't want to be rude. It didn't help that the greens were tasty, with the right blend of seasoning, complemented by the airiness of the cornbread, with just the right amount of sweet and butter.

"Ms. Hazel I must say I haven't had greens and cornbread in a while, but this was the best, thank you."

"Thank you, Calvin, Gavin," she replied with a gracious smile. "Now, if you get sleepy, gone take your shoes off and make yourself comfortable."

"We not gone stay long mama, we gotta make another stop."

"Y'all just got here, where y'all got to go now?"

There wasn't any place we had to go. Clarissa's excuse was personal.

"Ms. Hazel, may I use your restroom, please?"

"No problem. Clarissa show him the upstairs bathroom; this one here is on the fritz."

Clarissa smacked her lips like she was thirteen again. I looked sheepishly, walking behind her, respectful and such until we turned the corner and started walking the stairs. Tempted by the ass in tight jeans, I took the liberty of a pinch. "Chill," she replied cautiously. I smacked my lips, deflecting her rebuke. "Second door on the right…"

All alone, in this cheesy, pastel color scheme of a bathroom, I was careful to lift the toilet seat. I wondered what Clarissa was doing at the very same moment. When I finished, I took care to take a small wad of tissue and wipe the top edge of the toilet bowl, securing my sanitary place in life. After thorough washing of the hands and a face check, I left the bathroom just as I found it. A spry walk down the hall, I stood at her door, tapping it twice to announce myself. "Can I come in?"

"Don't get comfortable," she answered, looking through a book on her bed.

I walked over and sat with her in a quiet space filled with nuance and opportunity. The sudden need to live on the edge, to be random, seemed apparent for me.

"What's the craziest thing you've ever done in this room?" She looked at me with a confused stare momentarily, and then replied,

"Let you in it, with my daddy downstairs." I laughed a little as she smiled.

Still antsy to take advantage of a situation, I asked, "Is that it?"

She sarcastically answered, "Yep."

"I strongly disagree," I said, standing up in front of her.

She gave a consensual look and said, "I was gonna do this later, but fuck it." She sat up, on the edge of the bed, and began to unzip my jeans, while digging to get him out. The exhilaration of it grew an erection until I was completely out and firmly in her mouth. Her dedication, her glare, her stroke was perfect as we withheld our usual moans. I was 10 feet tall, grabbing the back of her head in praise. It was like, she felt free, giving head in her mama and daddy's house.

"Get up," I commanded, with a tone that meant business. Once she did, I took the liberty of unfastening the button and zipper of her jeans, pulling them down, along with her zebra print thong, to put her in position. Doing her best to be submissive and discreet, all at the same damn time, she grabbed her favorite stuffed animal, while bent over.

"Y'all okay up there?!" Hazel yelled from the bottom of the stairs

"Yes, mama! Go close the door," she whispered.

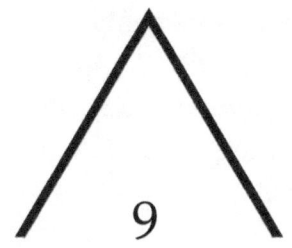

9

The Rapture

What started as some cat and mouse shit, boy meets girl, boy falls for girl, thus and so forth, turned to an actual love connection. Within a year of monogamy, we had become official, for the public. One night against the backdrop of downtown city lights and the balcony terrace of the Magnolia Hotel, for the annual faculty Christmas Ball, I found time to still away. Looking across the gathering of faces, drunk, but sure of a feeling, I confidently approached Clarissa, who was standing off in the distance, alone. She held a glass of champagne while looking down at Texas Avenue, possibly reminiscing or bored. She wore a form-fitting burgundy taffeta dress that received compliments all night. However, she'd grown tired of the attention.

"Risa..." She turned around with the brightest smile, accented by the amber string of lights hanging from a potted plant behind her. "You ready to go, huh?" Clarissa looked down and then hunched her shoulders, not sure if her classic impatience would offend me. "We can go if you want, it's cool."

Clarissa remained quiet, still smiling, but I was unsure of her state of mind. For no apparent reason, other than the cool breeze that occasionally brushed against her skin, or maybe being under the influence of the holiday spirit, she was compelled to speak her truth.

"I love you," she answered softly.

"What?"

A collision of two kindred souls, aligned in peace; I stepped closer, immediately kissing her, in full public display.

"I can't believe this."

"What?"

"I was coming to tell you the same thing."

Her eyes lit up, but immediately her face read *disbelief*, "Don't play with me, please."

"I promise to God, on everything near and dear to my heart, I was about to tell you the same thing. No lie, something inside said, *tell her*."

Time froze for two hearts, finally succinct. A single tear welled from her left eye. I took off my jacket to put it on her; "I do love you." We held a gaze, followed by an embrace, symbolizing another echelon of something new. We rocked back and forth to the music, despite the sounds of a cheesy cover band inside the banquet hall. For minutes, we went this way, isolated to some other place, understanding that the walls had ultimately come down.

Suddenly, Miguel came out of nowhere, spotting us in our world and asked, "You guys good?"

"Yeah, man, we're going home."

When we arrived at my place, Clarissa went to the bedroom to undress while I ran her a hot bath. The balcony influenced my impromptu move. "You taking a bath now?" I continued, checking the temperature every so often, going to the kitchen, to pour her a glass of wine.

"It's for you, babe." She sat quietly on the edge of the bed, amazed. "It's ready."

She stood from the edge, unclasped and tossed her bra to the bed, and slid her panties off. She walked into the bathroom, completely bare, inside and out. I took her hand as she stepped into the garden tub, with water, just shy of unbearable. Soap-suds and a glass of Merlot made for the beginnings of a beautiful night.

"Is the water okay?"

She looked at me, took a sip, and answered, "You're the best."

Gavin rose and left her alone to enjoy a moment. But underneath this lovefest, she thought of her son, still thousands of miles away, under the moon and stars of Malibu. She thought it could be a favor to relieve Jacob of the responsibilities of fatherhood. He could whore around with ease, and Bobby could finally have a wholesome family environment.

Forty or so minutes later, after the luxuriousness of warm bubbles and Merlot began to fade, she prepared to dry off, fuck and fall asleep. But she entered the bedroom, with Gavin standing by the bed, awaiting her arrival.

"Please lie down."

He removed her towel, only to lay it flat on the comforter. She climbed onto the bed, while he reached for the small bottle of warmed eucalyptus oil, at the ready.

"Please, relax."

"What are you doing, and what's that accent?"

"I do not know what you mean, madam, but brace yourself."

I poured the lukewarm oil at the nape of her neck, down to the small of her back; she laid submissive, seeming to appreciate my thoroughness to detail. Slightly embarrassed, she'd become wet, but thankful for the towel. From the angle she laid, it was impossible to drink wine, but she dared not interrupt my flow or her own.

"You okay back there?"

"Please relax. I've just begun."

Random moans prompted me to linger in areas, seeking the ongoing approval of her pitch. This sexually tinged fun was free and filthy. I worked her lower back, occasionally crossing the border by squeezing her ass at will, with occasional kisses. She giggled in pleasure, resting atop her forearms, while her legs spread. Piqued by the moment, I snuck a peek between her legs like a horny teenaged boy, teasing her inner thigh, inching towards her lips for just a brush with destiny.

"I see you, boy," she'd say, with no hesitation.

With concentrated forceful glides, I went the length of her thighs to the calves and the balls of her feet. Thank God, she oiled her feet.

Ten minutes in, I switched up and focused on just her upper back, shoulders, and arms. I enjoyed squeezing her muscles, in passive-aggressive dominance. At one point, she was snoring.

"Madam?"

She was unresponsive for five seconds until replying with a tired and lazy tone. "Never mind."

Not sure if she would follow my request, I sheepishly commanded, "Please turn over." Without speaking, she turned as requested.

Instinctively, I zeroed in on her breast, groping a willing participant. I took particular care on her nipples, prompt, and perky. Then I leaned in and began gently sucking, licking, and whirling my tongue around, until she gave in, with faint praise,

"That feels good." Again I smiled, with further, gentle kisses down her sternum, to her stomach, teasing her love handles, in anticipation.

"Madam, is everything okay?"

"Yes," she answered, with a crackling voice.

"May I continue?"

"Please."

With no reservation of mind, I dove into the valley, courageous and strong.

The rolling of her eyes and arching of her back was validation enough. Just above the ridge of her breast, her eyes were closed, with her head titled back and to the left. Her moaning was continuous, and her legs spread, with the balls of her feet resting on my back. A vigorous finessing of her soul, she pushed my head back as she climaxed into glory.

"Okay, ...okay," she pled.

"Enough, madam?"

"Boy, get up…"

Rising to wash my face, Clarissa continued to lie, exhausted from pleasure. Naturally, round two would take place, but for now, I looked into the mirror and smiled. "You a bad motherfucker."

When I returned, she laid on her right side, her body facing the bedroom window, washed in moonlight, as she began to fade away, until I slipped back into the bed, fully naked and erect, flushed with the curve of her body. She felt a playful thump but said nothing. "Madam, may I interest you in some dick?" I whispered just behind her left shoulder, with the tickle of my breath.

She laughed, "Why are you so silly?"

I remained silent, still in character, while she giggled. Patient for an answer, she coyly replied, "Go." My adrenaline filled the room. With the index and middle finger of my left hand, I took care to prep the situation, using her excitement as an aide. With my right hand, I held my staff, ready to lead into this covenant of one.

"You okay?" I asked, sliding myself past the threshold.

She grabbed hold to my left thigh in the process; "Yeah."

It was the beginnings of a match in frequency and body language. The pace increased to a cadence of a galloping horse, wild and free on an Oklahoma plain. Unfortunately for me, it was also the beginnings of a nut in just under a minute. I pulled back to a slower stride until the urge died.

Regaining my composure, I focused back on a crack in the wall, all to maintain my erection and earn a *nut*. However, for a flash, Pilar came to mind. I remembered the same care I took with her, the corresponding residual movements, void of love towards the end of our relationship. It scared me, the thought of making love in the same way. Instinctively, I rose from the side grind, proceeded to lay her flat, and resume. Unaware of my plight, she continued as a willing participant, with our eyes locked on one another, and our bodies in rhythm, producing a loud clap, like a Baptist choir singing acapella. My flow was evident with streams of sweat dripping from my brow to her face, a heavenly rain and baptism.

Clarissa's legs were raised high and wide in praise. A hundred pumps in, I changed yet again and commanded, "Get on top." Clarissa obliged, with a slow straddle, considering her inner thighs burned. This time, it was her turn to ride, as she mounted me with a straight back like a true cowgirl. But the rhythmic wave of her motion was so luxurious. She was now the captain of the S.S. Good Dick. She laid her hands on my chest, arched her back, closed her eyes, and drifted into a sea, free-flowing towards a breakthrough.

"Yes," she spoke, while her eyes remained closed, followed by soulful moans.

"Shit," I answered while I grabbed her cheeks.

Succinctly, our bodies raptured. Suddenly, I pulled out and released just between inner thighs, dangerously close to the point of no return. Clarissa rolled her body over to my left, as I reached for the box of tissue to my right. We laid on our backs, breathing in unison. Remaining in silence, atop damp sheets, calm befell the bedroom. I turned and asked, "You okay?" Clarissa continued her gaze at the moon, satisfied, or maybe unsure of an answer.

She replied, "I'm good..."

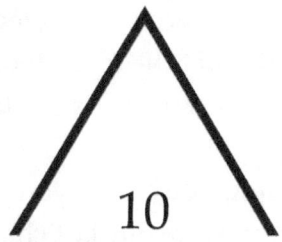

10

Transgressions & Iniquities

It was a minute before I mentioned Clarissa to Mama. Being infrequent with women, my parents gave me the nickname "Educated Playboy." When I experienced my first heartbreak, my freshmen year in high school, Faye and Bradford made it clear that education was first and foremost. However, privately and separately, Faye's words of wisdom went along the line of finding love when the time was right; "If you don't get a good education, you won't have a career, so how could you be a good provider?"

In contrast, Bradford's reasoning was much more straightforward; "Women come a dime a dozen." Dad's logic stemmed from being among Cincinnati's upper crust. His days as a county judge afforded him the luxuries of public life and the trappings of sexual interludes with staffers and interns. To Bradford, the dedication to higher learning could mean an excellent experience transcendent of color.

Long ago, Bradford's extracurricular activity had gotten out of hand. Faye's intuition proved correct when a string of incidental fuck-ups finally led to an admission of guilt. Faye toiled with the hurt and embarrassment of disrespect, the condescending glares at dinner parties, and off-color jokes by the other judge wives. Her one mission in life became steering me clear of the 'Adams way.' Anything slightly chauvinistic received the intensity of her tone and a pinch to my arm. She once scolded me for an entire day, for forgetting to open the door at the local department store. I never made that mistake again with her or any other woman.

"Hey, mom."

"Gavin dear, I thought you forgot your mother."

It was nearly a month since our last chat.

"Never that, just the life of an educated playboy."

"I see. Your father asked about you the other day; any plans to visit soon?"

"My bad about Thanksgiving."

"There's a first time for everything."

"How's Dad anyway? Still complaining as usual?"

"You know your father well."

Bradford Adams, the retired judge, avid golfer, and staunch republican, could be labeled in a word, opinionated. Even at the historical realization of America's first African-American president, his reservations stunk of party loyalty and conspiracy theory. "You are telling me a one-term senator, a *community organizer* with no real political experience, not even in Chicago, can rise through the ranks this fast? Think, son." I, being the liberal democrat, rarely saw eye to eye with Dad, but his accomplishments outweighed ideology.

"I may be able to get out there for Christmas unless y'all planning a trip somewhere."

"That'll be nice; we'll be here. Mexico's not 'til the summer anyway."

"Oh, Mexico, huh? Playa Vallarta or Monterey?"

"Some resort, with a ridiculous golf course," she laughed.

"That sounds like fun. I'd go."

"With us, old fogies?"

"I might bring a friend."

"New flavor, huh?"

"She's my girlfriend."

"Girlfriend? For how long?"

"Almost a year. I want y'all to meet her."

"A year?"

"I had to make sure…"

Faye supported me on most anything, except my love life. My problem was always consideration. After the abortions at Columbia, her silence only furthered my father's misogynistic spin on women. Besides, he was just happy to know I preferred pussy.

"You think you love her?"

I pulled away from the phone for a breather.

"What are you trying to say, Ms. Faye?"

"Okay, so you're upset now."

"I mean, aren't you happy I made it this long?"

"I'm always happy when you find love and keep it. When's the last time you did that?" Her quip was an uppercut to the gut.

"Okay, so yeah, maybe my track record ain't the best, I accept that. I'm learning."

"No judgment," she answered softly.

Her perfect indifference was gentle manipulation.

"It's all good, Mom, for real. But yeah, this feels different, I love her."

"That's beautiful, Gavin. What's her name, what does she do?"

Beaming with pride, it thrilled me to show and tell about my boo. Hoping my mama would be impressed, I answered, "Her name's Clarissa, she's a singer and songwriter." It was the first time my *flavor of the month* was not a sorority girl or some other bougie frame of reference.

"Oh?" Faye answered in that familiar bullshit tone. Unimpressed, she graciously listened and estimated how long this one would last.

"She goes by Renee."

"Any song I might know?"

"You remember that song, *Love is real*?"

Faye wasn't one to follow current trends, let alone the music of my generation, especially if it wasn't Chaka Khan or Stevie Wonder. Nevertheless, she continued listening to me, just like the six-year-old me discussing his pet turtle.

"Can't say that I do, does she still sing?"

"Yeah, with a band."

"Any kids," Faye continued.

It was the question that mattered most.

"She has a son with that actor dude, Jacob Finch."

"Wait, Jacob Finch from *Desperate Measures*?! I love that show," she cheered.

I immediately hated Jacob.

"Yeah, I've never seen it."

"How did you guys meet, was she on tour?"

Decoding her question, in my mind, it sounded like, *'how in the hell did y'all get involved when her last relationship was with a bona fide Hollywood actor?'*

"She's from Houston. We met in Whole Foods."

The memory of that day immediately washed out the contempt I felt.

"Awe, that's cute, Gavin. I can't wait to meet her."

"Glad to know you approve, mom."

"That's not fair, son…anyway, Pilar, how is she?"

I cringed at discussing a former flame.

"She's an ex, that's how she's doing."

"No need to get smart, I'm just making conversation, glad you moved on."

"I have indeed moved on, Mama."

Both Gavin and Clarissa's introductions were mildly successful. However, Clarissa's ease of heart continued to shine, choosing one fateful night to make a request of the band, for Gavin's sake. Of course, after the drinking, smoking, and a two-hour rehearsal, she gained the inebriated courage.

"Guys…got something to tell y'all."

"You're going solo, I knew it, I knew it," Fabian, the bassist of the band, joked.

"Don't tell me you got knocked up by the professor," Titus the drummer followed.

The fellas enjoyed being reckless, but the relationship we shared, though just a few years, had been solidified by long nights, playing in smoky dives and seedy clubs, sometimes for free or nearly next to nothing. We overcame the harsh realities of the road, the unprofessionalism of shady club promoters, and the humility of performing for a room with ten people. So, for this reason, I thought that the fellas should see Gavin as more than just the guy who showed up to gigs and walked me to the car.

"Don't be an asshole, T," I shot back. "Gavin and I, since we're a thing, I'd like to bring him to rehearsal sometimes…if that's okay with y'all." The guys were silent for a moment, before mocking me with sappy cheers of approval. "Oh, that's so sweet, you wanna bring boo to the dungeon," Zed, the guitarist of the group teased. As the saying goes, 5% of a joke has some underlying truth in it. Zed's carefree mockery masked the once deep-seated feelings he held for me, during our brief Spring fling when the band first started. When I decided to break it off in pursuit of other more pressing matters, he played it cool, but I knew it hurt.

"As long as he don't come in here, suggesting shit, he cool with me," Titus continued.

"Does he partake like us?"

"I'm sure he don't give a fuck about weed, Zed."

"I'm just saying, our weed be special, though."

I never gave it much thought, until that very moment. We drank together, many times into the wee hours of fuckery, but drugs, drugs never made it passed the light of day. My past was too damning for prime time. At a point when I was learning to be vulnerable, a misunderstanding could derail this newest chance at love.

"He's a big boy. I'm not his mama."

Now that close friends, family, and acquaintances knew about us, all that was left was this journey of compromise, and the experience of happy highs and disillusioned lows. Our first misunderstanding came from a statement Gavin made. During a dinner party at Miguel's, with the aid of free-flowing alcohol and a marijuana cipher out in the garage, this eclectic mix of sophisticated intellectuals, was dangerous.

"No fucking way I'm crossing dicks," Gavin answered while holding his red plastic cup of rum and Coke.

I, being a free spirit and seasoned in the ways of the world, thought it was unfair. The idea of a woman being loved and sexually enjoyed by two men, being something nasty, pissed me off. "But I'm sure two women make way better sense," I snapped. A lukewarm glass of Chivas fueled the tension in my tone. Miguel and Gavin smirked, while Miguel's wife Paula, cheered me on.

"That's selfish bullshit, guys." Paula enjoyed my Black girl *passion*. Having met me just a few times, she always saw me as a sister-friend. She invited me back into the house, assuming to the kitchen for more cocktails, but instead, we veered to the bathroom down the hall.

"Girlfriend, close the door...gotta little something, something." I hadn't done a line in years. Besides the primos I smoked with the band, I swore off nose candy, at least in its intended form. Paula's sneaky look, while closing the door, humored me. The excitement filled a tiny space, when Paula reached for the vile in her bra, revealing a small glass cylinder reflecting the bathroom light. My poker face hid the terror of a choice I'd make. "Wanna beam up?" Paula danced to the sounds of peer pressure, waving the vile in her hand, wanting an answer.

"You're a rock star babe, but I gotta pass...weed's enough these days."

"C'mon, have a bump with me, Clarissa, please?"

"I don't want any shit with Gavin."

"So, don't tell his ass, I sure as hell ain't telling that motherfucker!"

After ten seconds of well-placed laughter, my body language held firm, but Paula, being the bull-headed and persistent '80s party girl, stayed the course. "Fuck it. I'll go first." Immediately, Paula dumped a small amount on the bathroom sink. She conveniently reached into the medicine cabinet for a ready razor blade, and masterfully prepped her line. She bent down in one fell swoop, producing a hearty snort that reminded me of all things L.A. Afterwards, Paula wiped her nose a bit with a slight smile and prodding eyes.

"Fuck it," I proclaimed.

"Yes, baby!"

Paula prepped a line for me with the same enthusiasm. She stood back, making room for my joy ride, as I walked into the available space, shook my head in hypocrisy, and then bent down to pay homage to the truth. All the storied memories came rushing back, harmoniously, burning my right nostril. When I rose from the ashes of a filthy baptism, every part of me was in mourning. With the rush of blood and stank of peer-pressure, I glanced at my reflection, in hatred.

"Ready to go back and deal with these selfish little boys," Paula joked. I held my head down with a smile, disguising the disgust.

"Our little boys," I answered. We walked the hallway, out to the backyard patio where the guys remained. Gavin glanced at me, knowing he fucked up. I looked away, but he decided to play coy, walking towards me for reconciliation.

"You all right?"

"I'm good."

Gavin didn't accept that. I was already floating to the sky, but I mustered the nerve to forgive, even though his misogyny stuck like Houston humidity. His comment reminded me of the assholes in L.A., the label execs, and no talent having White boys who spoke inappropriately around me with no regard for my feelings.

A few days later, on a Tuesday afternoon, Gavin was on the balcony grading papers while I grappled with the idea of coming clean. I walked onto the balcony and decided to reveal the past and speak of Charlotte. I took to the lounge chair next to him and sat quietly, waiting to be acknowledged.

"You still mad?"

Gavin took another puff from his stogie. His question lingered like the smoke he just blew. "I'm cool, but we need to talk about something." He repositioned himself in the lounge chair for the news to come.

"The other night, that comment you made was some real homophobic bullshit I'd expect from guys down here."

"Hold up, homophobic? I'm not homophobic."

"You're not? What was that shit, *I'm not crossing dicks with another dude?*"

"What? I ain't menaging with another dude, point-blank."

"I used to fuck with a chick in California, like, she was my girlfriend."

I paused to let those words sink in.

"So...are you Bi-? I mean, if you are..."

"I fell in love with a woman."

My tone was evident by his reaction. We were quiet, waiting for the other to speak.

"Honestly, I was talking out my ass that night. I'm not homophobic. I'm sorry for offending you." He waited for me to reply, but I remained quiet. He continued with, "So how long did this relationship last?"

I looked up, out at the cityscape, still thinking of Charlotte and how things used to be. The harshness of the breakup was silly, uncalled for, and initiated by an unwillingness to sacrifice an addiction to fame.

"It was long enough."

It would seem highly unlikely for a straight dude to pass up a chance with two women. If Gavin ever entertained the idea of a threesome, he blew it.

"That's why I was upset."

"Well, I'm not homophobic. I like what I like."

"So, another chick sleeping with us is cool, right?"

"Where's this going?"

He knew where I was going and chose to play dumb. Sadistically, I decided to believe him, even though I was momentarily embarrassed to love him. "Please," I fired back.

He smacked his lips, appearing to be frustrated before saying, "So what you want me to say? Yes, I've fantasized about being with two women, should I understand being with you and another nigga?"

As much as I disliked him at that moment, I appreciated his truth. The time would come, either by admission or luck, when I'd eventually have to talk of my son's custody, my history with drugs and alcohol, or that Charlotte could still get it. "I'm good man, I'm good," I spoke, as I walked back into the apartment. Surely, he questioned the likelihood of our relationship after that day. With stogie in hand, he re-lit it, leaned back, and crossed his legs.

We remained quiet for hours, separated only by the space of his 1,500 square foot apartment. The television blared on, blasting the theme music to *The Love Boat*, while a comfortable, cool breeze blew through the living room via the open balcony door. I lounged on the sofa with a nice glass of South African red, slightly pissed, but mature enough to stay put and figure things out. This was a benchmark in our relationship, our first real fight beyond a simple disagreement over tact and etiquette. This wasn't like the time he was taking a shit, and I walked in to get my hairbrush. No, this was the other side of love.

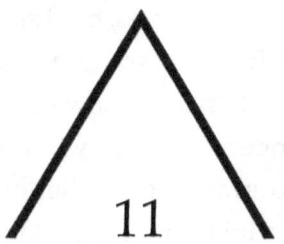

11

Let There Be Light

The springtime bliss of May 2009 was particular; Gavin and Clarissa had dated for over a year, growing leaps and bounds in exclusiveness. No longer living selfishly, their love for one another put them on pace with the world. With much discussion and deliberation, they purchased a townhome together, in the gentrified part of *Third Ward*, minutes from her childhood home. For friends and family, it was labeled a good investment, an easier explanation for shacking up.

Life was good; My latest book, *Cuff*, was steadily noticed by the right people and a broader audience. Clarissa also experienced a resurgence of her own. Within the year, she placed two jingles for major ad campaigns and three songs for recording artists on major labels.

Though the trial and error of monogamy had tried me, it was the catalyst to my rebirth. Being convicted, with no hesitation or reservation, I was ready to ask Clarissa for her hand in marriage. I would seek the blessing of Ezra Gentry, but first, the counsel of my dad.

"Hello, son," Faye answered, through the backdrop of running water. She was washing a head of cabbage at the kitchen sink, prepping for dinner. She would always start cooking at 6:45, something I never forgot. The nerves that bubbled in my gut made

me change my mind a million times, but I stayed. "I know you 'bout
to cook, huh?" I could hear her smiling, continuing to peruse the
cabbage, picking it apart as the lukewarm water flowed through
her weathered ladyfingers. A shallow Sunday eve, ripe with the
dawn of a purple and orange hue, she looked out the window,
over the backyard, reminiscent of the days when she would yell
out, "Gavin, get the table ready!"

"As always, son."

"How you been?"

"Blessed as always, and you?"

"I'm in a good space."

"Praise God…how's your friend, Marissa?"

"Clarissa. She's fine; I'm calling to let y'all know I'm planning
to propose."

"What!"

Immediately, the energy changed. Faye hollered for Dad in his
home office, replete with mounted degrees, awards, and annals
of law. Not much for a retired judge to do, he was either in his
decorated cave for hours or lulled by the serenity of a golf course.
My nervous energy and growing need for approval caused me to
be meticulous with my words. My father could be problematic and
quick to wrath by the peculiarities of mundane talk.

"Gavin."

"Hey, Dad."

Two months had passed since we last spoke. There was no beef;
we just didn't. After formalities, I wondered the words to come.
Judge Adams hated unnecessary phone calls. "I'm fine son…it's
been a while, huh?" The shade was standard, but my tolerance
was high.

"It has. Just promoting this new book."

"Busy is good."

The infrequency of his kindness made his words more valuable
than I'd care to admit. "Thank you, appreciate it." My voice
cracked like the time I asked, "Did mama tell you I defended my

dissertation" or "Did mama tell you I'm writing a book?" Even when Dad and I went silent, Faye was always the conduit.

"You ready to do this?"

"Yeah, that's why I called."

Taking a deep breath, I repositioned my phone and uncrossed my legs.

"What should I know?"

"How long y'all been going at it," Bradford asked.

Translated, he meant, *how long y'all been fucking?*

"It's been a year now."

Hopefully, he could respect the time I'd put in. He asked for mama's hand in half the time.

"You love her?"

"Yes, sir."

"That's all that matters."

"That's it?"

"Well...you sure you did enough fucking before you get married?"

We laughed, but Risa was enough. "One thing I'll tell you, son, if you don't do nothing else, always tell her the truth, rather she likes it or not."

I nodded as if sitting face to face with him, listening to a singular truth. "I will." My father's statement, as pure and direct, challenged me to remain vulnerable.

When it came time to woo Ezra, I mustered up two highly coveted playoff tickets for the *Rockets* versus *Lakers* game. My plan to impress him was unoriginal. But I scheduled a driver to take him to the Toyota Center.

For nearly twenty minutes, I waited outside, with the crowds, until a black Chevy Tahoe pulled up at the curb. The driver hurriedly stepped out and opened the door to reveal the Smokey Robinson look-alike, Mr. *"Lady-killer"* himself, Clarissa's daddy. When Ezra got out, he looked around with a slight dip in his stance, moving his body and head at the same damn time.

But when he spotted me, he flashed those pearly whites, bright enough to light up an evening sky. His bow-legged stride, weathered by time, was cleaner than a bill of health, with his jet black, short-cropped hair, and mustache, complemented by his matching mustard-colored linen short set and matching mock alligator sandals.

"Hey there, doc," Ezra gleefully greeted, while shaking my hand, with a slight brother hug to follow.

"Hey, Mr. Gentry, looking sharp tonight, don't get in trouble."

We turned towards the arena entrance, walking together like father and son, for the love of Risa.

"How was the ride?"

"Man, Jack, I could do that every day!"

"Me too…did you eat already?"

"Hazel cooked some healthy bullshit earlier…baked chicken and broccoli. I got high blood pressure, but I ain't worried; when the Lord says its time, it's time."

"After the game, we can get something."

"Yeah, man, Frenchy's be open late."

"Sounds like a plan; hopefully, these Rockets show up tonight."

Completely unauthentic, I was a Laker fan since childhood.

"Oh, you got the Rockets, doc?"

"They might do something; Kobe's a beast."

"Harden ain't no punk either. I got twenty says the Rockets take out the Lakers."

I thought it was innocent, knowing the Lakers would whip the Rockets ass anyway.

"Sure, I got twenty."

We walked into the massive lobby of the arena, fortunate to have seats a few rows behind the Rockets team bench, thanks to a couple strings I pulled. Again, impressed, Ezra spoke, "Man, Jack, I know you spent a pretty penny on these." I smiled at the unfolding of my masterful plan.

"Wanna beer, Mr. Gentry?"

The crowd was rapidly filling in, with the anticipation of the night, building.

"Make it a Heineken," he replied over the sound of techno music and the announcer in the background, announcing tip off in twenty minutes.

But by halftime, the Rockets had made it clear they'd come to play, and Ezra was beginning to talk shit. "I don't know doc, Kobe ain't here tonight." I just laughed, humored at the notion of him taking my funky twenty dollars. I didn't want to believe that Ezra could be petty, but I was prepared.

"It ain't over yet, we gone see," I replied.

But by the fourth quarter, the Houston Rockets were on their way to upsetting the Lakers. From time to time, Ezra looked over, petty as fuck, but I was amused. The Rockets beat the Lakers 99 to 87. The crowd erupted in shear hometown jubilation. My smile was broad, but I shrugged my shoulders as Ezra looked at me in shock.

"A bet is a bet." I shook my head, but he deferred the offer, responding, "How 'bout you cover my chicken, and we call it even."

Ezra reached his hand out, and a deal was struck. Moments later, coming down from the high, we waited for the crowd to disperse before making our exit. An hour later, we were standing in line at Frenchy's on Scott St. at 11:11PM, small talking about the game, but all the while I thought of the matter at hand. *Am I really about to ask for his daughter's hand on the patio at Frenchy's?* We were next at the register, both hungry and ready, despite Ezra's high blood pressure, and my standard of not eating after 9.

The young lady taking our order was visibly irritated about something, rolling her eyes and patting her head to avoid scratching freshly laid finger waves.

"Welcome to Frenchy's, can I take your order."

Ezra couldn't care less; "I'll take the five-wing special with some fries."

She input his order and asked, "What's your drink?"

Ezra, clearly not used to ordering fast food, asked, "What y'all got?" I cracked up, putting my head down to snicker.

The young lady smacked her lips before rattling off the available beverages, "*Coke, Sprite, Fanta…*"

Ezra listened intently until she mentioned *Dr. Pepper*; "I'll take that!"

He then stepped to the side for me to place my order, which took all of 3 seconds; "I'll have the same." The young lady rolled her eyes again. I paid, and we took the open table to wait for our orders.

"I still can't believe that game," Ezra said as he sat down. The warm breeze mixing with the aroma of hot grease and seasonings permeated the patio and set the mood for a comfortable, non-threatening conversation about the future. It seemed he genuinely liked me, more so for not being in the *business*. Maybe I represented permanence for once, a regular smart guy, not from L.A. and without any ulterior motive. I could be a savior.

"But you already know the Lakers gone win it all," I proclaimed.

"Maybe…is that another wager?"

"I'll check back after game 4."

We continued on, with Ezra discussing his days as a former janitor for the Houston Independent School District, nearly twenty-seven years. For him, retirement without his former work routine, made him complacent. "So, has my daughter got on your nerves yet?"

His question was a stark contrast. Just as I was preparing a diplomatic response, our order number was called out.

"I'll be right back," I answered.

I returned with a tray full of fried, crispy goodness. After placing the food down and getting situated, I felt it appropriate to proceed with the plan, but not before asking Ezra if he'd pray over the food.

"Dear God, we thank you for this food, and we ask that it be a blessing and nourish our bodies, in Jesus name we pray, Amen."

We began to tend to the business at hand, with our senses heightened and the fear of cholesterol, overruled. While Ezra sifted through his plate, I began. "Mr. Ezra, I gotta admit, I invited you out for another reason. I'd like to ask you something."

Ezra, being unaware, said, "Shoot doc."

"You know Clarissa and I have been dating a while now…"

"Yeah doc, you good?" He asked with a chuckle that followed.

"Very much so…I'd like the honor of having your blessing."

A look of astonishment washed over his face. He was speechless a few seconds, with nothing but the shine of those pearly white veneers in pure joy.

"Are you serious, my man?" The awkwardness was no longer the location in which I chose to tell him, but rather, the angle in which Ezra tried to hug me. A few patrons that sat nearby hadn't a clue what the celebration was for, but infectiously smiled. I was no longer anxious or nervous, thanks to Ezra.

"So, does this mean I have your blessing, sir?"

"Son, you have my blessing, as long as you pray about it."

Immediately, I became pensive, curious of his concern.

"Yes sir, been praying for a while, is there anything I should…"

"No, no, not like that. Risa been through a lot, that's all. Hazel and I prayed that girl through some things. That show business life ain't for everybody."

I gave a nod, but the ambiguity remained.

"As long as you love my daughter, unconditionally, you have my blessing, doc."

"I do Mr. Gentry, unconditionally."

"Honestly, Jack, you're good for her, you balance her out. She's happier, more focused than ever before. That's gotta be you, doc."

I smiled, even though I remained curious.

"Thank you, and I promise to do right by her, you, and Mrs. Gentry."

Ezra flashed those pearly whites once more and said, "Damn, I forgot, I gotta tell Hazel."

After driving out to Sugar Creek, to drop Ezra off, driving home was quiet and filled with ambition. In preparation, one matter came to mind; *the perfect proposal to Clarissa Gentry.* First and foremost, it had to have an element of fab, the kind expected for a worldly woman. It crossed my mind to reach out to the band, maybe even Denise for a softer touch, knowing I'd need the assistance of her inner circle to pull this off.

I contemplated location, dinner, music, presentation, and undoubtedly, color, clarity, cut, and carat. All I cared about was creating the perfect scenario, in which she'd say yes. *What day should I ask her?* She had a gig coming up the following Wednesday, which meant rehearsal on Tuesday and pre-game prep yoga on Monday. *Maybe after her set, yes!* But quickly, the thought of it was risky, especially in a room full of strangers. I couldn't live through the embarrassment of her saying no.

The more I thought about it, Friday seemed best. When she wasn't gigging on Fridays, we went to bars or dives in Midtown and the Heights, or whatever trumped-up trendy spot, hot for the moment. And then it hit me, *Tommy Tio's.* That was the first time we went out at night, dancing under the influence of alcohol and sharing the incidentals of our lives. The widgets in my mind began to turn, as a Mariachi band came to mind, just before getting on one knee and popping the question. *Is that corny, too predictable?*

Even though she loved and cared for me, quite possibly, my proposal, if done wrong, could represent an awkward end to our relationship. I knew Clarissa's innate ability to read bullshit well, and thus came the urgency to cross the t's and dot the i's.

In the twilight of the night, I laid restless, eyes darting back and forth, scanning the flashes of intermittent light from the bedroom windows, and the hum of the ceiling fan, with a million thoughts. The scenarios changed from the simpleness of Tommy Tio's to the lush grounds of Hermann Park.

By Wednesday morning, I settled on the restaurant for sentimental reasons. It made sense as a decoy. I'd gone to a jeweler on Monday, at the suggestion of a colleague whom I trusted. With her guidance, I decided on a one-carat solitaire cut, VS1, invisible set diamond ring. Proud of my $3,200 purchase, I forged ahead with the conceptualization of Friday.

Tuesday afternoon, I decided to call up Denise after snooping through Clarissa's phone to get the number.

"Hello?"

"Hey, Denise, its Gavin."

"Gavin? How did you get my number? Is Risa all right?"

"Risa's fine, we good. I ah…stole your number, I need help with something."

"You stole my number? What's up," she answered with a slight chuckle.

"I'm going to ask Risa to marry me."

I remained silent, gauging Denise's temperament.

"Oh my God, Gavin…for real, when?!"

"I'm torn between tomorrow and Friday. She's performing tomorrow night, but I'm skittish on doing it at the show, she might feel ambushed, feel me?"

"What does your heart say?"

"I was thinking about this restaurant, where we had our first dinner date; it would be nice to have you and other friends and family there."

"That sounds sweet, did you get the ring yet? That's the most important part, buddy."

"One-carat solitaire, invisible set…"

"Okay…Friday at the restaurant, I'll take care of the rest, give me a time."

"Really? Oh shit, okay, um, I'm thinking 8, nothing too late."

"9 is sexier, and see if they can arrange some privacy."

With just three days, six hours and nineteen minutes left, a proposal loomed, but being denied weighed heavily on my soul. Clarissa's predictable unpredictability had become commonplace and legendary. I considered the time I bought her a bouquet of roses, only to receive a contrived smile, or the whisperings of sweet nothings in her ear, reciprocated with granules of affection. Oddly, something simple as me fixing her a bowl of *Fruit Loops* in cold 2% milk on a lazy Saturday morning, could end up being head in bed.

My fear went beyond the doubtful thoughts that cripple fate. I called Tommy Tio's to speak with a manager for reservations and a private room for ten to fifteen. I wasn't sure if they even had a private room but remained hopeful. Afterward, I would call Clarissa.

When I called, my gut burned deep with anxiety, as if preparing to die. Looking at the ceiling in my office, I sat uncomfortably in my chair trying to psyche myself out, listening to the ringing that seemed to go on forever. After the third ring, I hoped she wouldn't answer.

"Hey," she answered groggy, waking from a nap. Stunned and nearly at a loss for words, I replied, "You got plans Friday?" The abruptness of my question was optimistic. It sparked curiosity, but not enough to prod.

"No, not right now…a vacation would be nice. You wanna take me on vacation?"

"Where you wanna go?"

"Wherever there's a beach…and a fucking strawberry daiquiri."

A destination wedding instantly came to mind, but where?

"Hold on a second." She took another call, while I waited nearly forty seconds to hear, "Hey, don't be mad, we just got booked for Friday at the *Sky Bar*." The randomness of it fucked up a plan.

"Oh, okay," I answered. The burn that once swelled in my stomach turned to a lump of fire in my throat. Nevertheless, having a sense of resolve, *all things destined would be by the will of God and me.* "I'll be there."

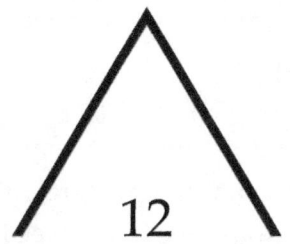

12

A Ram in the Bush

Classic *Luther*, *Prince*, and *Tina Marie* filled the upper room on a Friday night in Scott Gertner's Sky Bar. Thirty to forty-somethings, ranging from the stylishly bougie to the helplessly soulful, dressed to impress and hopefully hook up.

DJ Spruce rocked the crowd, while Clarissa sat in the back with the boys and a bottle of *Jack*, like any other time before a performance. But tonight was odd; she could feel it in her gut.

A thin film of sweat began to bead on her forehead, and for a moment, she distracted herself with thoughts of Bobby and their phone call, minutes earlier. Hearing the crackle of his voice was always enough.

Meanwhile, Gavin surveilled the joint, making sure everything was in play. He committed to a Friday proposal, following the band's performance. Up till that time, he and Denise planned for the execution of it all.

First, Hazel needed to remain quiet 'til after he proposed. She talked too damn much. Secondly, the band needed to be in the know, so they could play *"Ribbon in the Sky,"* as he approached the stage.

Getting close friends and family to commit to an abrupt Friday show was exact to pulling teeth. Ezra and Hazel were never the ones for late nights past 9PM and the 610 freeway. This occasion was worthy of pomp and circumstance, for merely knowing Clarissa's history with men.

Gavin was considerably a ram in the bush, a blessing in disguise. Hazel thought of him that way as a prayer answered. The wealth of his character, his pedigree, was good for Clarissa. No more were the random calls in the wee hours of distress, with Risa sobbing, "Mama, I'm tired..."

Of the many melodramas of Clarissa's life, Charlotte had been an outstanding tragedy. The revelation of Charlotte put Hazel on the edge of heartbreak when she overheard the commotion of a late-night phone call, filled with tears and curse words.

"I'm sick of this shit seriously, every time, it's about you. And still with the questions, though? Wow, Charlotte, we lived together and shared a bed!" Stunned by the admission, Hazel stood still. She immediately began rebuking the devil, pleading the blood, on the verge of a meltdown. With her hand over her mouth and eyes closed, the tranquility of her home had rocked. She remained outside the bedroom door, in the shadows of faint light, crushed by her daughter's choice in love.

The night Ezra told Hazel of Gavin's proposal plan, she cried from the depths of a mother's soul, redeemed. She was excitable in the audience, waiting for the noise of secular music, and the unsaved, with their glasses of liquor, to come to an end—the anticipation of engagement overshadowed filth.

I sat nervously, my right leg bouncing offbeat. At one point, Hazel, who sat beside me, offered a consoling pat to my back with a smile. But nothing could soothe this uncontrollable edginess. This manifestation was beautifully terrifying; I could drop the ring.

More curiously, I wondered what Clarissa would think, seeing Ezra, Hazel, Denise, and other close folks in the audience, without forewarning, much less, an invitation. Making a significant life decision, on stage, was the last thing to come to mind.

When Clarissa and band came forth, the lighting in the room scattered her vision, especially by the glare directly overhead.

The band members got in place, while the DJ continued rocking. "Risa...Risa!" Hazel called out. Clarissa immediately blocked the lights to discover her mother, father, Denise, and I sitting at the same table, just a few feet away. Of course, she immediately thought, *what the fuck?*

The dots didn't connect. Her mother and father hadn't been to a show in two years; *da fuck?* It was no one's birthday, no one's anniversary, nothing; *why tonight?* With a hearty smile and wave, she walked over and hugged all four of our necks, pleasantly surprised, at a gig. Maybe she was thinking, *this motherfucker is not proposing to me tonight.*

But yes, the unexpected, lucid eloquence of an occasion, was a marriage proposal. I hoped it could be a conceivable reason to love me for the rest of her life. So, if I proposed, hopefully, she'd act surprised, well up with tears of joy with her hands over her mouth, me on bended knee, and say, "Yes."

From the first downbeat to the melodic *Fender Rhodes* keyboard, Clarissa stood before us, forever the consummate professional. It was ironic to propose at a performance, thinking back to the night of the gala. This moment was unthinkable a year ago.

I doubted everything when we started. She scraped my soul clean, and I tried forgetting her. Curiosity prevailed, and I realized my entire adult life heavily relied on charm. My only substance had been the blessing of an upper-middle-class childhood, and my acceptance by White academia and the literary world. But did I know how to love?

Time and patience answered all things. I learned Clarissa's quirks, her unrelenting hate of food touching other food on her plate, the buttons to push when she went diva mode, and to some degree, the demons that still haunted her. But most of all, Bobby liked me. From our first phone conversation, he understood that his mom had a new friend.

As the set played on, melodies and applause rang out, and I lost myself in the music. Aside from Hazel's annoying smiles and pats on the arm and back, my nerves got the best of me. Every song she sang, affirmed that the end was near.

"Is everybody all right tonight?" she asked, with a million-dollar smile, hands raised, with more beads of sweat. Forty minutes in, she was preparing to wrap the show with her signature rendition of Shirley Murdock's *"As We Lay."* Prepped and ready, I knew just as soon as she hit that last high note, I was to get up, walk towards the stage, and once in front of her, I would drop to one knee and propose.

"Hey y'all, we got some special people here tonight, and it ain't even my birthday." Hazel chuckled, with another tap to my knee. "First and foremost, please show some love for my parents right here, sitting near the front, looking all good; Daddy, how you get Mama to come out this late, you know this ain't no place for a child of God." Again, the crowd laughed along with Ezra as Hazel shook her head and smiled. "Sitting right next to them, is my very best friend in the world, since sophomore year at Jack Yates y'all...show my girl Denise some love." More applause followed as the band continued playing softly in the background. My nerves were shot by now. The anticipation overshadowed the proposal.

"Sitting by Niecy is my boo thang for over a year, and that's a personal best for me, y'all." My anxious energy came to a head in a singular moment like this, dangerous, freeing, and ambiguous. "Y'all, please show love for my boyfriend." Oddly, it sounded like an introduction to the stage. The band knew to begin playing *"Ribbon in the Sky"* after Clarissa finished the set, but to me, I was summoned to a proposal. In a flash of absent-mindedness, I stood up and began walking, wholly committed, and numb. Titus looked at me like *what the fuck?* Even Clarissa was stuck. The crowd cheered as if being in on the plan, but to me, it was just us in the room.

"Babe, you okay?" Clarissa asked over the microphone, as I slowly approached her. I just smiled, at a loss for words, but more abrupt was the band's immediate transition to *"Ribbon in the Sky."*

Clarissa looked back with her hands on her hip, befuddled as fuck. "Y'all just gone go to Stevie?" I walked, painfully rigid with boyish charm. When I finally stood in front of her, I leaned in for a kiss, then kneeled to one knee. The audience erupted, some rising to their feet, all with praise.

I was feeling the pulse of the rhythm on my entire right side. I fumbled to grab the ruby red velvet, ring box in my side pocket. She put her hands over her mouth in disbelief, with genuine tears that welled for the changing tide. In those secret places, she wondered if the day would ever come, someone committing to her, and her shit. God knows Clarissa did things to piss me off. But I hung in there like a pledge.

When I held the jewelry box in my hand, the sounds of the audience against the soft melodic backdrop of the band, seemed to drown out my proposal. I could only laugh and look at them until making a hand gesture to quiet down. Hazel shed tears, engrossed in this joyous fanfare. Ezra clapped his hands, with a hoot and a holler, shining those pearly whites. Denise was emotional, not for the usual bluster of marriage proposals, but for knowing her girl. It was redemption for the years of bullshit wrapped in fame. Maybe now Bobby could have a family, and I could make this house a home.

"Clarissa Gentry…will you marry me?"

"Oh my God, …yes."

A roar followed. I rose, beaming with pride, evident by an unadulterated French kiss. My right arm was wrapped firmly around Clarissa's back, with her leaning her body weight onto me. For a glimpse, I felt the wash of celebratory admiration, standing next to the former R&B star.

"I thought I was gonna faint," I leaned and whispered in her ear.

She just looked up and smiled, replying, "You got me good, dude."

After what felt like five minutes of straight applause, we walked off stage into the audience to be greeted by family, friends, and strangers, all vying for the chance to say congratulations. For the days ahead, we lived a new narrative; engaged.

Clarissa and Denise shared livelier conversations, with phone calls that went for hours, in the hopes of creating the most memorable extravaganza she could've never imagined. "Bitch, what color is your dress gone be," Denise joked.

I, on the other hand, was less vocal but excited. I shared with Miguel, who sat behind his ram shacked desk, replete with stacks of papers and a giant *Starbucks* cup half-filled with lukewarm latte.

"Hey, you got a minute?" I asked while knocking on his door.

"What's up," he answered, swiveling around in his black leather chair.

I hadn't told Miguel of any plans leading up to the proposal for fear of being swayed by the logic of a disgruntled married man. Miguel wasn't much of a proponent of marriage, especially when making vile remarks about Paula or flirting with the department administrative assistant.

"Yeah man…ah, just wanted to let you know, I popped the question this weekend."

"Get the fuck out of here, yeah? Congratulations, man, she said yes, right?"

"Of course, she did."

"Wow, you bagged a superstar," he responded. "Set a date yet?"

"I just proposed Friday…I can't even think that far ahead."

"How do you feel? I mean, man, you ready to do this?"

For some reason, his tone struck a chord. At thirty-six years of age, and with all my life experiences, for this one thing, I hadn't prepared. Even with parents who'd been married over thirty years, my father's infidelities made me doubt my ability to do right.

"Miguel, I've whored around, excuse me, *hoed* around, for the better part of my adult life, and I can honestly say, without a doubt, she's the one."

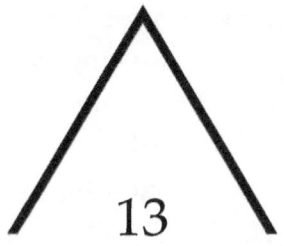

13

The Truth Shall set Them Free

"Whatever you do, don't be sloppy, you know you sloppy," Denise advised. I confided in Niecy, all the secrets of my life, even the shit with Charlotte, causing her to ask, "Did you eat her out?"

No topic was off-limits, and for that reason, I confessed, "I love him, but I want Bobby back too."

It sounded calculated and soulless. "You not getting married for Bobby, right?" I was quiet, clear on every word she spoke, but reluctant to answer.

"It ain't even like that. I love Gavin. I just want my son back; we can be a family now." I paused, for some snap ass reply from Denise, while reaching for the bottle of Merlot. Truth and alcohol, a dangerous blend, could be the misunderstanding and the potential downfall to any friendship.

"And how am I sloppy, though?" Denise walked away, mindful of a blowup. "Nah, bitch, how am I sloppy?"

Denise took the bait, walking back into the kitchen, and simply stating, "Charlotte, bitch." Denise walked away again, while I shook my head in disbelief, but speechless.

Back in 2004, on a September Saturday morning, driving down La Cienega Boulevard, I had the top down on my brand-new silver *Lexus* convertible, under the beam of a Fall sun. Charlotte and I were fiending for *Roscoe's Chicken & Waffles* after a vigorous fuck, thirty minutes prior. On the armrest, our hands clasped together, a supposed look of love. Yet, it wasn't until we reached the restaurant parking lot, that the fragile things about us, begin to break.

Charlotte reached for my hand, a small gesture of love symbolizing a two-month relationship, with one month of that being nightly sleepovers. But I pulled away, different from the earlier moments in the car. She was stunned, but courteous and calm, as I played dumb. When we were seated, and alone, she asked, "What was that?" I had a look of indifference.

"What was what?" Charlotte rolled her eyes and smacked her lips, leaning back in her chair, fucked up.

It was from that point on, she questioned the truth, and our situation. Charlotte had fallen while I was simply taking refuge. For months, love remained in the shadows by managers protecting a brand—the effort to keep things quiet, from paparazzi, fucked with Charlotte's sensibilities. For the times that she licked away the pain, with her sensuality and care, for all the moments alone wiping tears away, I was dismissive that day at Roscoe's.

Throughout our relationship, when the fun and exploration faded, I saw the writing on the wall, but Charlotte read it before the ink could dry. Fed up with my demands, Charlotte selfishly and courageously, bailed without warning. I came home to a note on the kitchen counter after being on the road a few days.

Dear Clarissa,

This was supposed to be a face to face conversation, but fuck it, maybe I'm scared, or just tired. We've been masquerading for you, and I know you have a public life, but I'm not ready to live like a mistress with someone I love. Your career is important, Bobby is important, but how long do you get to play with me, like I enjoy being secondary? What would you do, be honest? Why aren't you risking it all, especially for someone who has been with you through the bullshit? I know Jacob is a piece of

shit and having an openly gay relationship may not be high on
your list of priorities, but I wish you well, I love you, and I regret
it came to this

    I still love you, Risa,

    Charlotte

My way was always unfinished and broken, customary of the pain and regret in my adult life. Even with success, I didn't belong to anyone, to be loved forever. Fans could only fill the void of acceptance, but never take away the hurt of being alone. However, Denise was concerned with my growth. Denise thought Gavin was right for me, despite thinking he was suspect.

I considered my BFF's words, agreeing that perhaps, I was full of shit. I walked into the living room where Denise sat, looking through her timeline, and asked, "Why you think Imma hurt him? Charlotte ain't the same; this a real situation."

"I know you think that, and I know you have a love for him, but do you love Gavin, like, for real, for real?"

I made a face to her audacity. "Do I love him, why you keep asking me that?" It was awkward, but I smirked and shook my head again, followed by silence.

"You need to tell him you want Bobby back; it's only fair. Besides, what if he doesn't want kids?"

"Denise, they talk on the phone, Bobby likes him, Gavin knows I have a son…"

"But does he know why Bobby's with Jacob and not you?"

"When the time comes, bitch."

"All right…that's what I'm saying, sloppy."

For hours, we sat on the living room floor, drinking more Merlot and listening to *Chaka*, reminiscing about life at Yates, but a question lingered on; why did I leave L.A.? The embarrassment of falling from grace was not enough to leave a 5-year-old boy behind. Inevitably, time would've healed my despair, but fame had spoiled me. I could no longer be 10 ft. tall in southern California, much less the record industry. At least in Houston, I could hide from regret and reacquaint myself with life.

The next day, after seeing Denise off to De Soto, I made a call to Gavin, hoping to chat about the wedding, but more so, the matter of Bobby Finch. In my mind, I rationalized, that previous conversations with him about children, and the idea of making a family, were fair game.

"Babe," he answered playfully.

"Babe, let's get lunch; we need to start talking about wedding plans."

"I proposed Friday…"

"Yeah, but the sooner, the better; nothing major…like, where do we want the wedding, how many people are we thinking of inviting."

"I think we should have it in Jamaica, on the beach, what you think?"

"It's an idea."

"We could kill two birds with one stone; wedding and honeymoon, right?"

"Hmmm, interesting."

"Is that corny?"

"No…let's make a list first, your family, my family, my friends, your friends."

Hours later, when we finally met at Tommy Tio's for customary rounds of frozen margaritas, no salt, chips, and queso, and our combination plates of choice, he figured it a carefree Wednesday, with no idea of what his fiancé had planned. I would ease into the topic, being mindful that the climate had to be right, after his second drink.

"So, Bobby…" Gavin began to nod his head, following my words with a slurp from the last of his cup. He continued looking into my eyes, unsure. "I've been thinking about us, as a family, and what that would look like." Gavin remained quiet, with an inkling of an idea. He assumed it was about the wedding and how I wanted Bobby in it, but my tone changed. "We've talked about him…I don't wanna pressure you or make you feel obligated, but I'm sincere about wanting my son back in my life full time."

Gavin continued nodding his head in agreement. "I understand."

I hoped he could imagine fatherhood, chastisement, Saturday morning haircuts, and Pop Warner football games in the Fall. Maybe Bobby and I were the missing pieces to his life, and for that, he could appreciate the proposal. And yet, Jacob Finch, the "A-list" actor, with his probable big-time lawyers willing to fuck up a good thing, lingered somewhere in the backdrop.

"I'm not opposed to him living with us," he offered.

"Wow, that was easy."

"Why would I have a problem?"

"I mean…"

"How could I love you and have a problem with him," he interjected.

Right then and there, the last of a wall surrounding my heart began to crumble. I looked at Gavin, believing this was finally true love.

"But what about dude?" He added.

And just like that, the warm, fuzziness of the previous moment was broken by the reality of sole custody. I looked at him, wishing to say *'shut the fuck up,'* but he was right. Jacob held all the cards.

"I don't know…I don't care, I want my son."

"Didn't mean to be a Debbie downer."

"It's okay, you're right."

Gavin motioned for our waiter, "Can we get another round, please."

I appreciated his gesture, but no matter how buzzed I felt, the truth was more sobering. For the remaining time, we continued sitting, conversing, pretending that all would be well, with nothing more than the joy of impending nuptials. When the next round came to the table, Gavin lifted his glass and said, "Like my mom always says, leave it in God's hands."

Besides the hoopla of wedding plans, we agreed on *Wheeler Avenue Baptist Church*, as a plan B. Of course, Denise would be matron of honor, and Miguel, the best man. All we needed was a date.

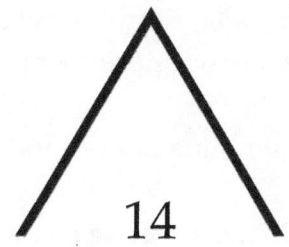

14

Prodigal Son

Christmas plans with Bobby gave me life. After talking with Jacob about Gavin, we arranged to have my son brought to my Venice Beach hotel by 11 that morning, Christmas Day.

We laid in bed with the TV quietly playing in the background, and a nine o'clock beam of sunlight peeking through a drawn curtain.

For the many months of long-distance phone calls, this time, Bobby was meeting his future step-daddy.

Gavin wanted to make a good first impression, thinking of what to say, and how cool it needed to sound.

"You wanna hit a mall or something, right quick?"

"Awe, look at new stepdad."

"Whatever."

"We usually go to the mall; he picks what he wants."

"Oh, …okay."

"What?"

"Where's the element of surprise?"

"At the register."

"You mind if I get him something?"

The vetting stage was over, but he continued proving to me why he belonged in Bobby's life.

"That's cool."

Thirty minutes later, after showers and bagels, he grabbed his laptop, looking for the perfect gift for a nine-year-old kid. "Does he like sports-related stuff or video games?" He feared Bobby's reaction, imagining the rolling of eyes and the smacking of lips, at a shitty gift.

"He loves Harry Potter, anything Harry Potter."

"Hmm," Gavin answered.

"He's a nerd."

"No, it's cool, I'm just, like, those are some big ass books, he reads all that?"

"My boy is a serious nerd."

"Cool…hope Jacob ain't beat us to it."

"This is why we go to the mall."

"Touché."

By noon, Jacob called, saying he arrived; I instructed him to meet us in the lobby.

"Hey, we're here."

"We're sitting to the left when you walk in."

"Oh, you and your man?"

"You're such a fucking cornball, bye," I answered, after waiting an hour.

Five minutes later, They walked in. Jacob had the look of a bona fide, Hollywood prick, with his $200 messy haircut, plain black *Versace* t-shirt, and tapered jeans. He flashed a smile and removed his *Ray-Bans*. Bobby's eyes lit up when he saw me, running and jumping into my arms. Gavin and Jacob's eyes glanced, with polite head nods.

"What's up Bobby birdie," I called.

"Mom," Bobby complained.

I fawned over him, as Gavin witnessed the embodiment of a mother's love. Instantly, he understood everything.

"Guys, this is Gavin, my fiancé." Bobby walked towards him with an outreached hand, as an official welcome.

"Nice to finally meet you, Gavin."

Gavin smiled while shaking his hand, "Nice to meet you as well." Jacob stood off in the distance, arms crossed with a plastered smile to his face.

"When are you getting married, mom?" A classic Bobby moment, when tact was unnecessary, I looked at Gavin and smiled, hunching my shoulders.

"Bobby, tone it down," Jacob commanded.

"All right, buddy, I'm outta here…I'll come back around 8ish?"

"Make it 10, it's been a while," I shot back.

Jacob stood in silent protest with his head bent, but I hadn't seen Bobby since last summer. The least he could do was be gracious. Gavin looked sheepishly away, opting to reach for his phone, checking for notifications.

"Fine, call me at 9 when you're heading back. Bobby, I'll see you later behave."

"Bye, Dad."

"Nice meeting you," he offered to Gavin.

Jacob dashed out the door, like a scene from one of his movies, and here we stood, a newly constructed family, in L.A.

"Y'all hungry? We gotta get something to eat."

"I ate already," Bobby answered.

"You don't want *In-N-Out Burger*? What about you, mommy," Gavin asked.

"Mommy does, but who's buying?"

Both Gavin and Bobby raised their hands.

Hours later, after hitting the Beverly Center, spending $481.09 on three items, and going to *In-N-Out Burger* as promised, we decided to stroll the promenade at *Fisherman's Wharf*. Back when Bobby was a toddler, Jacob and I would wear disguises to shake the paparazzi, for long walks down the beach at dawn. It was a simpler time when the world was full of love.

Bobby walked between Gavin and me, looking the part of a family. The vibe was chill enough for Bobby to ask, "Are you gonna have another kid?"

I looked down at him, concealing my shock with laughter and spoke, "Bobby!"

Gavin, not being bothered, continued to stroll, and smiled, answering, "Your mother is the best."

"The best what," he giggled.

"Bobby!"

"Your mother is the best at picking boogers!"

"C'mon man, that's gross," Bobby remarked.

"That was gross, Gavin."

"I don't know about y'all, but I want some ice cream now."

"Me too, mom, can we get some ice cream?"

We continued walking a few minutes more, before spotting an ice cream shop up ahead. When we arrived, Bobby immediately rushed to the front to explore the flavors behind the glass encasement. Gavin spotted an open table and grabbed it.

"What flavor you want?"

"Peaches and cream."

After receiving our orders, we sat together, looking like an instant family in an unfamiliar space. Gavin seemed peaceful with this 'family day out,' but I wondered how our lives in Houston would play.

"So, Bobby, what if you came to live with us in Houston?"

"I can?"

"I mean, do you want to? We have to ask daddy first."

Gavin sat quietly, listening to the conversation. Nearly a year went by before telling him about the DUI and the custody case. The vulnerability in my eyes told him everything. Exposing my episodes with cocaine and binge drinking, and losing my son because of it, felt naked. He won't admit it, but he judged me. For a time, he seemed more withdrawn, and his words, sharper. So, I snapped one day.

"Hey, if what I told you made you uncomfortable, or like, I'm unfit to be with you or whatever, let's stop this whole thing now before we get too deep." Had he left, it would've crushed me.

"You could even be my best man at the wedding," Gavin added.

"Okay, but can I wear a tuxedo?"

"What color," I asked

"Plaid. And mom, your dress could be black."

Gavin and I looked at each other, speechless; this was too easy.

"Let mommy think about it, okay?"

One week later, I was finally meeting the Adams, as sort of a tour before the wedding. Unlike Gavin and Bobby, who spoke a few times on the phone, Faye and I hadn't. The level of anticipation was probably different between us. I thought of our meeting as nothing more than proper Christian formality, while Faye may have felt that I wasn't even a Christian. Surely she dug through my resume. The scandal-ridden articles about my infamous night on Sunset were plenty. Bradford, on the other hand, was probably more proud of the piece of ass his son snagged.

We flew to Cincinnati, a day after New Year's, to his old neighborhood. It was a beautiful backdrop of moonlight shinning over a modest, two-story home on Oak Knoll Dr., with white Christmas lights sprawled along the front of the house. The lawn was probably well-manicured under a layer of snow, with coned shaped bushes peppered with icicles, leading to the front door. This tree-lined street was all the things my upbringing was not. I wondered about his childhood from the moment we stepped out of the taxi. Where was his corner store, and had he ever experienced the ungodly goodness of a jumbo pickle with a peppermint stick in the middle? Or did he ever slap box in the street, under the burn of a hot July? Nah, this was some Cosby shit.

Gavin hadn't been home in quite a while; as a matter of fact, his last time was just before meeting me. He blamed obligations, like speaking engagements and book signings. In fact, had it not been for our commitment, he might've found a reasonable excuse. But on this night, January 2nd, he was accompanied by his future wife. He prepared for all the stories Faye would tell of his awkward adolescence, over her world-class chicken and dumplings, a New Year's dinner tradition. He also prepared for his father's slick mouth.

"Hello," Faye answered in a sing-song tone, opening the door.

"Hey, Mom," Gavin replied as they hugged.

I stood patiently, waiting in 43° weather, studying Faye's face; *she looks like Nancy Wilson.*

"And the superstar..." Faye continued.

"Hello, Mrs. Adams, finally nice to meet you," I offered, as we hugged.

When our eyes met, there was an honesty between us, a sisterly understanding of some kind, even if she had suspicions of me.

"Where's Dad?"

"Right here," Bradford answered, coming from behind the door.

They hugged like old friends.

"How was your flight?"

"Relaxed...Dad, this is Clarissa."

"Well, well, young Diana, how are you, miss lady?"

Bradford instantly turned into a flirtatious mess. I'm sure he searched my digital resume, admiring my choreography and scantily clad choices in clothing. All I could do was laugh.

"Welcome to Adams' manor, and Happy New Year."

"Thank you for having me; same to you."

Without being obvious, I looked around, thinking of my own family, wishing to smell the stale leftovers of my father's *Newports* mixed with *pine-sol*, and whatever grease from whatever pork in the frying pan that night. But I understood the importance of meeting his parents.

"Gavin honey, take you and your fiancée's things to your room, the chicken and dumplings are just about done, get comfy, you're home now."

Gavin looked slightly shocked like *we sleeping in the same bed?* In Adams' manor, young ladies of any kind, in his room, under their roof, was make-believe. His A.M.E. mother and woman of God, Faye

Marianne Adams, established an understanding years ago, when she walked in on him, jacking off to a *Jet Magazine* 'Beauty of the Week'.

And still, I'm sure he considered all the sexual shit he could do, under his *Magic Johnson, Larry Bird* Converse poster on the wall above his twin-sized bed. Looking around his room, you could see the memories and all the years of crumpled *Kleenex*.

Meanwhile, back in the family den, left of the kitchen, as Faye prepped the finishing touches to dinner, I was surrounded and sunken, into a plush and worn brown leather sofa, watching a rerun of "227". Bradford sat relaxed in his recliner, caddy-cornered to me, legs kicked up, with gray tube socks that showed the bulging outline of bunions. His careless demeanor spoke of his prolific legal career, retirement, and golf on Tuesdays with a former mayor. He didn't give a fuck who *Renee* was; this was his got damn house.

Faye moved with ease, setting the table for first impressions. Her classic blue enamel pot simmered of seasonings like paprika, onion powder, and bay leaves, presumably from her mama's Greensboro, South Carolina recipe. A golden-brown pan of cornbread sat on the counter with a whiff of buttery lust, waiting to be devoured late into the evening.

"Is it cold enough for ya?" Bradford asked, breaking the ice.

"Colder than usual, for a southern girl."

"Yeah...last week, we had almost two feet of snow; I told Faye, baby...I need you to keep me warm at least one of these nights." It was awkward humor, leaving me no other choice but to look amused.

"My, my, hope she came through."

Just then, Gavin walked into the room, at the tail end of Bradford's crassness.

"What he say?"

"Oh, I was telling her how I made your mama shovel the driveway and sidewalk last week when that blizzard hit."

"Don't believe that; Faye ain't shoveled snow since '76."

With empty laughter and small talk, I wished for the warmth and comfort of a bed, any bed, with Gavin beside me. I'd grown accustomed to the contour of his body and body heat, my secret lullaby. Discreetly, I looked at pictures on the wall, on the mantle, some of him, and the Adams as a family. It pleased me to see other moments to this man, as the layers began to fade. I even giggled at a photo of a pimpled-face Gavin, with a *Jheri curl*, braces, in a red and blue striped *Le Tigre* polo. In another photo, Faye was rocking those ungodly, over-sized prescription frames, in a teal-colored, ruffle neck dress with pearls.

Gavin sat down beside me on that twenty-plus-year-old couch, slightly awestruck. Renee was in his mama's house, and hopefully, his bed. "You all right, babe?" he asked lovingly. From the look on my face, he could tell I was tired and ready for bed, but I trooped along.

"I'm good...I'm ready for this chicken and dumplings!"

Not even a minute later, Faye called out, "let's eat!"

We sat around the dining table, under a dimly lit, old-fashioned brass chandelier, popular for the early 90s. An odd yellowish, floral wallpaper surrounded the room, accompanied by a polished Cherrywood dining set and curio they purchased in 1988. They were the thriftiest of people, something that never passed down to Gavin. Bradford was so cheap, he'd cut open toothpaste tubes, after being curled for a week. He only bought American made cars for him and Faye, every ten years. They only went on vacation once a year, and out for dinner twice a month. In some ways, the divide that persisted between father and son was Gavin's expensive taste.

"Gavin, honey, will you say grace?" Faye asked.

"Make it quick," Bradford followed.

We all grabbed hands, bowed heads, as Gavin said his trusty dinner prayer.

"Dear God, we thank you for this food that we are about to receive. We ask that you bless it to our health and bodies and that you bless the hands that prepared it, in Jesus' name, we pray, Amen."

"Amen, pass the fiddles."

"Guest first, Brad."

Faye served me a hunk of cornbread, followed by a healthy helping of chicken and dumplings. I began thinking of the last time my parents and I sat down for dinner, at an actual dinner table, and not T.V. trays. I could understand his bougie ass ways, even more.

"So, Clarissa, what's your family's traditional dish for the holidays?" Faye asked. I looked up, thinking, *what do we do?* Then I thought about Christmas time, and how daddy and I would sing carols all day, into the evening. Or how on New Year's, mama would cook black-eyed peas with ham hocks, while *Bobby Womack, The Isley Brothers,* and *Earth, Wind & Fire* played on.

"Mom loves cooking black-eyed peas, New Year's Day."

"Oh, I love black-eyed peas, especially with turkey necks, girl," Faye replied.

"When's the last time you cooked black eye peas?" Brad asked.

"And when's the last time you cooked," she shot back.

"Game, set and match," Gavin joked.

I continued being polite, smiling when necessary, a chuckle here and there. I even enjoyed the downhome savory taste of Faye's dish, immediately thinking of home. Right now, I'd be sitting on the kitchen counter, while mama whipped up a grilled cheese sandwich for me. I was thankful for the 180 degree turn our relationship had taken in the last few years. Through the grace of God, I hadn't died, and mama hadn't given up on me. "Mrs. Adams, you have to let me get this recipe, this is so good." Gavin smiled, continuing to eat.

"Oh, thank you, honey, it's an old family recipe, you'll get it after the wedding," Faye answered with a wink.

I gave the nod, responding, "Fair enough."

Then Bradford asked, "So do we have a date?"

Gavin and I looked at each other, at a loss, but then he answered, "We're thinking this summer, maybe Jamaica, as a destination wedding." I looked at him like, *'oh really.'*

"Ah, Jamaica, that sounds so nice honey, I can't wait," Faye answered.

"Can't wait for what?" Bradford asked.

"For the wedding!"

"Who said anything about us..."

"You can leave your ass here, I'm going to my son's wedding, in Jamaica or the moon!"

Gavin and I both kept our heads down, snickering, and it was from that moment on, I knew she was okay. We talked about Faye's knitting club meetings every third Saturday of the month, Bradford's lousy back from sitting as a judge all those years, and the time Gavin snuck out the house on a Friday night, his Junior year. "This ma'fucka dared to take my brand new '91 Cadillac DeVille for a ma'fucking spin, two in the morning," Bradford recalled. Seventeen-year-old Gavin returned home three hours later, and his heart sank when he saw all the house lights on. "When I walked into the house, I didn't even look at them. They had on robes, sitting on the couch, waiting on me." Their son had become a man in the twilight hour, sneaking to Amber McLaughlin's house for his first taste.

I enjoyed this family time, thankful to meet his parents, but at some point, the questions would come if they hadn't found the answers through the internet already. And just then, Bradford being Bradford, decided to get personal when he asked, "Did you ever meet Prince?"

"No, not personally, but I sat a few rows behind him at an award show in 1999."

"He has the most beautiful hair I've ever seen on a man," Faye offered.

"Remember that concert we went to in '83," Bradford asked.

"That wasn't me," Faye replied.

Immediately the dinner table was unbearable until Faye said, "Oh yeah, the 1999 tour."

"Mama, you play too much."

"Hey, I'm getting old, I forget sometimes."

When dinner was over, Gavin and I offered to clean up the kitchen, while Faye stored leftovers. Gavin washed dishes as he handed them to me to put away in the dishwasher.

Bradford said his goodnights and went to bed long before we finished. I took note and wondered if Gavin could become just as selfish in our marriage. He had his ways with cleaning up around the house, usually taking days to wash dishes, or cleaning up the bathrooms only when guests were coming over, but he cleaned.

"Y'all, thank you so much for cleaning up, I know you're tired now."

"Yes, ma'am," I answered.

"Yeah, we ready for bed," Gavin interjected.

"Clarissa, you'll have the guest bedroom," she replied.

Gavin's face went cold, he wanted to say something, but I tugged on his arm. He looked down and smiled and answered, "All right, mama, have a good night."

"Goodnight, you two," she replied and walked off.

Gavin shook his head while I walked behind him to his room. Slightly pissed, he stood by his bed, staring at it, then he sat on it and said, "Go close the door right quick, let's trade, remember?" I saw that familiar devilish gleam in his eye and said, "No, you go to bed, and I'll go to mine. Your mama gone think Imma hoe."

"Five minutes."

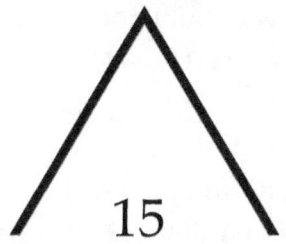

15

Where Two or Three are Gathered

"Girl, you coming down before we fly out?" With a bottle of Merlot and a box of *Cheez-Its* on a leisurely Sunday morning, it was the couch, me in sweats and a tank top, looking at *Wheel of Fortune* and discussing wedding plans. Six months since the visit to the Adams, we decided on Jamaica for June 25th, at the *Mystic Ridge Resort* in Ocho Rios. All essential details were sorted, from the resort appointed officiant to the beachside reception dinner by tiki light. The guest list was an even twenty, a majority of that being my side. And as promised, Bobby would be a second-best man in a plaid tuxedo, while the rest of us would wear white linen to match a Caribbean vibe.

"Bitch, did you make sure everybody got they ticket straight?" Denise and I had been talking since 11:37 that morning, critiquing the finishing touches to a fairy tale. And to think, over 15 years ago, both of us swore off marriage, for fear of being like other women. But as fate would have it, Denise got married and divorced, and I engaged with second thoughts.

"Did you get your dress, Niecy?" I was nervous and anal, like my days on tour. More than anything, the visual was most important.

"Girl, I've had my dress since after we agreed on the shit... relax and calm yo ass down." A beautiful pause followed. It was just the thing to set me straight.

115

"Oh, so I ain't tell you, but I got hit up for another favor."

"No, Risa, what she want now?"

"She wants her sisters to sit together on the front row."

"But for why?"

"She milking shit, it's okay, though."

The situation was the milking Faye was doing, of a situation. Going back to the night, we arrived at his parent's house, after being so graciously received, and even fed, things turned south, literally and figuratively. After dinner, with the sleeping arrangements set, Gavin decided to live vicariously through his adolescence. Those 'five minutes' he asked for, were costly.

"C'mon, five minutes."

"To do what."

"Just come, I promise it's worth the five feet."

I was hesitant but walked over and stood in front of him.

"Take your pants off."

"Boy."

"Risa, stop playing."

I looked at him, but not before saying, "Man, I'm ready for bed, you keep playing."

He flipped my top button, while I stood in stubborn protest. He pulled my jeans down, playfully, revealing a hot pink thong. "What are you doing?" I whined, knowing his exact plan. He looked up at me and smacked his lips.

"You know what it is." As usual, when it came to cunnilingus, I complied. Slowly and methodically, he teased the waistline of my thong, stretching the elastic, and occasionally, letting it snap back. I watched, wishing he'd get to it. More teasing with kisses around my belly button, my thong was eventually removed.

A subtle lick, followed by a soft blow, were the beginnings of foreplay, but the way I moaned, put gas to a flame. Every twitch of my back or thrust of my hips, made him dig deeper. Before I realized it, I was palming the back of his head. "You like that," he growled, looking into my eyes. And then, seizing the moment, he pulled me around to the bed, switching places, and now, entirely on his knees and I, on my back. With his right hand, he held my left thigh up, while I continued guiding his head, with eyes closed. A low hum from the A/C covered the mischief, as he became lost between my legs. He went robust, wild, and free, so much so that I decided to watch. Suck after lick, kiss after nibble, five minutes no longer mattered.

"Ooh," I whispered, as his lick went south.

However, four minutes of horseplay later, and without fair warning, Faye realized that she'd forgotten to tell us about the faulty shower knob, and how we needed to jiggle it for the hot water to work.

With a weak knock, the door opened; "Oh, by the way..." Gavin's adrenaline rushed back to like '88, when it was him, two sheets of Kleenex, and a *Jet Magazine*. He did his best to throw my left leg over his head, and quickly shield my naked lower body with the comforter. But when Faye walked entirely in the room, she could smell something was fishy, no pun intended. She paused to analyze why my jeans and panties were on the floor like I had no damn home training.

Gavin decided to be stupid, fast. "And Father, we ask that you honor this prayer..." Faye even bowed her head, as she continued looking for clues.

I couldn't hold it any longer and began snickering but added, "Yes, Lord."

"In your son's name, we pray, Amen," Faye answered along but felt compelled to add more. "Dear God, I would also ask that you remind my son and his soon to be wife, that this house is sanctified, blood-bought and filled with your holy spirit and that he honors his mother, that his days be long upon the earth, in your dear son's name, we pray, Amen."

We all answered "Amen," him still on his knees with a greasy mouth, and me, butt-ass naked. Faye was so disappointed, she forgot to tell us about the shower knob, and for the next two days, besides the lukewarm showers we took, Faye's vibe was even colder. On the day we were flying back to Houston, with the taxi driver waiting outside, Gavin leaned in to kiss her cheek, but she curved him, settling for a hug. It was nearly a month before they talked again.

"If she asks for anything else, tell her ass *'unavailable,'* Risa."

"I think that was it...this shit need to be over anyway."

"Over?"

"Niecy, this shit is getting stressful."

"You don't have to do this."

"I love Gavin; he loves me. We are doing this. You wanna be in the wedding, or not?"

"Look, don't come for me. If you are having second thoughts, it's okay."

Gavin, on the other hand, was an unusual groom. He would now be Gavin Beverly Adams, Rice University Professor, New York Times Bestselling Author, and husband to Clarissa *Renee* Gentry. Every step of the way, he was hands-on, especially with our vows.

"We should say our own shit."

"What's wrong with traditional vows?"

"Nothing, if that's what you want."

"I mean, what do you wanna change? I'm sure both our parents said the same..."

"That's exactly why we should create our vows," he interrupted.

"Hmmm."

"If you don't wanna do it..."

"I'm not saying that...I hadn't planned on saying anything different."

"What promise can you make for the sake of our marriage, think of it that way."

"I promise to remain the person you met," I quipped.

"That's a given, Risa. Put that in words."

"I promise to call you out on your shit and give you head once a month."

"Great, that's a start," he replied sarcastically.

"Professor smart ass, you do it, show me."

"Aight…let me think."

Gavin cleared his throat for theatrics, looked to the sky, then took my hands in his and began. "I promise to love every fiber of your being, with every fiber of mine. I promise to be vulnerable and to let my ego die, even when challenged to do otherwise. I promise to be by your side as life takes us on a journey of exploration and fulfillment. And until the day we part ways, either by death or disagreement, you are love."

I stood there, the classic Aquarian, able to disguise emotion with a tilted head, and said, "And I promise to love you so good, that you will forget all the other bitches that ever came before me. I promise that my love won't let you be on some bullshit, 'cause my love is pure, perfect, and kind. And I promise that if you love and respect my ass, don't lie, don't cheat, pick up behind yourself, and admit you're wrong when you wrong, my love will forever be yours."

For nearly five seconds, we stood in silence, with looks of indifference, until Gavin said, "…fuck out 'a here."

We laughed like cool kids, understanding that matrimony would be whatever we wanted. In two days, we were boarding a plane for *Miami International Airport*, meeting young Bobby, along with Jacob's assistant, on a private chartered flight, courtesy of Jacob's money. In his mind, the cost of getting Bobby there was a wedding gift. Denise and her sons would fly out a day later, while the Adams were already sipping Pina Coladas, waiting for everyone else.

In the wake of the occasion, last-minute details were reworked, from the seating arrangements to the group activities. Denise handled sending out invitations, to the complete list months ago, but it was hell being sensitive and selective. Between our families and friends, and being mindful of the cost involved, of the sixty-seven invitations sent, twenty committed to paying their flight and accommodations. Hazel was slightly pissed that family members who talked shit about me back in the day, wouldn't see me married off, in all the glory of justification. Her only child was becoming a woman now.

On Gavin's side, his list included Aunts Teresa and Hannah, both from South Carolina, Cousin Kim, who he grew up with in Cincinnati, and a couple of frat brothers from Columbia. Miguel was the best man, so Paula came along, to his disappointment.

Besides Denise and her sons, I was expecting Uncle Darold and Aunt Dottie. Also, Aunt Francine and Cousin Antoine, along with my former manager Yancy Tillman, and good friend and back-up singer, Tai Foster.

The stage would soon be set, as loved ones and friends would witness the culmination of trial and error and love by default. For the many years that it took to get to this moment, long nights alone, with tears that flowed forever, Gavin Beverly Adams and Clarissa Renee Gentry would be man and wife, but first, an itinerary of adult fun was in play. Gavin researched resort offerings, touristy shit like parasailing, zip-lining, seaweed wraps, and banana boat rides, but something called hedonism sparked his interest.

The first night there, we were cordial, having dinner with the Adams at *Bellisimo*, the resort's version of an Italian restaurant. It was awkward initially, but the linger of a misunderstanding soon became water under the bridge when Faye saw little Bobby. "Who's this handsome young man?" I was pleased with the reception of my son. However, Gavin's focus was the hedonism party, set for later that evening. He gave me the eye, meaning, *'let's wrap this shit up.'*

A few hours later, after saying our goodnights and tucking Bobby in, we were chauffeured by golf cart to the much anticipated, mystery of a hedonism party. I couldn't care less, considering my days up in the Hollywood Hills, when mounds of cocaine and opioids flowed into full-on orgies, with A-list actors, singers, studio and record execs, and their mistresses. The lush vegetation, cobblestone walkways, and an ocean breeze mixed with Dancehall music filled the night with lustful electricity, popped off by an earlier bottle of rum.

The closer we got to the party, the music grew more festive, more pronounced, with a more extensive bass line leading to the unknown. I looked at Gavin, watching his eyes dart back and forth at the collage of seduction. When the driver stopped at the front entrance to the reception area, two women dressed in hotel uniforms, welcomed us with genuine Jamaican smiles. Just beyond, we could see a crowd, mostly White, with ages ranging from millennial to *what the fuck are you doing here*? Regardless, curiosity had us walking through the gate, into a crowd, only concerned with all things pleasure.

With our hands clasped, we continued towards the bar, intent on maintaining a decent buzz, when suddenly, a delicate whiff of jerk chicken crossed our paths. We looked at each other and smiled; "Don't judge me," he spoke. We looked around, and none were concerned with judgment. The twenty-something group of frat boys, in *Von Dutch* trucker hats, bare-chest, swim trunks and flip-flops, jammed alongside the middle-aged women with bras that hung to their navels. This was "no-fucks," personified.

"Are you feeling irie?" the host yelled, in a strong accent over the sound system.

We screamed, "Yeah," to the vibe of *Buju Banton*, tiki torches, and Mary Jane, creating the perfect atmosphere to forget.

I lightly nudged Gavin to get his attention. I gave the nod in the direction of an older White guy, who was probably in his sixties, dancing and dangling, completely naked with a "Black" chick half his age, with her breast spilling from a bikini top and ass that swallowed up a thong.

"You cool with this?"

"Please…you not trying to leave."

"If the shit is crazy, we can go," he shot back.

I knew Gavin wanted to see something pop off before the wedding day. I, on the other hand, was happy to be with him for a new chapter, including Bobby.

After getting drinks, Gavin noticed an attractive group of "Black" women, hanging together, poolside. When Gavin got near them, he gave the nod to the only brother in the group, while the ladies spoke back.

As usual, one of the ladies recognized me; "Oh my God, Renee?" I smiled in confirmation, and the ladies screamed and clapped, offering hugs and kisses. But there was a member of the group that especially caught Gavin's eye.

"Y'all, this some interesting shit."

"Girl, I'm like, your biggest fan...I went to every concert. I know every word to every song. I can't believe this," she cried.

"Wow, I appreciate that, thank you, what's your name?"

"I'm Shanice, and this is my boyfriend, Clarence. That's Greta, Ava, and Zuri."

Zuri was the mystery girl, he eyed. He was nonchalant, but every chance he got, he groped her 5'11 frame, thick and curvaceous...with his eyes. Her two-piece, black and white bikini, was barely there. She played along, noticing the occasional glances, and a brewing vibe. Her fully-grown hips and full C cups were undeniable. And yet, Gavin was doing his best to respect his fiancé.

"We're all from Atlanta, Zuri's from Dallas."

"Texas in the house," I cheered.

This new group of seven had become an instant clique, with drinks in hand, looking at the wackness. Clarence nudged Gavin.

"You smoke?"

"Hell yeah."

Clarence took a joint from his fancy fanny pack, lit it, took two pulls, and passed it to Gavin. I smiled, while the ladies chanted, *'we gettin' fucked up, we gettin' fucked up'!* It was now a cipher. The party patio was full of folks, young and old, rocking out, throwing care to the wind, as rum punch and other elixirs flowed like rivers of impulse. With a warm ocean breeze and classic reggae roots music, the ganja blazed under the midnight sky.

"Y'all, we need a jacuzzi," Greta randomly said.

"You wanna get in a jacuzzi after these ma'fuckers?" Ava asked.

I was having fun but hadn't planned on hanging all night. I figured Gavin would initiate an exit, for a stroll on the beach, alone. But two joints in, and a few drinks later, Gavin's bromance with Clarence was lit. They walked around, pointing out white girls with fat asses while we chilled in a nearby cabana. By the time they finally caught back up with us, they were high and drunk.

"Clarence, don't embarrass me," Shanice warned.

"Babe, you tripping, I'm fine."

"Did you smoke the shit up?" Ava asked.

Clarence reached in his knock-off Gucci fanny pack and pulled out joint number three. He handed it to Ava, who suggested, "cannonball, anyone?"

Everyone looked at her in shock and laughed, but Zuri answered, "Me." The laughter turned silent when Ava took a hit and turned to Zuri, who then opened her mouth and closed her eyes. The seduction of it got me wet, just a little. After she exhaled what Ava gave, the group clapped and cheered.

"Who's next?" Zuri asked.

"I am."

The group 'ooohed' and 'aahed,' but Gavin crossed his arms, doubting my gangster. Zuri took the joint from Ava, pulled, and blew in my mouth. But as she exhaled, our lips came dangerously close, until touching, which became a full-on kiss.

Time stopped, confusion sparked, eyes darted back and forth, and all Clarence could say was, "Oooh shit." Shanice put her hands over her mouth, while Ava's remained wide open. Gavin just sat and watched, unsure of what to say, think, or do. He was smitten by the kiss, mainly from his love of lesbian porn. Not since his summer internship in '97, had he been remotely close to a threesome. The upwardly mobile socialites he dated, didn't play that. He'd known about my Charlotte phase, but that was history. And yet, right before his eyes, a five-second chew between strangers tweaked a situation.

When I unlocked, I sheepishly looked up at Gavin, while wiping the corner of my mouth. The group began clapping, Zuri hid her face, and Clarence was dying to say something slick.

"Is it time for truth or dare, shit."

"You good?" Gavin asked as I sat beside him.

"Are you good?"

"We getting freaky on vacation?"

"Whatever."

Tension from Gavin's jealous vibe couldn't stop the lust in the air. Now, Zuri and I glanced at each other from time to time, while Gavin played the side. Some of the other patrons tried mingling with us—even the naked older man, dancing and dangling, moonwalked past our cabana. But when the DJ dropped Dawn Penn's *"You Don't Love Me,"* it immediately prompted me to perform a special dance for my man. I stood in front of him, winding to a slow and seductive beat until I was entirely between his legs. He wanted to stay petty, but when I turned around and put a grind on his lap, he *woke up* and gave in.

"Don't act like you don't like it."

"You ain't slick," he answered back.

I smiled, turned around, and straddled his lap for a dutty wine. Shanice and Clarence were in their world, while Ava, Greta, and Zuri playfully danced together, until Zuri saw my select show, and decided to join in. She broke away in a rhythmic walk from the other girls, getting up close to my back, while I was between Gavin's legs.

She leaned in, whispering, "I eat like I kiss," kissed me on the cheek and danced back over to Ava and Greta. I fell forward, laughing under the influence of pussy, weed, and alcohol. Gavin was now a third wheel, a rarity in his life.

By 3AM, the patio was thinning out. More than a few patrons found themselves either bent over a trashcan or flat on their backs, in drunken bliss. The ladies decided to call it quits to avoid sweating their hair out. We hugged each other, the fellas dapped, and we all went our separate ways, but not before Gavin saw me whisper something in Zuri's ear. His jealousy was curious, and yet, numb.

"Can you make it back to the hotel, you looking wobbly, champ," he teased.

"We riding a cart, I know that much."

Like clockwork, a resort employee drove up in a green, eight-passenger cart, but again, only for two. When we arrived at our suite, we undressed for hot showers, from the filth of a good night. I told Gavin, "Clean up real good."

He stopped, looked back, and replied, "What's that mean?" But I kept walking. Still confused, he walked into the bathroom, turned the shower knob, and began examining his face in the mirror. I could imagine he thought of Zuri, cause I did. But he was getting married soon, and needed to learn to walk away from the booty. When he climbed into the shower, the steaming hot water washed over him as a pause from the day. His exhausted mood had been from a bunch of nerves, sexual tension, and too much *Appleton* and *Red Stripe*. It was time for a release.

Twenty minutes later, he emerged, ready for bed, and the rest of his life, with me. As he toweled off, he walked into the bedroom, where I sat patiently, watching a local commercial for bleaching cream. I looked at him with a loving gaze, in my bra and panties. He walked over, leaned in, and gave a kiss. Suddenly, there was a knock at the door.

"Did you order room service?" he asked.

"Go see who it is."

With a confused look and towel around his waist, he walked to the door, looked through the peephole, and immediately cracked a smile. He then looked back at me and said, "For real?" I calmly shook my head to his boyish amazement. When he opened the door, there stood Zuri, in a sheer cover-up and new bikini. Without a formal greeting, she walked in as Gavin backed up. She gently pushed him against the wall, closed the door, looked him straight in the eyes, and commanded, "You first." She ripped his towel off, went down to her knees like a lady, and took charge of a situation. Conflicted, Gavin turned to me, one hand on Zuri's head, the other in the air, as to say, *'I did nothing.'*

I smiled with my arms crossed and answered, "Wedding gift."

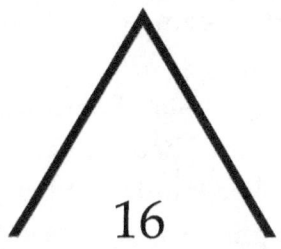

16

Blessed Quietness

On June 25, 2010, the glory of love swayed with the clouds. The crash of waves and anxious energy ebbed and flowed, and the Adams and Gentry clans would soon join by holy matrimony. Guests were seated in twenty-five white wooden folding chairs, tied with white satin bows on a scenic pier that overlooked the eastern cove. Resort attendants graced the attendees, wearing tuxedo styled uniforms in a God awful green, still with impeccable service, handing out face towels, and chilled bottles of water.

As planned, Faye sat alongside her sisters, neither of whom had ever traveled outside the United States. A beachside wedding moved Faye's older sister, Teresa Hammond, a retired school teacher and widow, that she cried uncontrollably, with streaks of mascara and sunlight running down her face. "Stop that damn crying," Hannah commanded. Hannah, the baby of the three, was the "spitfire." Back in the day, on Farham Road, she was the neighborhood shit talker, and the least expected ever to get a man.

Hazel and Ezra were thrilled, especially Hazel, who was now vindicated by God. It was Aunt Dottie, who kept up mess about my "Hollywood life." The embarrassment of my D.U.I. arrest kept Hazel in the house for three months. Even my return home was tension-filled, with arguments about my late nights that turned to disrespectful mornings, fresh with the stench of whiskey and weed.

"Dang, they need to come on, it's hot," Cousin Antoine complained.

"You know she a diva," Aunt Francine answered.

The amazing amount of hate I received from "family" over the years, for leaving Third Ward and Sunnyside behind, was sad, lowkey. Francine thought I was supposed to give her the money for a down payment on a condo, for the few times she babysat me. Antoine was disappointed that I never helped his rap career take off, despite not having talent.

"She probably in the back, smoking crack, snorting coke," Antoine shot back.

"Boy, you need to stop!"

What I feared most was the impatience of my guests and an ill-fitting bra. I wore a white linen sundress, my hair was pinned back in a bun, with an orchid tucked just over my left ear. Denise remained close by, attending to last-minute finishes, with sips of Riesling in between.

"I'm so proud of you, Bobby, thank you for being here with me."

"You're welcome, Mom."

"Does mom look good or what?" Denise asked.

"She's killing it."

Meanwhile, Gavin sat with Miguel under a tent nearby the pier. He seemed torn between the occasion and the business two nights ago. It was the nastiest of nasty, ungodly in description. An uninhibited thing of folklore, it was something a lying ass fuck boy would tell his fuckboy friends. Our mystery girl, Zuri, had become a living sacrifice in suite 133. Gavin remained pinned against the wall; toes curled. She gave good worship service, over every inch with love and care. Once he realized his free reign, he got aggressive, pumping a light stroke between her lips. Zuri gagged, opening wide to accommodate a king.

I sat in the lounge chair near the patio door, pleasing myself, watching in admiration, and patiently waiting for my turn. It reminded me of '99, on tour, with one of the backup dancers and the drummer boy. But on this night, it was different; this was one last fuck. I continued my gaze, while Zuri occasionally glanced back, as Gavin's eyes either rolled or remained closed. He hadn't had head this good since the night he told me he loved me.

Her hands gripped the wood grain while I honey dripped. Gavin was so close, so many times, he distracted himself as much as possible, but she was right, and he, thrown. *Squirt!* Unannounced, and on the left of her face, by courtesy of a pullout, he finished. She looked up and smiled as he apologized through a pant. Gavin leaned his head back in thanks, with his hands resting on his hips. I locked eyes with Zuri, commanding her to crawl over, slow and seductive, obedient, and willful. Gavin stood still, watching her body move with the grace of an untamed beast, wild and free.

When Zuri was entirely in front of me, I leaned over to my obedient subject and began a vigorous French kiss, with the anticipation of more worship. Zuri gently pushed me back in the lounge chair, parting my legs in the process, kissing my inner thighs, down to the center of the tootsie. This was regular *'fan love,'* but more erotic, sensual, and cum worthy. She had an unselfish tongue that spoke directly to my secret place. I let go, forgetting a wedding, the whereabouts of my parents and son, or the fact that my man had never seen this before.

We were a marathon of carnality, three bodies together, exhausted in ecstasy. Bedsheets and pillows were a mess, making for the look of an irresponsible, adult slumber party. If nothing else, this would be more memorable than the wedding. In a way, a new bond formed between us, as we graduated to the unknown.

Gavin wanted to tell Miguel everything, but it was too soon, too fresh. As meaningful the experience, it could taint the sanctity of the day.

"You ready, man," Miguel asked.

"I'm ready."

The occasional breeze blew thousands of miles away from responsibility. The resort officiant, an older gentleman, appearing to be in his fifties, wearing a white robe, walked over to Gavin and asked, "Are you ready?" Gavin gave the nod, and a resort attendant radioed to get me, Denise and Bobby.

The thought of becoming Mrs. Adams made Denise snicker. For a second, she told me she imagined us, eventually settling down somewhere in the suburbs, in Sugarland or Katy, Texas. Maybe, somewhere down the line, Bobby would have a little sister or brother. It was weird.

"May we all stand," the officiant spoke as music from an iPod and speaker, was cued. I sat patiently, in yet another resort cart, waiting to make the walk. My father sat with me, holding my hand, and doing his best not to shed a tear for his little girl. His joy was in the development I'd made over the years, dealing with alcohol and drug abuse, and inconsistent men. I was now going to be cared for and protected, as he'd done for Mama.

When we exited the cart, I feared to fall in my Jimmy Choo's. *I should've worn flats, damn it. Walk slow, be careful, don't you dare fall.* I held on tight to Dad's hand like I'd done so many times before, on the way to Ms. Betsy's corner store for a pickle and peppermint stick. "You okay, baby?"

I looked at him, afraid and brave, answering "yes." We continued the long stroll, looking at friends and family members in the audience, smiling and offering waves through the façade of confidence, but off in the distance when I saw Bobby, I began crying tears of joy, for my baby.

I took my last few paces, standing before the officiant as he said, "Who gives this woman away, to be wed in holy matrimony?"

Daddy smiled and answered, "It is I." Gavin walked over, shook his hand, and took my hand in his. With tears in my eyes, I could not stop smiling and looking at Bobby. Everything about the moment was love, in place of doubt.

"As we gather here today, to witness this union between this man and woman, we are reminded of the covenant God set forth between Christ and the church. The church, being the wife, and

Christ, our husband, and protector." Gavin stood with his hands in front of him, listening to the officiant and his proper Jamaican accent, and I wondered what was on his mind. "On today, God saw fit for you all to witness this union as a sign of love and commitment." I looked at Gavin with a smile, and then my mother, who wiped tears of joy from her face. This was the day that the Lord had made.

"Let us pray; dear God, we ask that you cover this union, that you be in their lives, and guide them as they embark on a new journey together. Bless them to be aware of challenges and to seek you for refuge." The more the minister prayed, the more it became apparent that this was happening. Gavin looked nervous as hell, with beads of sweat on his forehead. He clenched his teeth to hide his nerves, glancing at his father for support. "We ask that you keep them girded in your word, that they live a life of holiness, pleasing to your sight." Gavin swallowed, sheepishly looking up at me. Bobby fiddled with his thumbs, looking at grandma, while Miguel looked as if he desperately needed to pee.

Immediately after the prayer, the minister announced that it was time for the sharing of vows. In retrospect, six months ago, it was touchy for me, and my southern Baptist ways. In my mind, vows were like Bible scriptures. Minister Delroy, turned the microphone towards Gavin, prompting him to go first. He cleared his throat, looked me in the eyes, and began reciting the first verse to 'Love is Real.' Those in the audience, who remembered the song, started smiling, and some even cried.

'A dream came true when I believed, a look of love, I now could see
The past is gone, gave hope a chance, the fear of trying a new romance
Some days we loved, some, stayed away, but here we stand 'til this day
If doubt would ever challenge how I feel,
I'd look it in the face and say, love, is real.'

"Clarissa, I don't know where this journey will take us, nor will I have all the answers to the questions that challenge us, but what I do know is that my love has grown into this day. This day was written in the stars, even before you and I were born. God saw fit to design a universe in which we would meet, just two strangers from two different places, who met by accident but fell in love on purpose. And now that I've been given this gift, I promise to love you unconditionally. I promise to pray for us in times of difficulty and find the good in every situation that comes our way. And if it is the will of God, I promise to be by your side until my last breath, so help me God."

When Gavin finished, he smiled, but I was visibly emotional. He spent over three months crafting those words, hoping and praying that they'd mean something to me, that I would forever trust and believe that God ordained everything about them. I looked at him, more in love than ever, mouthing 'thank you' for what he'd written. Minister Delroy turned the mic to me, affording the same opportunity to speak. I stepped closer, looked lovingly into his eyes, and said: "Today is a miracle."

I paused for what seemed an eternity, as Aunt Dottie rolled her eyes, and Francine answered, "Hmm." This was my space in time to shame the devil and be freed of what ailed me.

"I never imagined finding the one man worthy of all of this," I spoke, as guests laughed. Gavin cracked a smile. "You arrived at the exact time that destiny would have it, and I purposely tried to hinder you from loving me, as punishment for a broken heart. You persevered like a man settled and determined. And all I can ask is that you forgive me before I become your wife. Do you forgive me?" A collection of 'awes' rang out, while Gavin playfully looked up to consider an apology. He gave the nod with a smile.

"It's undeniable what we have. You graced me with patience and a willingness to show me love all over again. You've made me whole, and for that, I promise to love you, in sickness and in health, till death do us part, so help me God." Gavin smiled, and I winked.

When it was all said and done, we were pronounced man and wife, Mr. and Mrs. Gavin Beverly Adams. We kissed, turned and waved like a *Lifetime* movie of the week, and proceeded back to the cart, with Bobby in hand. When we arrived, Bobby looked over at Gavin and said, "I guess I have two dads now." It struck Gavin just as the prayer did. All of it was real, the marriage, and now, the possibility of co-parenting.

"It's an honor to be your second dad," Gavin answered, with a hug. And just like that, a mission was set in place, by my will.

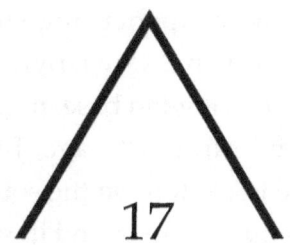

17

Choose You This Day Whom ye Will Serve

On a Thursday evening, after a week of finals before Spring Break, Clarissa called, hungry, but unsure. I was still on campus, but I hated picking for her choosy ass. I surprised her once, with an assortment of tacos from Tommy Tio's, after getting a typical, 'what's for dinner' text.

When I arrived with the food, she looked at it and said, "You should've called first." But this was after an argument, two days earlier, on my lack of spontaneity, within our eight years of marriage. I grew a thick skin for monogamy, but secretly, I was sick of the routine.

"It's not that big of a deal, just make a decision," I demanded.

Daily life in the Adams' home, although well off, was a safe ritual. We usually had dinner from the same three restaurants, and leftovers the day after. Thanks to invitations from friends and family, for life occasions, we'd never leave the living room. Virtually every aspect of the sparkle that drew us together replaced the realities of life and the peaks and valleys of being over forty.

The sex was okay, not quite like the honeymoon, but predictable like the days of the week. The first year was excellent, with some verbal scuffs, from a few misunderstandings. But, now, it was about maintenance. I was experiencing success with my third novel, becoming a celebrity in my own right. Being nominated for awards and having a growing fan base, numbed the pain.

On my latest promo run to Chicago, I did a meet and greet at Parson's, an upscale bookstore on the south side. The rain was crazy, but the line was out the door, and it was then that I realized my fame. The alpha male was finally on the biggest stage of his life and wanted to hide, but the money, though. This was the novel that made me a millionaire, with a lucrative book deal and Hollywood offers. My level of influence had also come with many invitations for random pussy.

That day in Chicago, I reunited with an old flame. As I signed books and took pictures, I'd occasionally look down to see how long the line was. About five bodies back, I spotted a familiar face. I was excited and vengeful. All the slick shit I could say, for a bruised ego, filled me with spite. But my life had changed, and I couldn't let the past take this moment. Plus, it could look bad for the press and Clarissa. *Just be kind to the bitch.*

"Colette..." She smiled, with an outreached hand, and my book curled under her arm. I felt vindicated just by her being there, wishing she'd answered my calls, all those years ago. I liked her, and she fucked it up.

"Yes, Gavin, it's been forever, my friend." *My friend, bitch?*

I smiled, as if nothing happened, as if *I never fought with a friend, behind yo' ass. Yeah, he was wrong, but you ain't have to leave the damn restaurant. I called yo' ass for a week straight, with no reply. And here you are, standing in front of me smiling and shit, like shit is sweet, oh funky bitch.*

"Thank you for coming; it's crazy out there. How you been…it's what, over ten years?" She looked well, in fact, nothing about her changed, still with every right to have left that day, and I knew it.

"Yeah, this is crazy, big-time author now, good for you." An awkward three-second pause followed before reaching for her book.

"Married? Kids?" I asked.

"Well, I was engaged, but it didn't work out," she answered with a nervous laugh.

Did you run out on him too? "It's for the best. But what about you, sir, Mr. married-to-a-famous-chick."

I hated references to my celebrity wife, being in the shadows, and having to be cordial in the process. She had one hit song. "Yeah, eight years now, time flies." I thought of what to write, wondering how to say it in a, *with all due respect* kind of way, but I chilled. *'To Colette, thanks for the support, I hope you enjoy!'* For a flash, I considered putting my number down.

"How long are you in town," she asked. The perfect question for the perfect storm, I was off the hook for a play.

"I'm leaving out in the morning. I'm at the Hyatt Regency; you wanna get something later, catch up?" She agreed, and by ten that evening, we were at the bar in Carmichael's, me and my second Long Island and she, with an old fashioned.

"Life makes no sense. I thought I wanted to be married, with a kid, a house in Evanston, shit like that."

"You seem to be doing all right, successful investment banker… no STD's."

"Whatever, fuck you," she laughed.

I had a patient vibe, placating regrets for the spoils of revenge sex. Head would've been beautiful, but hers was trash. It was too early to initiate sex talk, for lack of drunkenness, but I didn't have all night, my flight was 7 in the morning. So, I did my best to speed things up, with probing relationship questions, which led to sex talk.

"So, you're not seeing anyone?"

"I've not been on a date in four months."

"Wow, no dick that long? Bummer."

"Gavin," she replied in shock. "Ah, just cause' you getting that celebrity pussy…"

"Hold on; I'm a celebrity too, I got a celebrity dick now."

"Hmm."

"I mean, I could lend you something…"

"Boy, I don't do married men, number one, number two, did you just shoot at me? We just gone go there, huh?"

Colette held her ground, waiting for an answer, while I wondered why my celebrity status hadn't magically kicked in. She flipped and asked, "Do you know how to be a celebrity? I mean, we know each other, but we don't. We dated in college, that's it. If I were a scheming ass bitch, I could take my phone out, snap a picture of us and social media your ass into oblivion. You should think about Renee." A pause followed after she berated facts. Clarissa didn't deserve the embarrassment of being thrashed on *Bossip, The Shade Room,* or some tabloid haranguing of our lives.

"So why did you come out today, why are you here now," I asked.

She finished the last of her watered-down drink and answered, "Because I'm happy for your success, the past is the past, and every woman who admires your talent doesn't wanna fuck. It was nice seeing you, be well." She pushed back from the bar, gave me a pat on the back, and walked out; *Bitch.*

Later, after paying the tab and having the last of my drink, I ubered back to the hotel, took a long hot shower, hopped in bed, and fired up the laptop for a round of pornhub. But just before getting it in, Clarissa called. I was pissed.

"Hey, babe."

"Hey."

"What's going on?" I asked with the volume muted, searching for videos.

She knew about my porn thing, and I knew about her special little vibrating friend, *"prissy,"* a pink vibrator she hid in the closet. Though our sex life had tapered, I never imagined that she'd cheat on me, even with ample opportunities. "I think I found the one I want," she answered, referring to a black Range Rover she found online.

"Are you getting it?"

"I can wait 'til you get back," she answered.

"You sure? Anything could happen between now and Saturday."

"If it's for me, it'll be waiting. How was today, anything exciting?"

I'd grown a tad irritated. Already 11:15 at night, I wanted to bust a nut, but she knew I'd be up. Most nights, neither of us went to bed before midnight, with me working on a book idea, grading essays, or watching cable news.

"It was a trip today. The line went out the door. People stood in the rain."

"Amazing, babe…"

"I know…it's crazy."

"So, when you finally leave Rice and have all this extra time on your hands, don't get on my nerves 'cause you bored."

We were living the good life due in part to the success of my latest book, and Clarissa's revived songwriting career. Last year, she wrote a smash hit for a Latin pop star from Argentina. It got nominated for a Latin Grammy, and the publishing checks were back heavy, enough to splurge on a new toy, cash. But of all the trappings of success, the one thing she wanted most was motherhood.

About a year after the wedding, we talked about getting custody of Bobby. We met with an attorney who would file a motion to rescind the parental rights as it stood, for her chance to be made whole. But due to a technicality and Jacob's pettiness, the case was dismissed.

Again, she relived the regret of over a decade ago. The depression nearly derailed our marriage, to the point that we thought of separating. For a time, she couldn't articulate her feelings out of fear of sounding selfish. And yet, a blessing in disguise, she wrote songs of love and melancholy, which birthed a top ten R&B hit, giving her new notoriety in the business. The calls began to roll in again, and despite her deepest desire, she at least had a voice.

Every chance she had, she flew to L.A. for Bobby, watching him grow into a curious teenager, with hopes of becoming a film director. She was there for every birthday and both graduations from elementary and middle school. During the summers, he'd fly down to Houston for a few weeks to overeat on *Pappas Barbeque* and crawfish from *BB's Cafe*. We bonded as a family, with Bobby and I developing something close to a father-son relationship over time. There were moments that I struggled with step-fatherhood, fearing the day I'd hear Bobby say, "You're not my dad."

Now, as a successful couple in our forties, with sex in decline, two international vacations a year, we seemed to be at a crossroads. Clarissa was curious about the future. Throughout our marriage, we fought unnecessarily for rank, me and my big words, and she, with her power trips down memory lane. Arguments about the grocery list or who left the bathroom light on were commonplace. Ultimately, we accepted the belief that we'd never change, mentally, spiritually, or sexually.

In 2014, a situation occurred the night of Clarissa's fortieth birthday party in L.A. Old industry friends with simple habits revived the demons of excess and an impromptu sexual incident. After a night of drinking backstage at the Nokia Theater for a "Best of 90's R&B" concert, where she performed, her former road manager, Yancy Tillman, planned an intimate party at *The Beverly Hills Hotel*, with implicit instructions to go to bungalow 11. We agreed to play while in L.A., but I had no idea the kind of a night I'd have with the cool kids. When we got to the bungalow, five dudes were standing out front, all looking the part of a well kept, male model. The vibe was already off.

Darius, my *Ginuwine* look-alike of a friend, answered the door and gave me a hug that went on a little too long. "Girl, you late, we were waiting for you. And who this big fine thang," he continued. Gavin extended his hand and offered a firm grip,

"I'm Gavin." Darius began laughing, mocking Gavin's deep voice.

"Well, nice to meet you, Gavin, I'm Darius, come right this way."

We walked through the door, to the sounds of Mtume's '*Juicy Fruit*' while a smoke cloud filled the living room. Everyone was so L.A., fashionable and unbothered, but faded or about to be. Most of the ladies looked bougie, maybe in the business, or by association.

It was a celebration of a short-lived era when we were running around L.A. and the world, getting money, high on coke and weed, reckless as fuck. This was the senior class of '98, the year I graduated to fame. These were people I toured with, musicians, background singers, dancers, hair and makeup artists, and groupies.

"Darius played keys for my first band."

"Cool," Gavin answered nonchalantly.

The vibe was mischievous under dim lighting, now that the birthday girl arrived. Not even five minutes in the building, an old friend walked up, unannounced, hugged me, and asked: "Y'all wanna bumpety-bump?" I sheepishly smiled, offering a pleasant denial.

The women in the room ranged in age and attraction, from exotic to fuckable. I felt a wandering eye coming on but did my best to be respectful. And yet, the savages cared less. Through the smoke, with laser-beam focus, eyes connected with mine, some women, some men, but all clear. The positive vibration of raw sexual energy aroused the possibilities in my mind, and for that, I was home.

"You want something to drink, babe?" Gavin asked, as I caught myself and my thoughts.

"Yeah, that's cool." We continued towards the bar, where another old friend stood, playing bartender.

"Hey, bitch, I need a gin and tonic," I joked.

"Don't come in here demanding shit, fucking two hours later," Yancy replied.

"I ain't that late…"

"The hell you ain't, we was gone sing happy birthday and forgot to, oh late ass…"

"Bitch, you ain't shit!"

"Gavin honey, you sure about this, 'cause I understand," Yancy continued.

Yancy was like a second mother to a young starlet, new to the bright lights and late nights in the city of angels. He exposed me to the world of queer and was the first to know about Charlotte.

"Every time you come to L.A., you forget to call, and now this… you don't love me no more?"

Yancy was proud of what I'd become, remembering my lowest, darkest days.

"I was trying to be on time, but somebody needed an *In-N-Out Burger* badly," I answered. "It's yo' fault Gavin, fuck it…everybody, somebody turn the music down, everybody, quiet down. I want to say that the birthday girl has finally arrived, and even though she wants to blame it on her fine ass husband, we gone sing to her anyway, okay?! On the count of three…1, 2, 3, Happy Birthday…" They all sang in unison, while I humbly accepted the love of L.A., and shed a tear.

After all the birthday wishes, Tai and Georgia walked up and hugged me. Tai hugged Gavin and said, "Can we borrow her for a second?" He thought nothing of it, but now, he was left alone with the sharks. Darius walked over with one hand on his hip, with a blunt in the other.

He took one pull and said, "I heard about that wedding in Jamaica." Gavin wanted to laugh from his randomness but feared to spit Crown and Coke in his face.

"It was beautiful, brother, sorry you missed it."

Darius gave a side-eye and replied, "You just take care of sis."

Meanwhile, we convened in the bathroom, bunched up like schoolgirls, skipping class. We shared a bond as southern girls; Tai was from Birmingham, and Georgia, from Atlanta. A kinship of sisters who loved being free, being spontaneous was second nature for the *'Get It Girls,'* our clique name. It was the exposure to life beyond the south that made us unapologetically free.

"Y'all look so good together…he looks like he beat it up too."

We laughed as I replied, "I taught him some things." Tai, being most inquisitive, wondered if I'd revealed my ability to love all.

"Y'all ménage yet?"

"Can I keep my business?"

"I know you ain't playing me," Tai fired back.

"Girl, we had a threesome two days before the wedding."

"And you ain't call me?"

"It was a random bitch at some party, I wasn't expecting it."

"Well…you owe me."

Over 18 years ago, on tour, in Atlanta, Tai's then-fiancé, got the chance to meet me after a show, in my dressing room. But after shots and the beginnings of a game of truth or dare, I was challenged to kiss the fiancé, who then reversed the challenge, prompting Tai and me to kiss, leading to my first dressing room ménage.

"You don't even talk to that motherfucker no more. That's not fair, Tai. That's my husband." Tai shook her head while reaching in her bra for the vile of coke she had left. Not listening to a word, I said. She made a line on the counter, bent down, and snorted a reply, "How about, you just let me kiss him one good time, and you can watch."

Georgia and Tai both looked at me, while I responded, "I ain't drunk enough, bitch."

Tai made another line on the counter, "This is for you; I'll be right back." Georgia started laughing while I remained silent.

"You might as well beam up. You know how she is." Peer pressure is a motherfucker; I gave in to that familiar burn to my right nostril, awaiting the glory of God.

Five minutes later, Tai came back with a whole bottle of *Ciroc*, placed it on the counter, put her hand on her hip, and said, "What else you need?"

Georgia took a quick swig to the head, followed by Tai, and lastly, me.

"You know you ain't shit, okay?" I took a gulp, proceeded to walk out, but not before stating, "I ain't ready yet."

Tai answered, "We got all night."

I immediately spotted Gavin, surrounded by all the guys, and tapped him on the back, "We ain't staying long," to which he gave the nod.

"Ah, Ms. Thing, you ain't say nothing about being married to a professor," Darius chimed. "You getting that educated dick." The guys all laughed while Gavin looked uncomfortable.

Suddenly, Yancy made another request, "Hey y'all; Imma make some *'Adios Motherfuckers,'* who want one?" A line formed, with Gavin in it.

For the next hour, Gavin's guard crumbled, and now, I was the one playing defense. Throughout the hour, I watched as Tai lingered, making eye contact with me, waiting in the wings, while Georgia played spectator. Feeling desperate, I went looking for Yancy to bid farewell but didn't see him. I stepped outside, and sure enough, he stood off in the distance, talking to his boyfriend of the week. Not one to cock block, I went back inside, looking for Gavin, who was lit and magically flanked by Georgia and none other than Tai.

When Tai saw the desperation in my face, she gave an evil smirk and began grinding, with Gavin clueless to it all. Thinking fast on my feet, I got between them, but Tai moved Georgia, and it was still on. Both of us were now visibly in battle, both grinding to *'Love Like This'* by Faith Evans. A salacious warmth of body heat formed, and a trinity of sweaty bodies had become inevitable.

"How long you gone keep this up?"

"You know what I want," Tai answered.

Fed up with the shenanigans, I took Gavin by the hand towards the bedroom, while Tai followed. At this point, Gavin, still in the dark, was hammered and couldn't give a fuck. Georgia followed, too, but got pushed back out once we reached the room.

"Babe, you feeling all right, you wanna sit or lay down a bit?"

"Yeah, lay down, Gavin, you look flustered," Tai added.

"I'm good, y'all," he slurred.

With the door closed, I looked at Tai, with a warning, as I wiped Gavin's forehead and fixed his shirt. "I just wanted to give you a breather from that hot ass room."

Tai and I sat on either side of him, in a room lit by a soft red lampshade, as he gave a goofy-ass smile; "I'm chilling...the gay guys are killing me!" We laughed at his slurred speech while I wanted to speed things up.

"Babe, I'm gonna get you some water, stay right here." When I got up to walk out, I looked back at Tai in agreement, by pointing to my lips.

With a brisk walk, I went for the fridge, got bottled water, and began walking back, but not before noticing the commotion at the door. Yancy had run back into the bungalow, yelling, "Somebody call 9-1-1," as a stream of blood ran from his nose. Distracted, I immediately ran to his aide.

"What happened?" A small crowd gathered around him to get the scoop.

"Oh, punk-ass, bitch ass Terrell hit me, it's okay though," he answered, visibly shaken.

"Why he hit you, baby?" Unbeknownst to most in the room, Yancy suffered from domestic violence at the hands of his much younger man.

"Child, Imma be all right, give me that dish rag...all his shit going out tonight!" Those around him began cheering as I continued tending to a dear friend. "I'm so sick of these young niggas trying to dictate my life. One day you gay, one day you not, one day you fucking me...I'm tired, girl; these new niggas ain't shit." I continued wiping the continuous flow of blood, while the vibe had changed. The DJ tried to lighten up the mood with Khia's classic *'My Neck, My Back,'* and it was at that moment I realized I was gone too long. I put the rag and bottle down, ran, and bust the door open to discover Tai on top of Gavin, with her bra off, in a full-bodied tussle and French kiss.

"Ah, excuse me!"

"Girl…" Tai answered in shock.

"Babe, you joining us," Gavin slurred.

"What kind of fucking kiss is that?"

"We just got into it, nothing happened…"

"But bitch, your shirt…its off."

"It was just a kiss like we said."

Gavin was drunk, and incoherent, but heard the words *'like we said.'* He sat up as if hit by lightning, looking at our altercation and interjected, "What the fuck did you say?" We stopped to acknowledge his shock. It was at that moment that Tai and I realized we'd fucked up. Tai walked out, quiet as a church mouse, leaving me to face the music.

We remained in silence for what felt like an eternity, before I answered, "Tai tripping, I don't know what she…"

Gavin raised his hand, with the bit of dignity left, and commanded, "Don't lie to me."

Another pause followed before I answered, "It was a stupid, stupid thing, I'm sorry." Gavin later learned more detail of the agreement we made, which changed the dynamic of everything, causing not only a decline in an already declining sex life but his trust for me. For nearly two months, we went without sex, while Gavin's ego healed.

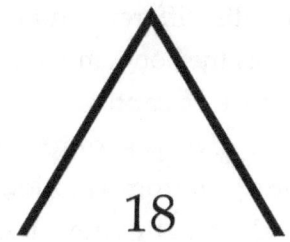

18

Be ye Transformed by the Renewing of Your Mind

They say time heals all wounds, but damn, four years after that night, things were never the same. We eventually got to the point of needing marriage counseling. Everything about our marriage required a reboot. All the fights, arguments, and silence had become evident in the way we touched. Affection was now withdrawn, behind misunderstandings, unresolved. Our salvation was outside of us.

"Would you be opposed to marriage counseling?"

"What's wrong?"

For years, I adapted to Clarissa's inability to be genuinely empathetic. But I felt like a bitch, always bringing shit up.

"What I do now?" she asked. The frustration of explaining had become the shive to my side. Her constant victimhood was an easy out, with me usually bowing to save from arguing.

"You don't think it's odd, our sex life? The lack of affection towards each other?"

She remained quiet, still doodling a verse to a new idea in a notebook, dividing her time between it and the truth.

"If that's what you want."

"So, everything's cool?"

"Are we in trouble 'cause we fuck less, Gavin?"

"Maybe, maybe not, it's different, though."

Once upon a time, post the honeymoon, there was genuine love between us. Back when I was captivated, it was nothing to stop what I was doing, to text *'I love you'* or for Clarissa, who was new to *Instagram*, to post our pics from vacations, random nights out to dinner, or whatever she felt. But now, the spoils of money and the sophistication of fame made vulnerability difficult. Mr. and Mrs. Adams held on for those who admired our story, who looked at our union as a model marriage, and for those who thought we wouldn't last.

My attorney referred me to a counselor, and without pushback, Clarissa agreed, and we had our first session on a Tuesday afternoon in River Oaks. We were pensive but committed for different reasons. I needed the truth, and she needed me to chill.

"Let's start with you, Clarissa…give me your side of things," Dr. Olga Seelenfreund, offered. Sitting comfortably across from us, Dr. Seelenfreund seemed a spry young soul of between fifty-five to sixty, with an uncanny resemblance to Dr. Ruth Westheimer. With black, round shaped glasses, and shoulder-length, grayish blonde hair, the lines on her face didn't just show age but time. Her soft tone and conservative flair indicated a session that would be mild-mannered, engaging, and non-invasive. Clarissa, however, was defensive, with arms and legs crossed; it was embarrassing.

"We don't have a problem per se, maybe our communication is off at times, but isn't that normal? I mean, who doesn't disagree from time to time? Whose marriage is perfect, right?" A pause followed, Dr. Seelenfreund looked over at me for a response. I remained silent, mostly afraid, but deeply hurt. In my mind, this meeting was supposed to be something more, something honest and pure, not a reason to be guarded. Even as a private man, I was willing to be transparent with a stranger, untangling a web of deep frustrations.

Back in November of last year, I noticed her increased phone interaction. Whether it was *Candy Crush*, checking emails, or responding to text messages and group chats in *GroupMe*, she was always with it, like a dude minding his notifications.

Finally fed up with curiosity, I took a swipe at snooping, from a screen message I read, while she showered. Presumably, untrustworthy, she often laid her phone on her nightstand, rarely in the bed. This specific time, it was in bed, on her side, but close enough to see some bullshit. Right as I was dozing off, a succession of notifications came in, and I was nosey. The sender's name was *Aria*, and the message read, '*Don't forget to bring that candy, sweet and juicy, TTYL.*' Thinking it to be one of her girls, I didn't give it much weight. But I should have. Aria Ramirez was an acquaintance from yoga class, who'd caught Clarissa's eye. They exchanged numbers, unassuming at first until Clarissa invited her to a show I couldn't make. After the show, they drank with the boys, and later, without the band, for their version of a nightcap.

"Gavin, can you articulate for Clarissa, what concerns you most?"

I looked over at her and asked, "Have you fallen out of love?" She smacked her lips and shook her head in disbelief. Maybe she loved me for all the wrong reasons, and I just played along.

"Maybe I need more love." Another pause, her answer lingered in semantics.

"Can you expound on that?" Dr. Seelenfreund asked.

There were many possible interpretations, but I responded, "Would that be Aria?" A striking silence, Clarissa was stunned as fuck, and Dr. Seelenfreund, in the dark.

"What are you saying?" Clarissa asked, attempting to save face.

"I saw those text messages…"

"What text messages…why were you on my phone?"

Visibly upset, the matter was no longer the truth of a thing, but how the fact came to be. Feeling violated, Clarissa shot back, "Is that what this is about? Some chick in my fucking yoga class,

Gavin?" The master manipulator, I'd fallen for the question tone-tactic many times. It was a trick she learned from shady music execs with broken promises. However, it was useless after I read a thread that spanned several weeks. There was a text from Aria that read, *'You were so good tonight, maybe I should kiss the kitty before every show!'* I dared not reveal my hand until due time. "You can play that game you play, but I read the whole thread, even up to her last text two weeks ago." I pulled out my phone, providing a picture of the thread for proof. It read, *'Can you please shave? It's ridiculous.'*

You could hear a pin drop. Dr. Seelenfreund struggled with words, while Clarissa continued looking down. She didn't say a mumbling word, but a single tear rolled down her face, admonishing her sins.

"Maybe we should reconvene at another time? Let's get our thoughts together," Dr. Seelenfreund offered.

"No, it's okay," Clarissa answered.

"Aria was a friend; we started hanging out when Gavin and I were drifting. It was a stupid excuse to be spiteful…" She stopped and looked up at me. My disgust wasn't another woman, but another woman without my knowledge or presence. There were other times since Jamaica, even after the L.A. incident, but always with consent. Clarissa would say that it was to keep an eye on me, but it was more about her lust.

"You already know how we get down. You could've told me." The good doctor, still in the dark, needed clarification.

"I'm not sure if I understand…what do you mean, Gavin?"

"We have an arrangement."

"An arrangement?"

"Gavin and I, from time to time, have an open relationship."

"Oh, with other men and women?"

"Women."

"This has been your entire relationship?"

"We had our first ménage a trois, two days before our wedding."

Dr. Seelenfreund's face read, *'oh dear,'* while she scribbled notes. Then she asked, "Clarissa, before you and Gavin were married, had you ever been in a lesbian relationship?" We looked away but thought, Charlotte. "I was briefly in a relationship with a woman, yes." The doctor gave the nod and continued, "Do you consider yourself to be a lesbian?"

"No...I like what I like; that's it."

"Sexual preference can be labeled. I'm a heterosexual man," I remarked.

"Brand new..." Clarissa shot back.

What was once a moment of repentance, quickly turned to pushback. Vindication burned deep and slow, with an emotion, somewhere between hatred and denial. "I couldn't care less about a label, but what is she to you? Is she your refuge in the time of a storm." Now, entirely big mad, I felt entitled to a rant, but the doctor jumped in.

"Your anger is warranted, Gavin. But let's be tactful. This session is not a means to an immediate end, but rather, an understanding of our choices and how they've affected us." Clarissa wiped another tear, still looking down, and offered an apology.

"You know I love you; you know that...I'm sorry for disrespecting you. I feel like, when you're mad or moody, you're not affectionate. Honestly, you think we stopped having sex because of me?"

"Would you say the point of origin is Clarissa, Gavin?"

I took a deep breath, paused to choose my words, and answered, "When we lost the custody battle..." Clarissa immediately looked up, with pain and tears. "You became another person after that. The depression changed our home; everything about us took a shift." Clarissa, blind to how I felt, looked at me, in silence. It was genuine, refreshing, and heartbreaking. I thought good husbands took shit.

"How do you feel about Gavin's remarks?"

"I can't argue, depression was there. I love my son."

"Be clear and be present. Your partner is talking to your heart."

"Is there something I…"

"Let her finish, Gavin."

"No, you didn't do anything…I just wanted us to be a family."

"Can you not have kids of your own?"

We looked at each other, at a loss. It hadn't been a significant discussion, maybe a thought, after getting Bobby back, but she was in her forties now. She worked hard to keep her body snatched and her skin glowing. More stretch marks were off the table.

"We never talked about that. We always knew Bobby was the missing piece."

"How do you see this marriage going forward? Is it based on the eventual custody of Bobby? What if you don't get Bobby?"

That was the question that lingered most in her mind, and perhaps, the reason for the infidelity. The void she felt, filled with pop offs like Aria, were strangely younger and needy. Jarring was the belief that deep down, she'd used sex to calm the absence of motherhood.

"I love Gavin, regardless of ever getting custody…he's been my rock for nearly ten years. We've been blessed to see each other's growth on this journey, and ultimately, I was selfish; I should learn to share," she added for humor.

"Gavin, how do you feel about Clarissa's comments?"

I was still processing the truth while in my feelings. For all the wandering eyes that lent themselves to a conversation, all the small talk that usually led to discreet rendezvous, all the wanderlust that my pedigree produced, I purposely ignored, for the authenticity of love. "I'm mad, but really, more disappointed." In the eight years of our marriage, the most I'd done alone was flirt in the club and tried fucking Colette in Chicago.

"Maybe we should look at the dynamic of this relationship and consider rather it remains open or not," the doctor offered.

I had no reason to object to the arrangement. Naturally, the average heterosexual man is capable of being desirous of other women, solely by physical attraction. When my eyes wandered, it was never, *I wonder if she'll love me more profoundly* or *could she be my soul mate?* It was, *I'll fuck the shit outta her*, or *I bet she got some good head*. Purely animalistic, purely selfish, the arrangement was indeed the icing to the cake. However, Clarissa's need to be in control was the main reason her fling was short-lived. Clarissa's doggish demeanor teetered on lesbian domination, causing Aria not only to stop calling and texting but drop the yoga class.

When the session was over, the car ride home felt tense and awkward. We rode in silence, all thirteen minutes, with just the sounds of 97.9 The Box. When we arrived home, we went separate ways, her to the office to write and I, to my man cave to watch *MSNBC*. But in that time apart, our minds began to spin, and collectively, we processed everything that led to the session, wondering what remained of our union. In the aftermath of the truth, it could've been easier to get separated and eventually divorced, but we knew each other's value to our lives. We were painfully aware of fear, having gone so deep into the water, baring our souls for love and commitment. Neither of us wanted to start over again, nor felt confident in trusting someone new.

Clarissa tried writing but thought of the session. She wondered about the days ahead and silent treatment. All these years, living life on her terms, had come to a halt. She now understood the responsibility of being responsible. Not wanting to change the dynamic of our lifestyle, she began to play with an idea, something that had more structure but remained true to who we'd become. She immediately went downstairs, to my cave, for a discussion.

"Can we talk?"

I put the sound on mute, still with a slight attitude.

"Go ahead."

Clarissa walked over to an armchair caddy-cornered to the sofa I sat on, took a seat while clearing her throat, and said, "Maybe we need something official, something like our thing, just us." Still unsure, I gave a *'what now'* look. "I mean, you know I enjoy being with women, with you, maybe we should explore a different path." She paused, hoping I'd get the picture, but still, nothing. "I'm saying, what if we brought a chick into the fold?" My face changed from confusion to consideration.

"Like, this girl is going to live with us, or we fuck her on the weekends?"

Clarissa cracked a smile, "That's up to us." I sat there, feeling blessed and highly favored, masking my innermost joy.

"So how do we go about finding this third party?"

"I guess we'll know when the universe presents her," she answered.

Instantly, the possibilities were endless, and spontaneity had finally shown up. I imagined a home robust with variance, rich in magical, random experiences, that only a man of my cloth, could handle. And then, just as quick as I whisked myself away in lust, I was reminded of my erectile dysfunction. From time to time, the *boy* would act up. I never imagined the need for a little blue pill, but life was changing. If anything, I didn't want to let down two women. We continued in silence, aware of a benchmark in our history. As she got up to resume her writing, she said, "Think about it." I had already thought about it. A week after our honeymoon, I looked for Zuri on *Facebook*, *Black Planet*, and *My Space*. I could only replay that night in memory, but if I had my way, a repeat was bound to happen.

For the remainder of the day, well into the evening, I began a methodical strategizing of ways to get new pussy. My most comfortable access were the many female students who often flirted, but I never entertained shitting where I ate like other professors, Miguel included. Most of my female counterparts were Caucasian, Asian, or Indian, and well into their fifties. I thought of what this prospect needed to have to be worthy of our bed.

She must have an ass, grabbable, cellulite welcomed, but not too much. She doesn't have to be fit, but flexible though. I could bend the legs back and ride; I'll be all right. Of course, she must be bi-, preferably

"Black," but not a requirement. Maybe she shouldn't be "Black," they might catch too many attitudes between them, and with me. Nah, she should be "Black," though, that's comfortable. She must have a job, her place, car, with at least a 675 FICO score. And no kids, that's gone be too much work.'

Clarissa's preference was much more straightforward; she has to be a bad bitch.

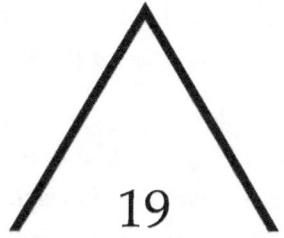

19

Judge not, Lest ye, be Judged

Denise objected to the idea. "Girl, no…cancel that. Either you love Gavin and be faithful, or live your life, simple and plain. Don't play with him."

I did love Gavin, and all the intimate places he filled. For him, I moved and had my being. But as with any journey, the press of an urge could always override intent.

So, I created a proposal, a guideline. It was a way to kill bullshit and confusion, early, and keep the focus where it should be…*me*. After typing it up, I dropped it on his desk and went to yoga class.

Proposed Guidelines
By Clarissa Renee Gentry

Before we do this, if we go through with it, there must be rules put in place. I came up with a few to help us. Why am I doing this? Because whoever we choose, she must meet our expectations, but she must know her place. These four rules will act as an agreement or understanding about this entire thing.

*1. **Convenience** – This is an arrangement of convenience, which means, whenever you get the urge, I get the urge, or we get the urge* *together, she will be the one we call, and we will know about the situation before it happens. You cannot fuck her and tell me after it happened.*

*2. **Understanding** - She must understand, first and foremost, we are married, and she is "our" side piece. She must also know that I am the 'Queen Mother' of this house. She is not my equal; she will not participate in any decision-making in this household. We will give her consideration when she is asked. She is a guest in our home until further arrangements are made. And she needs to be a full-grown woman, with a place of her own, transportation, working or in school, not trying to figure shit out. And no kids. Again, I am the Queen Bitch.*

*3. **Friendly** – It would help if the bitch were nice, with a personality. No boring bitches allowed. The first time she bucks at either one of us, she's out, no exceptions.*

*4. **Freak** – She shall eat my ass, pussy, suck my toes, nipples, and anything else I can imagine. And she'll be required to go to the clinic upon request. If she can't comply, she will no longer be necessary to the fold.*

These are just a few requirements I have. They are non-negotiable but feel free to make any additions you desire. Further, this arrangement shall not be discussed with any of our friends until we've committed.

Gavin read the document with a smirk on his face, with a few addendums of his own. The audacity, albeit cute, did not withstand the fact that they arrived at this place by infidelity. But he was game.

My 'non-negotiables,' not to be petty, were specific about body type. So, under the 'Freak' section of Clarissa's document, I specified, *'she must have an ample ass.'* I wanted to add, *'that I can fuck since you won't let me.'* I further added, *'Our side piece should be an equal sex partner. I do not want a sex slave.'* Under the 'Understanding' section, I wrote, *'Our side piece does not have to be African-American. We should be open to the one open to us.'*

The more I thought of things to add, the more interested I became. *What if we all fall in love, though? What if I fall in love with her and leave Clarissa?* Love had become the central theme, and for that reason, I added, *'She should be allowed to stay over one night a week. If things work out, we can increase the days.'* Whomever this woman would be, the intimacy of our home would be the eventual intimacy of our hearts. When I was satisfied, I laid the paper on the kitchen counter, in the usual spot for the mail and keys.

All that day, excitement and fear played in every scenario. *No crazy bitches in our house, but crazy bitches have the best pussy.* Nonetheless, I hadn't thought of how to introduce her. How would we introduce her? *'Yes, this is my wife Clarissa and our girlfriend?' 'Second wife?' 'Boo Thang?'* Maybe Clarissa hadn't thought about love. This arrangement served two purposes; keep my ass at home and keep things fresh.

I pulled my phone out and went to *Instagram*, searching for God knows what, in hopes of nothing. *Where would I find a chick willing to fuck two strangers, exclusively? She can't be somebody we know.* I didn't do clubs or hang out at bars much, except random visits to *Davenports*. I was a square, shackled by success and notoriety. Then it hit me. I randomly decided to go to Rice to run the jogging trail. Quite often, students and residents of the neighborhood would run that trail, at various times of the day, sometimes with dogs and children, and for me, it would look unassuming.

After changing into my running gear, I was heading to my old stomping grounds, partially feeling like a dirty old man. I doubled back, but reasoned, *I'm just looking.* Ten minutes later, I arrived at the campus, but instead of snagging a parking spot from campus security, I parked on the street, just off Main, like a regular guy.

The chirps of Spring brought back memories, when I walked the campus like a young Black god, turning down discreet sexual offers from young ladies, hopelessly charmed and curious. But now, I felt pathetic.

I began a lite trot, something between fast walking and jogging, to surveil my surroundings. None of it felt right, but I persevered. As I ran, there wasn't much traffic, maybe an older white lady here, an Asian guy there, mundane at best. But then I saw a shapely, redhead running and thought I'd flash a smile, something for her to bite. When our paths gradually crossed, she looked straight ahead. This plan was immediately dumb, but then I called Miguel.

"Yeah, man," Miguel answered.

"You in your office?"

"Yeah, what's up?"

"Are you busy? I'm in the neighborhood."

"Come on up."

I was slightly winded but appreciated the chance to walk the campus again. Forever an 'Owl,' I missed the days in Sewall Hall for department meetings or conferences with students. Even with the perks of celebrity, there was something sacred about getting up for work every morning.

When I got to Miguel's office, Bob Marley's 'Redemption Song,' played at a low volume, another vibe altogether. I wanted to tell him something but didn't know how to say it. And without the aid of scotch, I was more vulnerable.

"What's up." It was a week since our last heart to heart. I considered his advice but chose to move on. "All good, man, just hanging out a bit…sure you're not busy?" Miguel raised his hands and looked around to emphasize his point. I smiled, feeling less stressed about the conversation I wanted to have.

"Did y'all find a willing concubine?" Miguel asked.

"Funny, you should ask."

"What?"

"Where does one find such a person?"

"Go to a strip club. They're all in college."

It was ironic until it began to sink in, and slowly, the laughter faded for the reality of a plan. We both looked at each other, like, 'not a bad idea,' and gave each other high-fives.

"When do you wanna go?"

"Don't fucking include me in this shit, this is all you buddy, glad I could help."

"Come on, I need a wingman, support a brother."

Miguel rolled his eyes in hesitation. He was satisfied with his lackluster life and mediocre marriage, and he didn't need any rah, rah shit. He was okay with living vicariously through my reality, even if it reeked of excess.

"Man, with my bonehead, honey-do list she's got for me?"

"Sounds like chicken shit, but all right."

"Okay, so when you wanna go?"

"Let's go now. I know you know a place."

"First of all, I have a class at 3. Secondly, I do not frequent gentlemen clubs, but thirdly, there's a place on Richmond Ave., 'Sapphires,' I think... yeah, let's go tomorrow."

"Let's go when you get off work, tell Paula your working late, I'll buy all the drinks, and a few dances, come on Miggy Smalls!"

"I fucking hate when you call me that. I'll text you the address. I'm good for 5."

"You're a good man. God bless you."

On the car ride home, I wondered what to wear. The last time I'd been to a strip club was when my fraternity held its 100th anniversary conclave. Even then, I just spectated. If I had my way, she'd be a regular chick, not too flashy, maybe a tad green, but not a dumbass. But to be fair, I had to do research. So, I put on my Cavalli jeans, Etro button-up, and Fendi slippers, followed by a few spritzes of Clive Christian cologne and was out the door by 4:45PM.

When I arrived at 'Sapphires,' the parking lot alone, was a turnoff. Maybe the size of half a basketball court, there were only five cars parked, with Miguel's being one of them. When I walked in, I was greeted by a sliding glass window, with a young, Latina chick, possibly in her twenties, awaiting to conduct business. "Five dollars, please." *Filthy and cheap*, I gave her a hundred, paid, and went through a black door, leading to a dimly lit room with a bar and two stages at either end. Miguel situated himself in a corner, with one of the young ladies working there. *This shit is gross.*

The look and feel reminded me of a creepy basement, replete with poorly designed, pleather furniture and round tables that were off-balanced. A dank funk against the backdrop of cheesy strobe lights and the blare of Tone Loc's *'Wild Thing'* made me dash to the bar for a scotch, neat, hoping it would dull the pain.

It was no longer a good idea in a short time. Shitty brown carpet and even shittier orange, plastic, table lights, changed my mood to guilt. Miguel's delightful grin was that of a regular, like a motherfucker who always sat in that corner, with that girl sitting on his lap. "What's up man, nice," I joked. Miguel just smiled, making a hand gesture for me to sit in the available chair. "Gavin, this is Destiny, Destiny, Gavin." We shook hands like the first day of student orientation, politely awaiting small talk. Destiny, also Latina, looked either twenty-three, twenty-four, with long, gothic black hair and innocent doe brown eyes. Attractive in every way, her body, laid up against Miguel's, looked like a cliché.

"How long you been here?"

"Maybe ten minutes, and I'm thirsty," he hinted.

"Is there a waitress in here, I don't see…"

"I can go to the bar for you, babe, what you want," Destiny asked.

"Gin and tonic, please, and make it a double."

She got up and walked off to much fanfare, as we paused to inspect and ingest. I was slightly proud of Miguel, as we watched her navigate in six-inch platform heels and red lingerie. "You fucking come here all the time." Miguel scrunched his face in defense.

"Why would you say that?"

"You look comfortable."

"This is a relaxing environment."

"Right."

We focused our attention on the girl dancing the main stage, looking unenthused; I felt sorry for her. An older white gentleman strolled up for a dance, with a meager few dollars to throw.

Obliging the customer, she maintained her lackluster dance moves to Adina Howard's *'Freak Like Me.'* All I could do was look at her eyes when I wasn't looking at everything else. A distant and sad soul, this had to be college tuition or lack of ambition.

"What about her," Miguel asked.

"What about her?"

"She's kinda' hot, in a non-descriptive, shabby chic way."

"I'm good, trust me."

We continued looking at the show, when Destiny returned with Miguel's drink, and back on his lap. Looking around the room, none of the other girls appealed to my checklist. Miguel, however, was tickled pink. I could imagine him coming here every other Wednesday, with a budget of $80 on the entry fee, four drinks, and two private lap dances, with Destiny.

Just then, the house DJ got back on the microphone, "Give it up for your girl, Bubbles!" I shook my head. "Coming to the stage, we have the ever so sexy, the one and only, Melody…where you at babe, come on up." Expecting another skankish situation, I pulled my phone out to pass the time, while Destiny and Miguel played shits and giggles. With a few notifications from social media pages, I was giving this place thirty minutes, max. The music changed to a much slower tempo, playing Michael Jackson's *'The Lady in My Life.'* A seemingly unorthodox choice, I looked up for the oddity of it. Unprepared, I was smitten.

Standing easily 6' feet tall, with a blonde, flowing, weave or a wig that fell past her shoulders, this amazon of a woman went past my expectations. Her eyes, almond-shaped and Asian, influenced, sparkled against the floodlights, while she commanded the room with ease and just the flick of her hips. I put my phone down. All six guys on the floor, the bartender and the DJ, gazed at the glory of this light-skinned, Louisiana sexpot, shaking her moneymaker. I looked over at Miguel and Destiny, who both stopped to watch her. Her long, well-toned legs flexed with every dip or kick she made. When she gyrated her hips, her six-pack rolled in synchronicity. *Damn.*

With $85 in my wallet, I prepared to spend it, in the name of research. All I needed to know was whether she liked girls, but more importantly, how she rode the beat. It was decided, at that point, if the opportunity presented itself, I would request her company. *Clarissa might like this.*

And then, our eyes met; she locked in, and an unspoken conversation sparked for a few seconds, before moving on to the next patron. Miguel tapped me on the arm, flashed a wink and gave a thumbs up. This adolescent lust, exciting and reckless, was still fleeting. As a reserved gentleman, there was no intention to over extend myself and look foolish. I would make conversation, gauge her intelligence and maturity, and make a proposition. And as planned, I would call Clarissa first.

When her set was done, she disappeared, along with the energy in the room. Occasionally, I looked up whenever a body was in my peripheral. Miguel and Destiny were back canoodling. They excused themselves to go to the private area for one of Miguel's budgeted dances. Meanwhile, I was fidgety. Part of me wanted to text Clarissa to share the news of a prospect, while the other part said 'chill.'

Five minutes went by, with another regular chick on the stage, and the vibe, slowly turning to dust. If I didn't see her soon, I was leaving, with nothing more than the same cheesiness. I felt a tap on the shoulder, and fantasizing figured it was Melody, like a Hollywood movie, but instead, it was the security guard.

"Are you the G550 parked outside? A tow truck is trying to tow the car next to you."

I excused myself, into a breath of fresh air, free from the gutter of Babylon. I hit my alarm, got in, cranked it up, and proceeded to move. The tow truck guy obliged and continued to do his business on the Kia Sorento parked next to me. I parked, but not before seeing Melody walk outside, through my rearview and side mirrors. She reached in her clutch, just left to the entrance, and pulled out a Newport to light up. It was so sexy the way she held her cigarette; she felt right for the tribe. Before getting out, I checked my nose and swiped my eyebrows for form. When I got out, I looked in her direction, but she focused on her phone. Nevertheless, I was eager to talk up a dance for research. As I walked, nonchalantly, she was still entranced with the damn phone, looking like a teenaged mallrat. *Fuck it, get closer.*

"Excuse me, Miss lady, I saw you dance…that was good."

She offered a kind smile, "Thank you."

"Are you dancing again later?"

"You want a private dance?"

"Oh, okay, that's cool."

"No problem, I'll be there in a minute."

I walked away, assessing my play; *oh, okay, that's cool? That was so lame.* I sat back at the table, while Miguel and Destiny remained behind the partitioned wall, with her probably grinding on him. My mind raced, thinking about proper trick etiquette with this new chick. Even outside the prospect of a threesome, I wanted her first.

A few minutes more, and still no Melody, I was fidgety again. Even Miguel and Destiny had returned, him with a goofy and sheepish smile, and she, with twenty dollars. The clock was ticking on my patience when suddenly tapped on the right shoulder, there she stood, with seductive eyes that read *'you ready?'* I rose to follow, but not before Miguel offered a high-five, on the way to the mystery behind the wall.

Maybe the size of an average walk-in closet, the area seemed even darker than the club. There was a black leather loveseat that felt cold from the overhead vent when we sat down, but when she straddled me, her body heat made it all right. "I'm gonna wait for the next song, okay," she offered. I shook my head 'yes,' all agreeable and shit. Then came the small talk.

"So, you in school, or…"

"I graduated last year. I'm a certified massage therapist."

"Oh, wow, interesting."

"Yeah, business is slow for now, I'm building my clientele."

"Do you have a website or anything like that?"

"No...it's pathetic, I know."

"No judgment, I promise."

"It's a lot going on, but I ain't doing this forever. I want my son to..."

And just like that, an instant deal-breaker, per Clarissa's document. But with an ass like hers, an exception could be made. She continued talking, but the clamor of lust and truth muffled it even more. Finally, the song changed, she repositioned herself, with her back turned to me, crouched between my legs, teasing my sensibilities with ass. In full character, she whipped her golden tresses around, slightly slapping me in the face. It was intentional, yet playful, and welcomed. She woke the *boy* up, and I gripped her waist, along for the ride.

Her slow and convincing grind made her the perfect candidate for the fold. Her body, curvaceous, and sensual to touch, only heightened my imagination. The quintessential side piece, she had the look of ambition, but did she have the sex? Throughout my promiscuous journey, I crossed a few 'starfish.' But as Ini Kamoze's *'Here Comes the Hotstepper,'* played, she showed me a thing or two about riding the beat.

Still erect, and past embarrassment, her vibe matched immediately, beat by beat, stroke by fucking stroke. A rhythmic sun dance, I could hear the boom and bass of the song but concentrated on the moment in front of me. She was the embodiment of a *breather*, the smell of fresh-cut grass, after a summer rain. The deep, black of her pupils took me away from research and into the universe, hoping for a milky way. "You good," she asked, with a smirk. I smiled back, "Hell yeah." With every thrust of her hips, I ascended to glory, filled with adultery. She was grinding *o'boy*, so much so, I started counting; *'fifteen, sixteen, seventeen...damn.'* At that point, it was clear that she was on a mission to make me cum. But for the grace of God, the music changed, while the dick remained in limbo.

She gracefully removed herself from my lap, with a smile that suggested the ride was over, "That'll be twenty dollars." It was just business, but my thirst wanted more. I reached for my wallet, gave her $60, and proceeded to walk off. But when she noticed the money, she quickly bossed up. "Ah, you cool?"

Unsure of the question, I answered, "Yeah, why?" She looked down at the money, like, *'you paid too much.'*

"It's cool, get something nice for your son."

"That's cool, but I don't do charity."

"Nah, it's nothing like that."

"I mean, I work for mine, I don't need charity."

"It's cool, for real, I'm happy to give it."

"Well, sir, I can give you two more dances or something else."

'Something else' was more intriguing. I had time and space.

"What's something else?"

She walked up, stood on the tips of her platform pumps, and whispered, "Head." I raised my brow at the offer, but quickly remembered; I had something to do, first.

"Excuse me for a second, gotta make a quick call, I forgot something."

"Okay," she answered.

In keeping with the newly minted rules on extracurricular activities, I went outside for seclusion and called Clarissa for permission. It was the first initiation of an understanding, awaiting approval.

"Hello."

"Hey. You at home?"

"On my way."

"Oh okay, well I'm with Miguel, we went to this strip club."

"Strip club, hmm."

"What's that for?"

"Nothing, go ahead."

"I'm doing research…"

"Oh, when did we establish this?"

"When you gave me that list of rules."

"I just gave you that the other day."

"Are we doing this?"

I figured if she had the nerve to make up rules, I'd have the audacity to initiate them.

"Whatever. When are you coming home?"

"Well, I wanted to ask you something."

"Nope."

"Hear me out…"

"Stripper was not on the list."

"She got a fat ass, though, and I think she freaky."

"How would you know?"

I chuckled at this sudden change in mood; plus, she caught me.

"All right, never mind…"

"Don't try to play all disappointed and shit."

"I'm good for real. I'll be home in twenty minutes."

"All right."

"All right, bye."

When we hung up, I walked back into Sapphires, found Melody, and closed the deal. We walked out to my truck and drove around the corner. When we finished, I drove back, dropped her off, and went home. I parked in the driveway, thinking of what transpired. *How are we going to do this?* It was clear we needed to talk things out all the way, or the shit would fall to pieces.

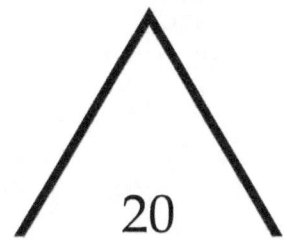

20

Ye of Little Faith

Wednesday morning, days after the strip club, I sat Clarissa down for a real talk. Given the dismiss of my first attempt, how seriously did she take this arrangement?

Around 9:30, I brewed a pot of coffee, scrambled some eggs with cheese, burnt some toast, and waited to have a conversation. Clarissa was groggy and half-sleep, but by 10, she could smell the commotion downstairs.

"What's the occasion?"

"Just wanted breakfast."

Clarissa pulled up a stool and fixed a small plate while I poured coffee. It was a careless morning meant for random plans like going to the movies or getting a mani-pedi in the Village.

"So…"

"So," she answered.

"Are we gonna talk?"

"About you trying to bring a stripper home?"

I took a sip, sweet with anger, and went numb to the antics of a discussion. "Are we doing this?"

She looked up at me, mouth full of eggs, smiling, attempting to finish every bite, and answered, "You thirsty these days."

"You like saying that shit. Who came up with this idea?"

"Yeah, it's not even a week, though, you already looking?"

"Ain't we on the same page?"

"We are, but can you chill?"

"That's funny. A bitch was snacking on your box a month ago, but I need to chill."

Clarissa was silent. The sting was fresh and understood, but she hated tit for tat shit.

"I get it, man, shit."

"You are trying to move on, but don't forget how we got here."

"I'm not trying to. I'm just saying, let it be natural."

"All right, check this, let's look for the bitch together. That way, you can stop the 'thirsty' shit, and we see what happens…naturally."

"Okay, but don't rush me."

Clarissa sought a word from Denise, about this thing, with the expectation of hearing, *'I told you so.'* As sadistic the need to be reprimanded, she preferred it from her than Hazel. The realization of this experiment was finally sinking in.

"Hello," Denise answered, in a tone suggesting a lousy reception.

"Can you hear me?"

"Hello," Denise said again.

"Girl, you can't hear me?"

"Oh, it's you, I thought your side piece answered, I was playing dumb in case she…"

"That is the lamest, corniest shit ever."

"Don't be mad; I be practicing, for this crazy bitch y'all end up with. I'm war ready!"

"Girl…I don't know."

"About what," Denise asked.

"This motherfucker tried to bring a stripper home."

"So. Y'all agreed to be about that life; no stripper allowed?"

"I don't want STDs in my house, my bed, my coochie…"

"You bougie as fuck, but yeah."

"I made an agreement we could follow together, no stripper bitches."

"Did he have anything to do with that agreement?"

A moment of reflection, she cornered me in a way that spoke volumes to Gavin's real issue; my unwavering need to be in control.

"He's a man, what kind of sense is he using? Any and all pussy is fair game."

"Any and all are the same thing, but anyway, you're not fair, just know that."

"Niecy, honey, you're divorced for this very reason."

Denise paused her words; usually, this is where she'd cuss me the fuck out, but instead, she asked, "Are you a lesbian?"

"Oooh, the shade."

"No shade at all...you don't ever need extra dick, but you want pussy."

"I'm not a fucking lesbian."

A five-second pause followed, we silently stood our ground, waiting for the other to explain. "You know I'm not a lesbian. How many times I been around yo' ass in bra and panties, I ain't never came on to you Niecy, and you know that." My tone had gone from surety to the crackle of consequence. Denise remained silent, listening to my chosen truth. "I fuck with girls, plain and simple. I love Gavin and his dick, but these bitches know how to eat my pussy, too, the end, and you know that."

"First, if you were a lesbian, I wouldn't give a fuck. So, if you're bisexual, say that, and it'll make sense to me, all of this. But you ain't gotta act like you letting bitches eat your pussy for shits and giggles. That's what a vibrator's for."

"I gotta vibrator too, bitch, and?"

"You gone do what you wanna do anyway."

"I love Gavin..."

"You love Gavin, but how much? Why do you need this arrangement, cause' that's basically what this is? He gets to come to the party, but the party's for you."

I put my phone down, shaking my head at a read. My faithful friend, my sister, wouldn't let me slide. Why do I have to be labeled? I'm free from labels. I live in a different world from these regular motherfuckers; I'm free.

Exhausted with emotion, I sought the retreat of my sofa, the remote, and a box of Cheez-its. No matter how much explaining, Denise was judgmental anyway. But deep down, I hadn't considered Gavin's feelings, concerns, or anything for that matter. I figured if he could handle that night back in Jamaica, he could feel a lifestyle.

Gavin was unaware of the level of hate I had for strippers and strip clubs thanks to my daddy, Ezra Gene Gentry, of Beaumont, Texas.

Over thirty years ago, when I was becoming a teenage girl, with rosebuds and the imagination of hips, Daddy sat me down and offered clarity on the world outside my bedroom window. A random and strange conversation, the topic was strip clubs, something that none of my friends or I cared for. He was adamant through his words, with occasions to spit in annunciation.

"A woman that carries herself like a woman, would never be seen in a strip club, you hear what I'm saying, Risa?" Fourteen-year-old me shook my head 'yes,' eager to keep a promise. "That's where some women go and be nasty, dancing on the stage, with no clothes on, and they probably got A.I.D.S."

I hadn't a clue what a stripper looked like, much less a strip club and pole, but I believed every word my father said. "And see, women like this, they break up happy homes, you know what I mean?" I shook my head yes, with absolutely no idea. "These women will take a father away from his child and husband away from his wife." I continued listening and looking into my father's eyes as he spoke so earnestly about something way over my head. But this was not a father-daughter talk, but more a confessional. Essentially, he was attempting to come clean and atone for the sins of July 30, 1988.

He and Hazel had words that morning, over his inconsistencies. He paid a bill late, resulting in a late fee, which caused an overdraft fee. He promised to take the chicken out of the fridge before work and forgot. Mama was fed up and read him like a book. So, in Ezra's classic passive-aggressive way, he chose the fellowship of the saints at 'Sugar Daddy's' on S. Post Oak, with co-workers. It was a hole in the wall strip club, probably with five strippers on the roster. For just $10, he could escape Mama's foolishness, for an afternoon of heavy petting and drinking. But by the time he came home, Hazel was already on the front porch in her rocking chair and rollers. He walked up the steps, fixed his demeanor, and spoke, "Hey."

"You got something you wanna tell me?"

"No."

"Sugar Daddy's called, you left yo' got-damn wallet."

She got up and stormed through the door, while he stood there, assed out. In their fifteen years of marriage, he'd never cheated or flirted with another woman. It was indeed his first fuck up, but it felt like the end of the world. He was so embarrassed that after he went to get his wallet, he didn't come back home, but to a friend's house. A few hours later, Otto, Daddy's friend, and a co-worker called to set things straight; "This nigga won't stop crying, what happened?" The next day, he was home, right after work, right at the front porch, looking like a hound dog, waiting to be forgiven.

"So, promise me, you'll never step foot in a strip club, much less become a stripper, cause' that's not the place for a young lady. You could end up a bull dagger."

"What's that, daddy?"

"Oh, see, now you done got me started…a bull dagger is a woman who likes other women, which means they don't have husbands, and they don't have kids. You want kids one day?"

"Yes."

"Well, keep yo' ass outta strip clubs!"

Supposed words of wisdom from a man I adored, I never stepped foot in a strip club, but instead, turned every hotel room and every tour bus into a strip club, every time. My sexual repression, as a Southern Baptist girl, eventually exploded in other ways.

But the more I thought about it, Gavin deserved favors, big time. That night in L.A., four years ago, with Tai, and now this shit with the yoga bitch, I owed him a strip club moment, with me by his side. So, I mustered the confidence to accept his pitch. I took the liberty of looking up Houston's more respectable gentlemen clubs to match my level of comfort. For nearly two hours, I googled and researched websites and distances from our home, all in preparation for a presentation. At the end of it, I was cool with four spots that seemed clean enough, but the closest place was an upscale joint in the Galleria, called "Longfellow's."

By the looks of the website, it was a massive place, surrounded by stucco walls, painted burnt orange. The wrought iron gates gave the impression that this place was probably really popping in the 90s, but only survived by grace and history. You could imagine the outlandish shit that went on, like orgies with the frat boys of a booming oil and gas Houston, fried on coke, fucking White, Asians and Latino girls with permed out hair and blue eye shadow. There was another picture of a chandelier, spiffy for a strip joint. I figured if he couldn't appreciate my effort, I'd at least enjoy the ambiance.

About 1:15 in the morning, we laid in bed, while Gavin watched an episode of *'Insecure,'* and I played *Candy Crush*. I thought of my tone before taking the best approach to a request.

"Babe?"

"Hmmm."

"So, I was thinking…"

"Yes?"

"Don't say yes like that."

"What?"

"If you gone have an attitude…"

"I'm listening, go ahead."

"As I said, I was thinking, you know, we started off…I started off on the wrong foot with the stripper thing, so I thought about where would we go? Like, if we do this naturally, the question is, where is this supposed to happen naturally? Neither of us works or go to parties and shit, mainly fundraisers. And so far, we haven't met any freaks at rich shit parties. We don't even go to church." Gavin listened intently, smiling at times, but hanging on every word.

"All I'm saying is, this is like our road to recovery."

"What are you trying to say," he asked.

"I'm saying, the strip club idea is cool."

"Okay, but one question."

"Yes?"

"We've been together ten years, over ten years and…I can't remember us needing this. And now, you seem ready, and I wonder, did you cheat on me before this last time?"

Deep down, he made a point, but even more profound, I masked the pain of my infidelity, with eagerness. He didn't need outside pussy like me, but my relaxed way irked his soul. There was never a need for this until I got caught, which means he passed up a whole lot of pussy.

"Never…and I don't need this arrangement either."

"But it's cool, though, right?"

"For both of us, right?"

I smacked my lips in protest. He had a smartass mouth too early in the morning, but it didn't matter. I could play along.

"Fuck it, let's go to the strip club, and if nothing comes of it, oh well," he chimed.

"Okay…just broadening my horizons, babe."

"I bet yo' ass already looked up places and shit, huh?"

I sat there, with my arms crossed, assured of one thing; we would not bring home any scallywag, skank ass, $5 hoe, with bullet hole wounds and stretch marks. Hell, we wouldn't be bringing back anybody unless I approved. But Gavin didn't know that, yet.

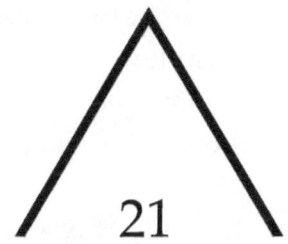

21

Fishers of Men

On Valentine's Day, after having had an exquisite meal and steady drinks at *Vaishya*, Gavin paid the bill, and we hopped in an uber, on the way to an experiment. Occasionally, he looked over at me, checking for a vibe, I guessed.

"You all right?"

"I'm good."

"We gone stick to the script, I promise."

"All right."

The script was the agreed time we'd stay in *'Longfellow's.* Anything past sixty minutes, and I was leaving. Number two, none of the strippers were invited to his lap unless, by me. And whoever we chose, her name couldn't be longer than three syllables, starting with *'La'* or *'Sha'* and ending in *'sha,' 'da,'* or *'qua.'*

Fifteen minutes later, we arrived at a black wrought iron gate, with an oversized 'L' in the middle. The scenery was a mix between Spanish and cheesy, with a water fountain that had neon pink and turquoise backlighting. The backdrop was a semi-modern, two-story building, circular drive, and porte-cochere, slathered in stucco and painted burnt orange, with even cheesier Spanish tiles on the roof.

A husky, red-headed White guy, maybe 6'ft tall, in all black, graciously opened the door for us, "Good evening." We walked through to a reception desk, where two young chicks, also dressed in black, stood with fake smiles. The portly one, with blonde streaks, appeared to be the manager.

"Welcome to Longfellow's, do you have a reservation for the evening?"

"Yes, it should be under Rudy Huxtable."

The other girl looked on the clipboard, with her index finger slowly gliding a list of names. "Yes ma'am, welcome to Longfellow's, right this way, please." Gavin looked impressed as we walked into the main room, dimly lit and two stories high, with balcony railings that went entirely around this cave of sin. The young lady led us to a roped-off area on the first floor, with two finely upholstered white armchairs, an intimate round table covered with a white tablecloth, and faux candlelight. "Your waitress will be right with you."

From where we sat, our view of the main stage was prime. The stripper on stage looked Brazilian, firm, and shapely. Her performance under white floodlights, washed over her partially naked body, to the sounds of Mad Cobra's, *'Flex.'* The beat went perfect with her rolling abs and hips, thick thighs, flat stomach, and pierced nipples. I played relaxed, legs crossed, eyes wandering around, with the slow tick of a tock. Gavin excused himself to the restroom, providing the perfect opportunity to throw shade. I had to text Denise.

'Guess where I'm at?'

'You at the hoe house?'

'Yeah, not bad, though. We on a time limit, and it's about 59 minutes left.'

When he got back to the table, he asked, "The waiter ain't came yet?" I shook my head no while easing my phone closer in.

"I'll be back, what you want from the bar?"

"Surprise me."

Again, left alone, and judgmental, we shared more sarcasm.

'Just make sure her cat and lace front on point.'

'Her cat, lace front, body, credit, all that.'

I was becoming a prick.

'I better not see a bump on your lip the next time I see you,' Denise wrote.

I cried, just as Gavin returned.

"What's funny?"

"Oh, nothing, dumbass meme."

Gavin looked like an uncomfortable regular, while another girl took the main stage. Not as voluptuous, she had an innocent, college girl look, and mid-grade ass. "What about her."

I just looked, with my phone still in hand, "She cute," which meant, *I don't give a fuck, cause no one is going home with us, you big dummy.*

"Let's get a private dance."

"With her?"

"Damn," he answered.

"You want me to pick just any bitch I see?"

"Don't start that bullshit, you gave this a whole fucking hour, and I agreed to it like a dumbass, and now you tripping."

"Ain't nobody tripping; I don't like her."

"Well, we ain't got that long, so."

"Okay, so the very next bitch."

"That's not what I meant."

"Gavin…"

He settled back in his seat with a slight pout. My little scheme was starting to crack. Whoever the next dancer was, regardless of attraction, regardless if he'd thought I was picking her to appease him, regardless of anything, I'd allow him a funky lap dance to shut the fuck up.

"Coming to the stage, is the lovely, the vivacious and beautiful, Nooni Baby," the announcer spoke. I laughed again for a different reason. Gavin looked pissed off and ready for the shit to end.

"What's funny now?"

"I have a cousin with that same nickname."

"Wow."

When Nooni Baby took the stage, her commanding presence, slow and confident, deserved attention. With a hand towel, she wiped the pole clean of DNA. Wearing a white laced bra and panties, with sheer white stockings attached to a matching garter belt, she accessorized with gold hoop earrings and blazing red pumps, six inches tall. On the low, her 80s retro theme was fly. Her skin was a deep brown that glowed against stage lighting. Her height and size were excellent, imagining those long legs up in the air, like a peace sign. Her beautiful complexion, athletic build, minus the weave, and most of all, that ass, did it for me. Nooni's ass was a mash-up of between Serena Williams and ungodly.

She waited to catch the beat, as *'Pussy, Weed & Alcohol,'* by the 5th Ward Boyz, started playing. A brother, easily in his forties, dressed in slacks and a buttoned, long-sleeved shirt, wearing glasses, walked up to the stage to break bread. We watched him throwing dollars, two at a time, like a regular trick, while I studied her everything. Briefly, Gavin looked over to see my reaction, watching my eyes dance in awe, with my legs no longer crossed, but both feet, planted on the ground.

"Don't be afraid to tip the main stage, ladies and gentlemen," the DJ offered. Soon after, a female patron walked up to throw ones at Nooni, who noticed, and turned to grace the audience with a back shot, before dropping it in her face. The patron, a White woman, who looked between stud and fish, and probably a regular, gave a slight tap to her right cheek and turned red with laughter and liberation by a Black ass. Gavin glanced at me with a look that read, 'see?' I rolled my eyes. Gavin then proceeded to reach for his stash, counted fifty ones, and got up to walk to the stage. He was defiant, with forty-nine minutes left to make a miracle.

When he got closer, the White chick stood there, tickled pink, but Gavin chose to intercept a play. He waited patiently as if using the only urinal in a big ass bathroom. In her peripheral, she could see him, but she played dumb for the sake of a chocolaty fat ass on stilettos. Gavin, being mild-mannered, looked beneath himself, waiting in line, tasting the dry burn of impatience on his tongue. In pure asshole form, he decided to walk up beside her, forcing her to acknowledge him with a shit-eating grin. He gave a *'fuck you'* nod and focused on Nooni. She caught his eye and made a transition, turning around to face him, still in character, deep grinding his desire. His brave stance won alone time when his opponent threw the last of her money on stage and walked away.

Victorious in lust, Gavin stood at the altar of grace, for the anointing to fall fresh upon him. Through the trial and tribulation of getting to this night, it was redemption. He dared to believe that this night was ordained, that his will may be done. He paid his tithe, one by one, while she smiled at his joyful giving, and leaned in close enough, probably to ask, "Can I get a private dance later?" Nodding his head yes, a real-life fantasy came true, while he stood there, full-on erect, with $23 in his hand. Then it hit him; for a man of his cloth, he'd been in front of the stage too long, looking thirsty. He threw the remaining money at her feet, while she danced on, stepping through scattered dreams.

When he returned to his seat, I looked at him and shook my head. "Thirsty right," he joked. I stayed silent from a quick snapback. Secretly, it bothered me how pleasant he was. For years, by spite, I dictated our sexual temperature. I initiated threesomes and random sex in odd places, not him. The most outrageous thing he'd ever started, besides head in my childhood bedroom, was giving me head in a limo, on the way to that 90s concert in L.A. But tonight, his swag was different.

But not one to back down, I was up for whatever the fuck he thought he needed, to love me. "Made you a little friend, huh?" He chuckled like the thousands of other patrons who walked through *Longfellow's* doors, falling in love through tips.

Why do men generously tip strippers, believing in love through currency? Somehow, he imagines that despite the hundreds of motherfuckers sitting behind him, with the same objective, he's the unique motherfucker.

Gavin's funky little fifty dollars was a business transaction, nothing else. "What did you think of her," he asked. I shrugged my shoulders nonchalantly and answered, "She cute, she *aight*." He laughed, not for the words or tone, but the rarity of seeing me jealous, and maybe threatened. "So that means you like her, then." I smacked my lips and rolled my eyes.

Gavin was now enjoying this careless night, instantly vibing with a stranger. But I admired Nooni's walk, enough to wanna give it a taste. But neither of us knew what to expect on this ride. Gavin glanced at my glass and asked, "You wanna another drink?" Already buzzing, I answered, "Yeah, the same thing." He looked around, antsy to find our waiter, determined not to walk to the bar. He spotted and flagged her down, but as she walked our way, so did Nooni. I saw her and began sizing her up. "Another round, please," Gavin told the waiter. Nooni stood patiently behind, awaiting her turn to serve.

"Hey, what's up," she spoke. Perhaps waiting for which lap to sit and chit chat on, I looked at Gavin, amused at the situation.

"You can sit here," he offered, quickly glancing at me. Nooni took her place on his lap and smiled.

"You're beautiful," I offered, to break the ice.

"Thank you." Gavin was happy, with a slight hard-on. His hands were resting comfortably on the arms of the chair, showing some respectable distance. I was chill, pleasant, and reserved. I figured we'd talk sexual shit, and he'd get a dance, maybe I'd get one, and then it'd be off to the comfort of our bed, just the two of us. But for Nooni, something else took shape.

"Are y'all a couple or…"

"That's my husband."

"Oh, okay," Nooni replied, feeling awkward.

"It's cool. I was laughing earlier because I have a cousin who goes by the same name."

That's when Nooni took the opportunity to investigate further. "Yeah, cause' you look familiar to me, is your name Clarissa?"

Gavin and I looked at each other, cautious of fans who shoot game for the come up. *Who is this crazy stripper bitch, sitting on my husband's lap?*

"I'm sorry, how do I know you?"

Nooni gave a nod and said, "Hey, cousin." Being mindful of crazed fans who imagine crazed things, I was now cautious of a situation.

"Cousin? How are we cousins?" Gavin awkwardly looked on as court began, and this fine ass woman remained on his lap.

"My dad was married to Dottie."

My eyes immediately grew; I got up and responded, "Kimberly?"

Gavin, being a full-grown, heterosexual man, and still with a hard-on, looked upset and surprised at the same damn time. He watched as we hugged and rocked from side to side, for all the years that went by without communication. He couldn't remember a time when I talked about a stripper cousin.

"Girl, the last time I saw you, you had to be seven?"

"Yeah, for granny's funeral."

"Oh my God, that was back in 2000."

We embraced again, and Gavin's erection, now gone entirely, was unnecessary. She was my family. Unsure of what direction the night would go, he tended to the last of what was in his glass, ready to go home.

"Girl, what is going on, what are you doing here?" I was blunt, yes, and maybe snooty, but it came from a real place. Before the fame, I babysat her from time to time, remembering those days I would braid her hair, putting barrettes on pigtails in Sunnyside. But when my career took off, so did our ties.

"I'm surviving. That's what I'm doing here," Nooni answered, flatly.

"Well, girl, no judgment, I can't believe this, when you get off?"

"I'm done unless y'all wanted a dance."

"Fuck that, let's get out of here and catch up, girl!"

The fucking irony of it all was like a sick joke being played out by God. We were leaving with my cousin, my twenty-five-year-old cousin, with the body of a stallion, and presumably, a sex drive to match. The clarity of the moment went from lust to concern, even though I knew Gavin wanted to stay. He wanted to explore opportunities for an agreement. But like a good husband, who listens to his wife, we called it quits with twenty-five minutes to spare. We decided to wait, as Kimberly went to the back to change.

"We took an Uber over, so pull up and we'll ride with you," I suggested.

Kimberly walked off to her car while we waited.

"Wow," Gavin spoke.

"What?"

"Imagine if we never came tonight?"

It was a profound slug.

I smiled and answered, "Whatever." About five minutes had passed before we wondered where she was, but soon after, she walked back up, with a defeated look. "What's wrong," I asked.

Kimberly just shook her head and answered, "My car is tripping again. It won't start."

"No problem, we'll get another cab, get you to your place, that's that," Gavin offered.

"But what about her car, we can't just leave it here."

"No, we could, I hate that piece of shit," Kimberly answered. "But nah, they gone trip if I leave it. Y'all go head. I can get a tow truck…"

"Nah, we gone wait."

Gavin did his best to hide a cracked face.

"Y'all smoke? I got some in the car."

His mood immediately changed.

"That'll work," he replied as we walked towards the lot. For some reason, my motherly need to nurture kicked in. Being selfish came naturally, but for all the years that Nooni was off somewhere, becoming a woman, without a 'big sister' to advise her on guys and heartbreak, I was reclaiming my time.

When we reached her white, 2003 Honda Civic, it was a sight to see. Two missing front hubcaps, primer paint on the front left bumper, and a *'coexist'* sticker on the back bumper, showed that the struggle was real. I cringed for Nooni's sake. Gavin, still horny and agitated, snuck peeks at Nooni's body every chance possible. She wore form-fitting, faded blue jeans with trendy, worn patches and a pink tank top.

When we sat in the car, with about seven pairs of shoes, a two-day-old fast food bag filled with trash, and some other unnecessary items not meant for a vehicle, Gavin and I did our best not to judge. I reminisced on my young adult days, trying to make sense of a cold world. Like Nooni, I didn't have all the answers but was stubborn enough to pretend. I could read her demeanor, a bit rebellious, even fearless, but all a front for someone in survival mode.

"Excuse the mess, I be on the go," Nooni offered.

"It's all good," I replied.

I knew she was lying. Nooni reached in her glove compartment, pulled out a *Swisher Sweet* and lighter, and lit that bitch. Aroma and smoke danced in a small place, as three souls prepared to be lifted. Nooni took the first drag and passed to me, sitting in the passenger seat. Nooni searched through her contacts for the tow service she used last time this happened. "Girl, this smells like some GX-14 shit."

"Yeah, that's some gas," she answered.

"Gas?"

Nooni laughed at Gavin's tone. It was a clear indication of the age difference between us. "It's not Reggie shit; I think it's purp." Gavin remained silent, avoiding any other statements that would date him. Nooni made her call, while we stayed in a cipher. Gavin took a hit, and coughed uncontrollably, while we laughed.

"Don't laugh at me, what's the name of this shit again?"

"So...you been dancing long?"

It was a question that burned in the pit of my soul.

"Ah, 'bout six months, it's temporary, though."

"No judgment, just wondering."

"I was in school, but my financial aid stopped last semester, and then I got fired."

"Oh, wow. What did you study?"

"Cosmetology."

"Oh, okay, so hair, makeup..."

"Yeah, but I wanna do makeup professionally."

Gavin, who had already taken flight, sat quietly, listening to girl talk, easily judgmental of her millennial storyline. It sounded typical of entitled motherfuckers, only concerned with *Instagram* followers and the next high. Sitting in the back seat of her car, he wondered how long the night would last.

Nearly a half-hour later, the tow service arrived. We called an Uber, and the tow truck followed us to her apartment. When we hit the road, Nooni and I sat in the back.

"Man, thank y'all for waiting."

"Glad we could help," Gavin answered, with shade.

For the remainder of the car ride, we giggled and caught up on shit since last seeing each other. Secretly, I felt renewed with a purpose and determined that Nooni would be a 'project.'

When we arrived at her apartment complex, driving through the gates, we looked at her surroundings; Gavin snickered at the complex name, *'Cat Tails.'* A group of dudes gathered around an old school slab, black on black, banging D.J. Screw. Kimberly made a call to the tow truck driver, "Just drop it off like last time." Almost in synchronicity, Gavin looked out the window, while I dropped my head, in bougie disgust. "Dang, y'all went up...all right bye," she complained. "Thank y'all again for everything; it was good seeing you. We gotta catch up."

"Let me get your number," I asked. After our exchange, we hugged once more, and Nooni walked off.

"Please wait, sir," I told the driver.

Gavin smacked his teeth lowkey, pissed at this over nurturing, motherly shit. We patiently watched her seductive walk to a door with a white sheet attached. She didn't walk in immediately. Her somber body language indicated something terrible, but Gavin reached for his phone to escape, while I continued watching, wondering what was taking so long. Suddenly, Nooni turned around, looking shit-faced, with paper in hand, walking back towards the car.

"What's wrong?"

"I just got evicted."

"Get in."

Gavin's facial expression read 'what the fuck,' but I ignored it. Even the Uber driver could see the tension. "Girl, that's too much, you've already done enough, Imma call my homegirl, I can stay over there tonight." For some reason, I was relentless. "I insist, plus we can catch up. I'll take you to your homegirl's tomorrow." Nooni just shook her head, slightly embarrassed. Gavin remained quiet, maybe feeling disrespected by my randomness. "I mean, I don't have any clothes, can't even get into my place…" Nooni's voice began to crack. It was at that moment, Gavin realized that she'd hit rock bottom.

"Go ahead and get in, we got you." Gavin's co-sign was everything.

Nooni wiped tears that rolled down her cheeks, shook her head, and answered, "All right." She slid back in next to me and got another hug. And just like that, the Adams received Kimberly "Nooni Baby" Ralston, in love. For the remainder of the ride home, we girls continued laughing, reminiscing about the good old days, when family was all we had.

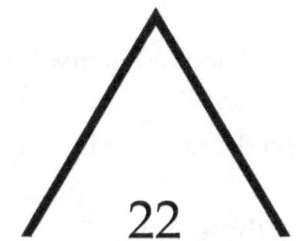

22

Suffer Little Nooni, Forbid her Not

The very next morning, after a night of highs, lows, and uncertainties, Nooni woke up in a plush queen-size bed in our guest bedroom. When I walked in, she was reaching for her cell, probably to check notifications; "Morning, girl, we 'bout to eat." Twenty minutes later, Gavin and I sat at the counter, wondering how long she'd take. It was breakfast, cooked in her honor.

"Wake her ass up for lunch then," Gavin joked.

"She was up when I walked in."

Nooni threw the covers back and went into the bathroom to piss and wash her face. She looked around, impressed by the décor and high-end finishes of a bathroom. White subway tile, brushed nickel faucet and knobs, with seafoam as an accent color. She was accustomed to cheap shit, sharing space with Dottie, up until she moved out years ago. I came back up and knocked at the door.

"Hey, cuz, you good?"

"Yes, girl! Bae-bae, this bed? OMG."

"Oh, thank you. We got breakfast downstairs, come get some."

"Girl, you got some shorts or something I can put on?"

"We already saw everything. I know you ain't tripping."

"I can't stand you..."

"Hold on."

I jogged down the hall, looked in my drawer, pulled out some grey boy shorts, and tossed them to her on the way back. Five minutes later, she walked into the kitchen, and it was suddenly uncomfortable.

"Are you okay with those shorts?"

"I was gone call you…" Nooni answered with a laugh.

Gavin remained nonchalant, reading an article from his phone, avoiding any eye contact with her ass, but it was inevitable. "Gavin, are those shorts too small to you?" He stayed with his poker face planted on the screen, pretending not to hear, "Huh, babe?" I smacked my lips, rolled my eyes, and looked back at Nooni, "Let's go to the mall after we finish." Nooni began walking towards the kitchen table, in front of Gavin, who snuck a glimpse at her abundant cakes and unconsciously licked his lips. He looked right back at his phone with precise timing, still mindful of other eyes.

"My homegirl gone pick me up around 3 when she gets off."

"You good."

"Yeah, you good," Gavin followed.

Gavin's support seemed genuine, considering the circumstance, or maybe he was warming up to his imagination. Somewhere deep down, in-house side pussy sparked a kind heart. I could only imagine late nights, me away at rehearsal, or early yoga mornings, maybe they'd slip up. Maybe, Nooni would accidentally suck dick while he worked on his next novel, or he would lace her with a five-minute pump on his way out the door. But that was my cousin, so, no.

Meanwhile, I was happy about the day ahead, with Nooni. I made plans for an impromptu round of shopping and lunch at *Moxie*. I was determined to investigate Nooni's life, feeling responsible for her wayward path. When I became *Renee*, between '98 to '02, I was lucky to be home for Thanksgiving or Christmas and maybe three to four weekends out of the year. Stardom had taken me to the outermost limits of reachability, causing disgruntled family members and the decline of phone calls that mattered. But this was redemption now.

By noon, we were out the door, in my new Range Rover, on the way to the *Galleria Mall*. Of course, I was extra, with my hair pulled back in a bun, edges snatched, with some popping hot pink yoga pants and a tank top, Louie shades, and Balenciaga sneakers. Nooni was impressed, but this was my chance to make it up to her. I especially missed her pre-teen years, when I was at my lowest and unable to help anyone. But by the grace of God, our paths crossed.

"I like your truck," Nooni offered.

"You wanna drive?"

"Hell yeah!"

We pulled over, switched sides, and instantly, Nooni fell in love.

"This my shit!"

Nooni pushed the ignition and felt the power of the throttle and the instant elevation from mundane to the liberated. The grip and feel of a wood grain and leather steering wheel felt like real money. Her reaction was pure and straightforward, just like she used to be. "Man, holdup," Nooni cheered. It was the first time in a long time that she'd escape, without the aid of purp and drank.

When we hit the road, Nooni seemed freed from the woes of being a single "Black" woman on the Southwest side of life. The 180-degree turn from yesterday gave her reason to believe that this was the day that the Lord had made. "Girl, don't get no damn ticket!" She smiled from ear to ear, in yesterday's clothes, "Girl, I couldn't even afford it."

"So, what's your plan?" In all fairness, I was hoping Nooni would tell me she wanted out of this bullshit life; otherwise, there was a plan of my own. "I mean...I just gotta sit down. I be living wrong." I gave the nod, like a shrink listening to a patient, but really, I was waiting for her to finish.

"This how I wanna live, one day," she continued.

"You can if you have a plan. You going back to school?"

"Yeah, if my financial aid got right."

"Well, I can help you with that if you want."

Nooni tried processing yet another blessing. This treatment felt foreign coming from a family member, much less a woman. But this was Risa, someone she hadn't seen in eighteen years.

"Cuz, you looking out, for real?"

"Say you'll go back."

"I'll go back."

Giving Nooni a second chance was the least I could do. She could move in, maybe six months to a year, just enough time to get things in order.

But then there was the matter of all that ass walking around the house. He needed to be clear that this was not an arrangement but family helping family.

"So, I was thinking. It's been eighteen years since we last saw each other; why don't you stay until the weekend. It's no pressure from Gavin and I. This'll give you some time to get things in order. But if you gotta go, I understand."

"Nah, it's...I don't know. We just connected, and you been so nice already."

"Yeah, it's weird, but I feel bad, Nooni."

"Why?"

"Cause' man, I could've been there for you when you needed me most."

"I ain't tripping. You were living your life. Shit, back in elementary and middle school, I used to brag about you all the time. We always been proud of you."

Her words moved me. And still, I felt obligated to steer her clear of the illusion of cool. She was a living sacrifice, for the times I chose lines of coke over a plane ticket home.

"Ah, that's sweet, thank you."

"We watched your videos on BET and MTV...I practiced your dance moves and shit."

She admired my rise to glory, and maybe even prayed for me when the lights began to dim. She probably remembered the news of the DUI arrest. I wished she would've reached out to me through Dottie, but after Dottie's divorce from her father, Dottie disowned Nooni out of spite of a failed marriage.

"Oh my God, you making me feel old as fuck."

"I used to ask Dottie about you, but she'd never tell me anything."

I was shocked at the revelation but knew Dottie could be a bitch.

"Why didn't you just…" I began, but stopped, to think, *how would she get my number from Dottie?* "I didn't know that. She came to our wedding in Jamaica.

"When did y'all get married?"

"2010."

"Oh, okay, yeah."

"Yeah what?"

"I stopped talking to Dottie in 2006; she and daddy got divorced in '05."

"Nooni, why?"

"She lied to daddy a lot, and on me. She told him I smoked weed, cause' she smelled it on my clothes one day. But I didn't smoke, it was niggas from my school I was with, but I couldn't tell her that."

"So, what did you tell her?"

"I ain't tell her shit. She got pissed off. I know how to keep secrets."

We laughed at adolescence, but underneath, there was a riff. Instead of a loving relationship between a stepdaughter and stepmother, who'd known each other since Nooni was three, it soured the more Nooni longed for her biological mother.

Kathy, Kimberly's mother, ran out on the family when she was just a year old. Strung out on heroin and alcohol, she clung to life in the *bottoms* of Houston's Third Ward, while Roy struggled with being a single parent. With no immediate female influence, Nooni received tough love from a man unfit to be alone.

"I think it's sad that y'all lost a relationship, but maybe, it's for the better; you needed to get away from that toxic shit." In my best efforts to console Nooni, I imagined the psychological scars left from cuts too deep to heal. Maybe she'd have a decent career by now, working in some office, wearing blouses, skirts, and professional heels instead of garters. She could've been a sorority girl from an HBCU, dating some dude named Rashid, but she seemed content. "Well, I'm good. I hope she good. I'm driving a Range Rover right now, so…"

When we arrived at the mall, a shopping spree vibe was to raise her spirits. It was nothing to drop a bag for retail therapy. So, first, we hit Louis Vuitton, where Nooni picked out sunglasses and a clutch, both costing more than her rent and what was in her bank account. Then it was off to Saint Laurent for $600 sneakers. Nooni's high-end collection of luxury items, before this, had been a Michael Kors and Coach bag. She had knockoff Louie and Gucci bags, but it was bum bitch shit.

"Girl, what you think about this," I asked, holding a Kenzo t-shirt against my body.

Nooni walked over to scrutinize, taking a glance at the tag, and answered, "Not for that price."

After a few more stops in the mall, we went on for a mani, pedi session at Paradise Nails, my little hideaway vibe. The girls at the shop always made me feel at home.

"Ah, Clarissa, you come here, your friend sits there," Lilly, the owner of the shop, commanded. We graciously followed suit, preparing to be pampered even more.

"So, you got a boo thang?"

Nooni burst out in laughter, feeling put on the spot.

"Single and ready to mingle."

"Wait a minute, with all that ass, you single?"

"Niggas my age ain't shit. Imma get a old nigga or a bitch."

Her non-filter amused me. In an alternate universe, she was partially perfect for us; young and sexy as fuck. All my questions slowly revealed the layers of Nooni, who was easing into grace. The stint at the mall, the drive in the Range, and now this, were all sensory overload.

"You mess with chicks?" Nooni gave a devilish grin as if caught red-handed.

"I mean, bitches hit on me at the club, all the time." In her world of entertainment, she must've felt like meat, sitting on hundreds of laps over the last six months, surviving for rent's sake.

"You way grown, huh?"

"I just like what I like."

"See, I'm at a loss now. My stripper cousin plays with coochie," I joked.

"Ah, I don't do the playing."

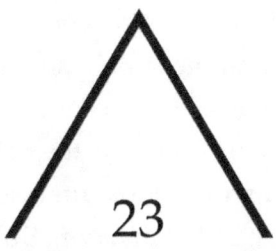

23

Favor

After a long day of playing catch up, we decided to get drinks at *RA Sushi*. We'd gone from the Galleria to a few more boutiques in between. Nooni's friend, Shawn, called, saying she'd be late picking her up, which worked perfectly for a couple more chocolate Martinis. "Girl, these go hard," Nooni cheered. She hadn't had many Martinis in her adult life. Her usual Long Island was enough to numb the pain of hands, groping at will. "This my new shit."

The randomness of the day was comfortable, remembering the times I'd look into her young eyes and smile, or braid her hair on the patio back in Sunnyside. I was awestruck by the woman sitting across from me, shapely and tainted.

Kimberly "Nooni" Ralston, got her nickname for the time she was born, 12:09PM, June 2, 1993. She was a bundle of joy for newlyweds, Roy and Kathy Ralston, but things changed. Kathy got a taste of heroin at a friend's house in the summer of 1994, and it was all downhill from there. Items in the family home came up missing, Kathy stayed out longer, and a little girl longed for her mother. Roy got frustrated, torn with committing to his wife and starting over again for the sake of his daughter. In the end, he chose his daughter over blind faith, and within six months of the divorce from Kathy, he met my Aunt Dottie at Red Rooster.

When I met Nooni, I was nineteen, and Nooni, three. Aunt Dottie and Roy would call me to babysit when I wasn't recording or performing at local clubs. I was becoming attached to a precious little girl, with big brown eyes and the brightest, hopeful smile ever. For over a year, I would look after her, thinking of the day when I'd finally have a child of my own. But when my career took off, quaint Saturday afternoons braiding Nooni's hair were traded for L.A. and the world. She didn't understand why I disappeared until the day she saw me on TV. But that was the only way she could see me.

After the second round of drinks, liquid courage gave me the confidence to talk the real shit I'd wanted to say since yesterday. I gripped my glass for one last taste, before making an offer Nooni couldn't refuse. However, just as I was about to speak, my phone began vibrating with a call from Gavin. For some reason, I chose to ignore it. Nooni saw who called but looked sheepishly away. In an instant, it felt like a betrayal, like a month ago, with the chick from yoga class. I knowingly planned to overstep my bounds as a wife and partner by offering Nooni at least six months' room and board without his consent. So, instead, Nooni agreed to stay until the weekend.

Later in the evening, after dinner and some binge-watching of 'Queen Sugar', Nooni went off to the guest bedroom while Gavin and I stayed on the couch, continuing to Netflix and chill. Gavin had no idea of my masterful plan, outlined in my mind. But first I prepared the situation. "You want some wine?" Gavin, already dozing off in between scenes, accepted. My carefree stroll was celebratory of what I expected; *an agreeable man.*

When I returned, I snuggled close, put my glass on the end table, and said, "I wanna run something by you." Gavin, the over thinker, knew I was plotting for something.

"Yeah, wassup," he answered.

I repositioned myself, cleared my throat, and replied, "I want Nooni to stay with us...not for long, just 'til she gets her shit

together. She's fucked up, and quite frankly, she gone be a hoe if
we don't intervene." He looked in disbelief and cracked up.

"What the fuck is funny?"

"She's going to be a hoe?"

"Look at her; she's fucking at-risk. You would let your cousin
strip, ass cheeks clapping?"

"Did she ask for help?"

His indifference pissed me off. For nearly five seconds, I stared
until he dropped his head. "Man, don't go poking your head in shit.
She might take it the wrong way." The fact remained; Nooni was
family. "I mean, it's your family, would I say no? I understand how
you feel?" He always knew what to say, or what I wanted to hear.

"You're still my husband. It's fair that I at least consider you."
Gavin gave the nod to my bullshit.

"So, what now?"

"I guess we tell her, see what she says."

"When?"

"I don't know, tomorrow?"

"So, how do you even say it, 'we wanna adopt you?'"

"Don't be a dick."

"I bet she turns you down."

"Why?"

"Any woman that strips for money has to be a go-getter."

"Profound."

"All right, you know what, we'll go out to dinner, and we'll
see. You cool with that?"

"Whatever."

The very next day, Friday evening, dinner reservations were set
at *Steak 48*, in River Oaks. It was a usual kind of dining experience
for us, but occasional for Nooni, either for a birthday or when
Beyoncé came to town.

When we were seated, we sat across from her, under dim
lighting. Nooni looked brand new, wearing an Alexander Wang
dress and Louboutin stilettos. "I think the last time I was here

was for the *On The Run Tour*…that was such a good show." We just smiled.

I struggled with the perfect time to ask a question. Asking too early could blow a dinner vibe. But the wait seemed unnecessary, so, after the waiter gave his spiel along with glasses of water, I threw caution to the wind. "This has been the most awesome and awkward few days I've had in a while." Nooni and Gavin smiled, listening on. "And, I've…we've been thinking about how we could help you out a little." Immediately Nooni interrupted, "Y'all done enough already. I can't pay y'all back."

"It's a blessing, don't worry about it," Gavin offered.

"You're family," I followed.

For a moment, I wanted to look at Gavin like, *you motherfucker.*

"I want y'all to know, I'm gone miss y'all, I mean, we'll keep in touch, but I'm gone miss spending time with you."

"Well, you don't have to."

Nooni looked slightly confused.

"We wanna help you get on your feet, so…how would you feel about staying with us, getting back in school again, stuff like that; it would be temporary."

Nooni sat still, mulling over the offer, while we waited for a response.

"Uhm, wow, that's nice of y'all, but I don't want y'all feeling sorry for me."

"We don't feel sorry for you. We wanna help you with your situation?"

"What situation?"

"I mean, you just got evicted, your car is fucked up, you stripping…"

"Stripping is not a problem for me."

"No, it's not, but we just wanna help, that's all," Gavin asked.

Nooni paused for consideration, even after being offended. The problem was her pride. Nooni knew I was right, but being put on blast stung a little.

"I'm not trying to be ungrateful or nothing, but I been through so much shit. I'm just used to surviving." Nooni became emotional. "I appreciate everything, but I ain't no bopper." The backfire of a genuine plea crushed me. It was the first time in a while that words hurt. Two women now sat across from each other, emotionally upset. Nooni noticed me go silent as tears welled in my eyes. Gavin began stroking my back for support, while Nooni looked regretful. "I don't mean to be a bitch; I'm not used to people helping me. I'm used to being hurt."

"Nooni, I have been to the pits of hell...and I survived. Why wouldn't I help you?"

"I just don't want you looking down on me," she cautioned.

"The last time I looked down at you, you were seven years old. A full-grown woman is sitting across from me. Be honest, though. You like stripping?" Nooni smiled and looked away. "I thought so."

"Look, I think our approach might be a little forward, but it's only to give you a second chance on whatever it is you think you should be doing if that makes sense." Nooni shook her head, yes. "We respect you and whatever you decide, but trust us; it comes from a good place." I wiped tears from her face, for an understanding.

"Well, let me think about it..."

"Okay," we answered in unison.

Her consideration gave me life. Without having to stretch toothpaste and rolls of tissue, or pump $5 worth of gas, on the way to a $20 payday, she could regularly eat, sleep, and rest her mind.

By the morning, Nooni could smell the beautiful aroma of sizzling bacon that fried, as sunlight cracked through drawn blinds. It was a new day worthy of a decision. Again, she found herself looking at the mirror, wondering what God's plan was. *Should I stay, or should I go?* In her heart she knew this could be the break she'd prayed for, with a new focus on getting that cosmetology license, and finally having a real career, but maybe, eventually, getting over the death of baby Jelani.

Back when the world was full of promise, her hopes of motherhood sustained the joy inside. It was the birth of her first and only child, a baby boy, Jelani Kareem Tyson. He was born on August 5, 2016, 11:10AM, at Texas Children's Hospital in Houston's medical center. None of my family was there for support, and I'd forgotten Nooni. Roy had passed years prior, to liver cancer, and Dottie had no intention of communicating. But sadly, just a week and a half, after the baby was brought home to a new crib, assembled with love, little Jelani passed from sudden infant death syndrome.

It ripped her and the baby's father, apart. Each blamed the other, and for a moment, Nooni even considered it a punishment from God, just like every other bad thing that happened in her life. She'd sunken so low in depression, that she gave up on reality, dropped out of school, further descending into self-pity. She was now unemployed and desperate. And after just a few months of staying with an aunt on her father's side, she'd grown weary of her prospects. So, on a dare from a friend, she drove her ass to Longfellow's and got a job dancing on a pole, to get the fuck up out of her Aunt Shirleen's house.

Gavin and I were already prepping to eat, with mimosas at the ready. "Morning, girl," I spoke. This time, Nooni wore a respectable nightgown, with arms, but the wiggle of ass through cotton twill was still evident. "Morning, y'all," she replied. Gavin, already with Houston Chronicle in hand and a cup of Blue Mountain coffee, did his best to ignore a sure thing.

Nooni even darted her eyes to see if he'd acknowledged her. She heard his reply, but *did he look up?* My back was turned, working in the kitchen, with my first mimosa in hand. "Food's ready." Both Gavin and Nooni got up, with Nooni ahead of him. Of course, it was opportune, to look at that wiggle, with a bite she casually pulled out. Pleased with yet another sighting, he glanced up, only to meet eyes with mine. *I saw everything, motherfucker.* He quickly looked away to scrambled eggs. "Ooh, this spread looks so good, babe," he spoke. It did; I cooked the old-fashioned way, especially when it came to my grits. I made mine with a splash of buttermilk, salt and pepper, some cheese, and ¼ of a stick of butter, smack dab in the middle. And still, I saw that bullshit.

After fixing plates, we sat together, ready to bless the meal. It was an array of good southern cooking, with biscuits, albeit from a can, grits, scrambled eggs with cheese, a stack of pancakes, a pile of bacon, pan sausage, and of course, mimosas. "You mind saying grace," Gavin asked Nooni.

Nooni looked up with a smile and began. "Dear God, thank you for this food we about to eat, we ask that you bless it to our health and bodies, in Jesus name we pray, Amen…and thank you for that bed I slept in last night." I looked over at Gavin, who looked back and realized a loss bet.

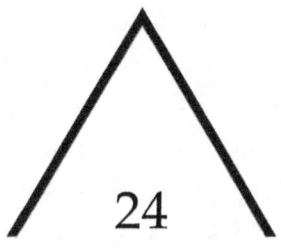

24

Redeemed

By Monday, we had a new member of the Adams family. Nooni was finally getting her belongings out of *Cattails*, after paying the past due rent of $675. I pulled the U-Haul van around to apt. 217, and with the help of the ladies, we cleared out what was most important to her; shoes, clothes, and wigs. With those items alone, the van was nearly filled. I did all I could to hide my usual shady facial expression, at the sight of emptied Cîroc bottles in the closet, but mostly, the look of adolescent irresponsibility, like my old apartment back in Chicago. Of course, there was make-up everywhere, old and new cylinders of lipstick, compacts, and multiple sets of eyelashes spread out like caterpillars on a bathroom sink.

"So, this furniture…" Clarissa shaded.

"We can leave that shit. I don't want it."

"You sure?"

"Where Imma put it? In the garage, next to the Benz and the Range Rover?"

"We should throw it out, so you don't get charged your deposit. But, Imma need help to get this to the trash bin."

"We can hire someone to do this," Clarissa complained.

"C'mon, a little hard work won't hurt you, princess."

"Imma break a nail."

"Me too, girl," Nooni followed.

Even though it was still the Winter, it felt like a warm Spring day. It was refreshing to be in the presence of two beautiful women wearing colorful, neon tank tops and black yoga pants. Adultery crossed my mind, with Nooni having the fatter of the asses. When it came to my sex life, back before it began to fade, Clarissa had leveled up my game. I never had a problem getting pussy, but she was the first to do things that no other woman in my circle did. Pilar sucked me off until I would cum on her face, but Clarissa was the first to swallow. That was the day I knew I'd never leave.

Looking at these beautiful "Black" women, bending, stretching, muscles flexing, sweat forming, I imagined a moment with us in bed. It would be a love supreme, a free flow of fluids, maturity, and mostly lust. And at some point, in this sexcapade, I would either be eating Nooni's ass or fucking it. In another scenario, Clarissa would ride my face while Nooni rode the dick, whichever happened first. But of course, this was all just fantasy.

Two hours later, the kitchen, dining room, living room, and bedroom were cleared. We were exhausted and hungry, so I made an impromptu decision for us to go home, shower up, and barbeque in the back yard.

When we arrived home, everyone agreed to a task for a spontaneous cookout. Clarissa made her kicked up baked beans from a can. I ran back out to get some steaks, burgers, and chicken, and Nooni made her grandma's potato salad recipe. We went our separate ways, first to shower, and later, prepare. When we got to our bedroom, Clarissa was feeling rather frisky and playful, grabbing at my ass, perhaps turned on by pheromones. I thought nothing of it, but when it was time to shower, unexpectedly, she joined. "Let me wash your back, zaddy." I gladly handed her my washcloth, then she made a lavender-scented lather, and washed her man's back.

For a moment, it was innocent, until she went a little lower, to the crack of my ass, the violation zone. I jerked away. "Stop tripping wit'cho funky ass," she commanded. I was reluctant, as she intentionally went deeper and slower between my cheeks, with emphasis on my asshole. "All right, it's clean now." Clarissa turned me around and began washing my dick and balls, tugging at me, with my hands on my hips, smirking at the gesture. She then let the shower rinse me off, as she got on her knees and gave thanks for the hard work I put in earlier. I appreciated her spontaneity, grabbing the back of her head, with her liberated, long strokes of gratitude. For a few more minutes, it went this way, until I pulled her up and bent her over.

It was beginning to feel a lot like 2008 when being random was normal. Before Nooni, we hadn't had sex in at least six weeks, and suddenly this happened? Meanwhile, Nooni laid in bed naked, partially covered by the seafoam colored comforter, after showering, looking at the 'gram, thinking about nothing but getting high and getting some new dick. There was a drought in her life too. The last piece of ass was from a former boyfriend that stumbled into Longfellow's a month ago.

Before that, she hadn't had sex in nearly a year, and had grown tired of Oscar, her blue vibrator, aka "Cookie Monster." She stopped on a picture of a male model for some clothing ad. His physique, skin tone, and look caused her to play with herself, just a quickie before cooking.

Nooni's sexual urges were strong; however, she was unable to find a good rhythm. So, she got up, got dressed, and made her way back downstairs. However, Clarissa had taken a little longer. Even after the shower, she played more until I became the voice of reason. "I need to get this food before it gets late."

Clarissa complied, but answered, "You owe me later." I obliged with a nod and wink, and walked out, pleased with this sudden revival. When I reached downstairs, I saw Nooni alone, sitting at the island, on her phone, as usual.

"I'm heading to the store. You need anything?"

"Some weed..."

"Really?"

"Really."

"I'll see what I can do," I answered facetiously.

I walked out thinking, *where am I getting weed from, and why the fuck you say you'll see what you can do?* Thankfully, Miguel came to mind. He was the only active drug user I could trust.

"Hey man, I need to get some weed."

"What kind of random call is this?" Miguel mocked.

"For stress."

As much as I shared with Miguel over the years, I was reluctant to bring up Nooni just yet. She was not a prospect but family, nor did I need any jabs from Miguel about the possibilities.

We hung up, and I went about my business on the way to Whole Foods. Back home, Clarissa and Nooni worked in the kitchen, listening to *Lemonade*, prepping sides for the cookout.

Nooni boiled eggs and potatoes, while Clarissa put together her concoction of brown sugar, honey and orange zest for her kicked up baked beans. It seemed surreal for Clarissa to reunite with Nooni, and now began the work of rebuilding. Days prior, Clarissa called her mother Hazel about Nooni and the decision to let her stay.

"Risa, you've always had a big heart, just be careful."

"Careful of what, mama?"

"You got this young girl 'round your husband. What she do for money, she got a job?"

For a time, I thought my mother had obsessive-compulsive disorder, the way she'd always overthink things.

"Mama, it's temporary. She'll stay a month, maybe two tops."

"You just make sure she cleans up; matter of fact, bring her over here."

"Maybe next weekend."

Honestly, there was no burning desire to run Nooni over to mama's just yet. Mama's nature was nice-nasty, charming, and condescending. Hazel would say things like, "You wearing that?"

or "I don't think that's appropriate for your body type." She never thought it necessary to be considerate with her words, which caused me to be secretive over the years.

"Mama, wanna see you."

"Oh, Auntie Hazel, she ain't gone remember me, though."

"Not with that big ass."

"You ever talk to Antoine?"

Antoine was Dottie's son from a previous marriage. Twan, as everyone called him, was exactly like his mother in look and deed, messy.

"Not since the wedding."

"Oh, sissy came too, huh?"

"Girl, just as messy as Dottie. I'm surprised he ain't try to holler at Gavin."

"Twan been sweet, girl. I walked in on him dancing in the bathroom with a bright ass, red thong on. I was eleven then."

"You ever hear from him?"

"He don't fuck with me. I don't fuck with him."

"Why they acting like that?"

"Fuck if I know. Daddy was tough on him, but he helped Twan get a car in high school, all that. One time he punched him in the chest when he rolled his eyes at Daddy. Dottie hated that shit. I think that was the last straw."

Nooni's family stories seemed to have a central theme; abandonment. She was just a child surrounded by fuckery; Dottie and her need to have a man, Roy, and his fear of raising a little girl alone, and a stepbrother desperate for answers. "Enough of this depressive shit; go look in that pantry and pull out that new bottle of Jack Daniels, we got work to do."

Meanwhile, I rolled into Whole Foods, picked up some expensive lamb burgers with feta cheese, some free-range chicken breasts and three wagyu T-bone steaks. Then I picked up a couple of bottles of Pellegrino sparkling water, for the culture. When I checked out, my bill was $210 for less than ten items. Then it was off to get some trees.

"What's the occasion," Miguel prodded.

"We're celebrating life, my man, just living our best lives."

"Whatever man, can I at least get some of this bag of goodies?"

"You got papers?"

"As they say, stay ready, so you don't have to get ready," he answered, with paper in hand.

Sometimes we get by with a little help from our friends, and thankfully for me, I had a friend with a weed connect and extra joint papers for the road. But what I didn't have was Visine. When I arrived home, the ladies could see that I'd started without them. "What up cousin, you good," Nooni playfully asked, noticing my bloodshot eyes.

"But I got you, though," I replied.

When Clarissa saw me in the kitchen, she had another approach. "Just felt like smoking today, huh?"

"Nooni asked if I could pick some up."

"Hmm," she answered, walking away to the back yard.

"Babe, what's wrong?" I asked, as I followed.

"I don't want her caught up with the same shit. The goal is to get her on her feet."

Her point was contradictory to the freshly opened bottle of Jack on the counter.

"Looks like y'all been partying, too."

"Always comparing shit; we drinking and working at the same damn time."

"We can smoke and work at the same dam time, too."

Clarissa smacked her lips while walking back in, buzzed, with a half-empty cup.

"She needs to see structure and responsibility around here."

"Okay…" I laughed.

"This is serious."

"Before she got here, you ain't even get out of bed until 10."

"I'm a damn millionaire. I can do that."

"We both are, that's structure enough."

"I want her to see something different, that's all I'm asking."

"And she will."

Later, after grilling, we ate beans that were slightly burnt, and potato salad out of this world. We all sat pleasantly filled, communing with a rolled joint at 6:35 in the evening. The sky, with its harmony of hues, gave me a sense of calm from the trials of a few hours ago. Music played from my portable speaker, and now and then, I mouthed the lyrics to songs I knew, while Clarissa would instinctively harmonize along with the music. When 'Da Butt' by EU came on, Nooni jumped up like, "Hey," doing her version of the dance with some twerk mixed in. Clarissa got up and joined, right behind her. When Nooni noticed, she instinctively bent over, giving aid to Clarissa's cause, thanks to rounds of Jack and Coke, and now a strain of weed called Cherry Pie.

I sat up to enjoy a slight freak show, with two fully grown bodies aligned to the cadence of soft-core porn. I watched with a poker face of indifference, holding the joint to my lips for a quick pull. Nooni and Clarissa momentarily whisked away to a time when young girls from around the way wore door-knockers and Reeboks, with biker shorts and feathered bobbed hairstyles. The ecstasy of music and memory was shown best by the looks on their faces. Pure Black girl joy, in unison, they'd say, "Hey…hey." Suddenly, a quick summer breeze blew through the patio, and we all snapped out of it. Clarissa smacked Nooni's ass before sitting down and looked at me with a teasing face.

"What you know 'bout that, young buck."

"That was daddy's favorite song, but he didn't let me dance to it, so I had to sneak."

"My goodness, that song is like…freshmen year at Yates," Clarissa reminisced.

The ladies resumed to the cipher, as I passed to Nooni. She took the joint and a strong pull, inhaling and holding for what seemed like ten seconds straight. Clarissa and I briefly looked at each other, while she exhaled a cloud of smoke and asked, "Anybody want something from the kitchen?" We answered no, as she walked away. I tried another sneak peek but didn't chance it. But it didn't matter, Clarissa was already on my case.

"You wanna fuck, huh?"

"What!"

"Nigga…"

"What are you talking about, seriously," I asked, but I knew.

"I saw you this morning," she replied.

"You saw me this morning, what?"

"Don't lose your mind, that's all I'm saying."

"And this is regarding what?"

"That's my cousin. You're my husband, that's that."

"What are you worrying about babe, just keep doing what you did in the shower."

"Oh, so if I continue to do what I did in the shower, we good…"

"You always extra, Risa…always."

I continued looking ahead, slightly frustrated, but mainly sick of her spot-on intuition. *How does she do that shit?* It was never my intent to do anything with Nooni. I admired her body, and maybe, I'd jack-off when it got to be too much, but never would I act on my urges; I was A.M.E. raised.

When Nooni came back, she had a fresh red *Solo* cup filled with more Jack and Coke, and another lamb burger, her new favorite. "Y'all, these burgers go hard." Clarissa was happy to see her cousin discover something new, while I remained quiet, with intermittent gulps of my drink and the inherent, heterosexual desire to appreciate everything about lust. "I know this is temporary, but I could get used to how y'all live."

Clarissa smiled at her kind words, but I, feeling petty, answered, "Welcome home."

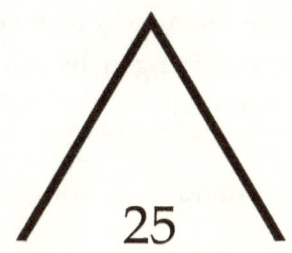

25

Abomination

For the past three months, we were a family, each with the responsibilities of home. Nooni would cook, making dishes like her hot sauce chicken dipped in buttermilk, or creamy cheese grits and applewood bacon for breakfast. Our newest luxury was regular, home-cooked meals. Even after cooking, she'd clean the kitchen, sometimes with our help, with me washing dishes and Gavin having the look of someone helping, while sitting at the kitchen table, watching us work. Depending on the day, she'd go to yoga class, or walk the trail at Memorial Park, with me. She kept her job at Longfellow's, but actively looked for other work. She even registered for the Fall semester, at Houston Community College, for a cosmetology certificate. Within a short time, she was beginning to see the possibilities.

One day, we had a conversation about motherhood. She never met Bobby, but enjoyed my stories, watching or overhearing our phone conversations, but she kept the hurt of her loss, at bay. As vulnerable as she'd been the last few months, she wasn't ready to heal from the pain of her life.

But one afternoon, on a whim, she decided to go to her favorite lingerie shop, *'The Brazen Brassiere'* off Richmond and Shepherd, and surprise her favorite cousin with a gift. With the money she'd been saving, she purchased a couple of new outfits for work, and a sexy black, sheer negligee and matching lingerie for me. As soon as she got home, she found me sitting in the den watching *'Judge Judy.'*

"Girl, I got you something."

"What you got me, girl."

"Hol' up," Nooni responded, looking in the bag and pulling out the lingerie.

"Ooh, bitch,"

"You like it?"

"Yaaaaassss, thank you."

"I got something too," Nooni followed.

"Yes, bitch."

"For real?"

"It's cool...I don't do fuchsia, but it depends on how it looks on you."

"Okay, hold on," Nooni answered, running off to change.

Nooni's pure, stripper joy, was the spark in my day, adding to the arrival of my best friend, Denise. Her flight would land that evening.

Before I could even see Nooni, I heard the clip-pity-clop of platform heels, quickly walking over travertine tile. When Nooni reached the den, she had the widest smile, waiting for approval from her big cousin. Without saying a word, she twirled for me, offering the fabulousness of her get up. "This shit fly, right?"

I was more impressed with her body, but offered, "That shit hot."

"I'm wearing it tonight."

"Oh, I thought you were off. My girlfriend is flying in from Dallas."

"Y'all should come tonight. I can get y'all a table."

"Yeah, she's not really into strip clubs, neither am I."

"For real? That's where you found me."

I stuttered for words, but little did she know, that night was a field trip wrapped in appeasement.

"I lost a bet on some bullshit...I let him win."

"What was the bet?"

Again, I was at a loss, crafting a lie on my feet.

"He likes to say I'm not freaky enough like I'm boring and shit. He just wanted to look at some ass, so I let him. It's the price you pay to make a marriage work."

"Boring? Nothing 'bout you is boring."

"I know, right?"

"So, you ain't never been to a strip club before that night?"

"Girl, when I was on the road…the strip club was anywhere I was."

Nooni was intrigued by my recollections of fame and the spoils of excess. Her popularity was an Instagram account, a stage, and a pole.

"So, did you do cocaine and shit?"

"Dang, that's kinda blunt."

"I mean, ain't that what y'all celebrities do?"

"Well, I'm not proud of it, but I tried some."

I lied. I devoured that shit. At my lowest, coke had become my personal Jesus. I copped so much of it that my dealer gave me the nickname, *'Candy Girl.'*

"I bet you was fucking celebrity niggas, too, huh?"

"No…I mean, if you include Bobby's father, that was it."

"What's his name again?"

"Jacob Finch."

"For real?! I remember in the news, they was saying you had got pregnant, but you was trying to keep it a secret; oh my God, I use to watch his show too," Nooni answered in fandom.

I wanted to leave it right there, thinking of other topics to insert in the conversation, but just as I attempted to, Nooni probed again.

"Did you do freaky shit, like, you know, crazy sex parties and shit?"

"You really pressing me, huh?"

"I'm saying; I like hearing about behind-the-scene celebrity stuff."

"So, what's the freakiest shit you ever did as a stripper?"

"Uhm…nothing with a customer, but them girls be on some shit in the locker room."

"Like what?"

"They be doing coke. I tried it once. My heart was speeding so fucking fast, that was the first and last time I did that. But uh, I let a chick eat me out in the locker room."

"Oh?"

Nooni began laughing, slightly embarrassed.

"Okay, wait…you ain't never kissed another chick? All them fans?"

The chit chat was cutting too close to the truth, so I lied.

"Nah, it wasn't too much of that going on, I mean, my female fans would say they love me, but I took it as fan love. Now the guys, that was a whole other story. All I can say is, thank God, Facebook, and Instagram didn't exist back then."

"Hmm, it must be nice to have a choice of dick, like a buffet," Nooni joked.

Immediately, I thought of Charlotte, the one love that got away. Under different circumstances, we'd still be together.

"I'll tell you this, though, that life was like going 100 miles per hour, every day. Falling in love and trying to have a career, was next to impossible. My life, right now, is just how I like it; slow and easy."

"Good for you, girl, cause I'm waiting on mine, whoever he or she is."

"That's the second time you done said that. You mess with chicks, huh?"

"Oh, I'm Bi."

"Since when?"

"Girl, since high school."

It was information overload, from a woman who used to sit between my legs as a little girl, getting her scalp greased and hair braided. Now, standing before me, was a full-bodied freak, well versed in pussy.

The vibe of the room changed, and secretly, I was bothered. How dare I have any thoughts about my cousin, with those thighs that led up to that ample ass, and those full African titties slathered in shea butter.

"Okay, girl, this is just way too much for me today. I wanna remember Sunnyside Nooni, who played with dolls and ran outside all day, sweating her hair out, right after I braided it."

"My bad cuz, I ain't mean to freak you out," Nooni answered with a laugh.

"I'm just fucking with you. You do you, whatever that is."

"Thank you. So, you wanna see if your friend is down to come tonight? My manager is cool as fuck. No charge on nothing, Imma cover the bottle; I get a discount anyway."

"Damn, it's like that?"

"I'm the best dancer they got. Tony sees the money I bring in; plus, he don't wanna fuck with me. He knows I know about him getting one of the dancer's pregnant, a month ago."

"Oh, wow. Well, let me ask Denise first, she might wanna stay in tonight."

"Plus, if y'all come, I'll put a show on for y'all," Nooni spoke, as she walked away.

All that afternoon, I couldn't escape the visual, sound, and feel of my fireside chat with Nooni. A singular truth squashed the judgment I had for her life choices; we shared similar cravings. Choosing to ignore the conflict, I called Denise for an answer about the randomness of a night at Longfellow's.

"What do you wanna do tonight?"

"Don't know, thought you had something planned already," Denise sassed.

"We do the same shit; you get in late, we go to the bar and get lit, come home and crash."

"I thought that was our thing, you cheating on me?"

"Bitch, for real?"

"So, what you wanna do, damn…"

"I know this is gone sound random, but my cousin, who lives with us…"

"Cousin?"

"It's a long story, girl; you wouldn't even believe it. But anyway, she's a stripper and…"

Immediately, Denise bust out laughing.

"What?"

"I'm sorry…I'm so sorry," Denise answered with laughter.

"Don't be laughing at my cousin."

"Girl, it's whatever. You wanna do some thot shit, I'm with the thot shit then. What's her name, Sparkles?"

"Kimberly."

"No, bitch, her stripper name…"

"Nooni Baby."

Denise hung up, leaving me shocked and humored. I called right back, and Denise answered with more laughter.

"Niecy…"

"I'm trying, babe, I'm really trying," she answered, through cries.

Now, there was a real concern. Knowing Niecy, since back in the gap, 1989, Lockwood Skating Rink days, she could be an asshole. Supposing she couldn't get over the giggles, something terrible was bound to happen later that evening.

"Okay, for real, you gotta be nice, this is my cousin, she young."

"Imma be nice to Nooni…baby," Denise mocked.

This went on for five minutes.

"So, is Gavin going?"

"He's in Cali on business; he'll be back Monday. Tonight's a girl's night anyway?"

"You don't think he be looking at her around the house?"

"I already caught him. He ain't slick, but she gotta fat ass."

"Uh-oh," Denise replied.

"Uh-oh, what, bitch?"

"Don't get fly, bitch. You know what."

"That's my cousin, Niecy. You don't remember when I used to babysit her?"

"Wait…little Kimmy, with the big brown eyes? Okay, yeah, she stays with you now? You still said she had a fat ass, though."

"Because she does."

"No! You always play dumb like that."

"I don't know what the fuck you talking 'bout, but what time you land, I need a nap."

"Whatever," Denise answered.

She was right. I had issues with being forthright when put on blast. Even when confronted with evidence, like our days at Yates in Ms. Baylor's social studies class, when Niecy noticed my stare at Ms. Baylor, I said I was daydreaming. Still, years later, after we graduated, I admitted to having a crush on Ms. Baylor. "But I ain't gay, though."

Later that evening, after picking Denise up from Hobby Airport, we swung back to the house to get Nooni, who was getting ready. "Like I said, please be nice, okay? She's been through a lot. Save the shade for another day."

"You're such a fucking lie. You the one."

"Whatever; be nice, hoe."

When we arrived, I called for Nooni, who promptly walked out a few minutes later, with a bounce to her step. When Denise saw her coming from a distance, she replied, "Nooni grew up…" She wore acid-washed, skinny jeans that hugged every contour of her lower body, a neon yellow tank top that showed ample cleavage, and black patent leather platform heels that hoisted the booty. "Y'all ain't tribbed yet?" I hit Denise on the arm, just as Nooni got in.

"Hey, ladies."

"Girl, do you remember Denise? She used to come over sometimes when I babysat you." Denise turned around to wave, with a wave back from Nooni.

"Were you the one that wore that orange fanny pack all the time?" Immediately, we bust out laughing.

"Damn, you remember that?" Denise reminisced for a moment, back when her fashion sensibility, hairstyles, and pimply, oily skin, weren't entirely on point. She remembered for an inkling, the little girl in pigtails, who loved Doritos and Capri Sun.

"Oh my God, hey baby, look how pretty and grown you are now," Denise added.

"Thank you," Nooni responded. "Y'all ready to turn up?!"

"Shit, I'm ready, girl, they got niggas up there too, right?"

"Ah, all girls, sorry. But I got y'all a V.I.P. section!"

"Cool. We gone look like some lesbian ballers." Denise shaded.

"You are so stupid," I answered.

I turned *'Diamonds and Pearls'* up a tad as we pulled out the drive, on the way to Longfellow's. It was a catch-up ride, with Denise being inquisitive, maybe to be messy, but Nooni obliged. "So, what y'all do in the back, between dances?" It was the third stripper question. By this time, Nooni began multi-tasking, emailing her new playlist to the house DJ, texting her co-worker to get the table ready, and checking her Instagram page for likes on her latest post, #423. Although homeless, and slowly building her life back together, she had 5,690 followers, checking for her latest outfits, hairdos, and heels. And now, with access to my Range Rover and home, her posts were way more lit.

"It's whatever backstage. I'm mean, girls usually chill 'til they get called."

"That sounds boring. Can we come back there?"

"Niecy, enough."

"It's all good; oh, by the way, what kinda liquor y'all want, they texting me now."

I looked at Denise, not sure what to say. Crown and Jack was my usual go-to drink, but I was open to something new.

"Can you suggest anything?"

"Y'all ever had D'Usse'?"

"Nah, you Niecy?"

"Uh-uh, let's try that shit, it sounds good."

"Especially when you put it with lemonade, girl."

"We finsta get fucked up, huh," I joked.

We cheered at the prospect of a drunken girl's night out. It was a while since Denise and I kicked it for a weekend, liked we always did before stardom separated us. Now both in our forties, every chance we got, we shared a zest for life and the acceptance of no longer being relevant.

When we arrived, the valet took the Range, and we walked right in. Nooni wanted to make sure everything was just right for us, "Imma see y'all in a little bit," she offered before trotting to the back. We were seated, looking at the other men looking at us. I felt gross all over like I'd never been there.

Denise, on the other hand, was waiting for the bottle. "Girl, one of your nephews gotta White girlfriend, and the other one talking to a Mexican, what did I do?" I laughed, attempting to shake the mood.

Tonight was a 'thank you' for all I had done. The section, the bottle, the V.I.P. service, was coming out of Nooni's pocket, but she didn't care. God had given her favor. Not in the last few years, had anyone looked out for her in this way, but more importantly, without wanting something in return. Had it not been for the grace of God, that night, there's no telling where she'd be right now.

When the bottle, with a bucket of ice and glasses, arrived, I received a text from Gavin, 'Where you at?' I looked at his message and thought of what to reply. 'I'm with Niecy, just picked her up from the airport. We went for a drink.' I hated lying to Gavin but found it easier to do. Equally, I learned to subdue the feeling of guilt, just as I'd done with my yoga buddy. But underneath it all, it was unnecessary deceit. *Why am I lying to him?*

'Did y'all eat already?'

'We'll get something later, Nooni's with us.'

'Okay.'

I flipped my phone over and switched the sound off to avoid any further obligation. It was a weird, unnecessary form of cheating. I turned my focus back to the stage, forgetting those things which were behind. "They got food here?" Denise asked while looking around for our waiter. I was more interested in the liquor set on the table.

"I don't remember them having food." Denise looked at me, confused.

"You've been here before?"

"Nah, I mean, I don't remember if Nooni said they had food or not."

"You been here, bitch."

"Quit playing," I answered, shaking my head no, with a smirk.

I reached for the bottle of *'yak'* and poured myself a double, with two cubes of ice. Denise followed suit, adding a splash of lemonade to hers. When she took a sip, she proclaimed, "This shit good, try it." I reached for the lemonade, as Nooni walked up to check on us, in her new fuchsia-colored lingerie. Denise saw her walking, turned to me, and said, "Nooni Baby," in a seductive voice, while I flipped her the bird.

"Hey, just checking on y'all, making sure you got everything."

"Girl, this with the lemonade, phenomenal," Denise proclaimed.

"I know, right? If y'all need anything else, let me know. I'm going up in ten minutes."

"Thanks, Nooni, this is nice," I answered.

Nooni walked off, and we marveled at the perfection of her ass. "She do gotta fat ass," Denise chimed.

For the next ten minutes, we people watched, enjoying the scores of men who looked out of place and extremely thirsty. This gathering of men, who came to fall in love with random women they had no chance with, was stupid. *Look at these idiots, probably all married, with kids and church responsibilities. They ain't shit.* Denise continued drinking her favorite new concoction, splitting her time between the girl on stage, and the guy in the red t-shirt, who wouldn't stop looking at her. "Clarissa, 3 o'clock, the dude in the red t-shirts, with the *Y.M.C.A.* mustache." I turned to look at the guy who seemed tall, even while sitting. He had Wesley Snipes' complexion, with a greased up, bald head, and creepy smirk.

"He might got some good. You gone let him talk to you?"

"Not with that musty ass mustache."

The DJ announced Nooni, "Coming to the stage, we have the vivacious, the incomparable, the bootylicious, Nooni Baby…where you at sexy?" We anticipated her, and the freedom to look, in a strip club. In a short period, Denise could see the trouble brewing ahead.

Back when I dated Charlotte, Denise was right there to hear the woes of her friend's lesbian relationship, and the pain of trying to be one image for the record company, while denying my true feelings. Whenever there was a big blow-up, Denise would get a call about it, no matter the time of day. She even met Charlotte one summer and found her to be not only beautiful but the calm to my storm. But I could be hoeish. When it was made clear of my bi-sexual nature, Denise, being accepting, gave me the freedom to comment on the women I'd see. "Girl, this new backup singer, I'm a have to inspect that…" or "I can get head from seven different bitches, for each day of the week, fuck Charlotte." So, she struggled with the notion that this arrangement would work in the name of family.

Two glasses of cognac provided the perfect filter for me, watching my little cousin gyrate on stage for money. Motherfuckers arose to pay tithes—her glow up was the love of the saints. I was now a fan of someone else. I got up to walk down to the stage. "Imma go tip her," I playfully mocked. It felt good, not having to be the star for a change.

When I got close enough, I waited my turn, as three Latino guys and an African-American woman, who looked butch, stood their ground. But Nooni noticed me and summoned me with her finger. I smiled, and the people looked back, making way for me to the alter. When I got to the stage, I started throwing money before Nooni could do anything. It was cute. Nooni got right to work, dropping it low, while Denise looked on, shaking her head. I could not stop smiling, while Nooni flexed her butt cheeks, *left-right,*

right-left. Then I finally did it; I reached out and grabbed Nooni's right cheek, with a firm grip. At that very moment, something changed the dynamic of our relationship as cousins, and we knew it. I stopped touching or throwing money and walked back. Nooni hadn't noticed until she turned around.

Seven minutes, two songs, and $321 later, Nooni walked off stage with another set to do in thirty minutes. She took a few puffs from a joint, a molly she had in her purse, and the shot of tequila she ordered. By this time, Denise and I buzzed with our complimentary bottle of yak. Nooni decided to come back out to hang with us, but when she got there, she first had to complete a task. "You left early, girl; I ain't finished." I blushed, and Denise saw it.

"How you make your booty do that," I asked.

"Practice...but I owe you a dance." Denise looked over like, 'what now?' "Girl, you good, I just wanted to throw some money, baby." But Nooni, still standing, didn't take the excuse for an answer, and straddled me, nearly kicking the bottle over. Denise laughed in shock while I covered my face.

Nooni was grinding on me while I sat, unsure of what to do. I was still shocked that I grabbed her ass. But soon, she hit a rhythm I could get with. It was slow and sweet at first, but then she sped it up, just like before a nut, then she slowed it back down, leaned over to my right ear, and said, "Thank you for saving my life."

She then came face to face with me and gave a soft peck to my lips, but the peck lasted longer than average, between cousins. I was flustered and conscious of being inebriated but parted my lips. Nooni took the signal as an invitation, and a slow bubble gum chew followed. I could feel Denise looking at me, eyes wide, hand over her mouth, straight watching this unbelievable shit happening. *I'm tripping right now. I am really tripping right now.* But instinctively, I grabbed Nooni's whole ass, gripping both cheeks at the same time, as water began to flow. The moment lasted seven full seconds too long by any standard. But casually, when the kiss was over, Nooni said, "All right y'all, I gotta get back. See y'all later." She got up and walked off as nothing happened. Denise and I, stunned, looked at each other in silence, for the same length of time as the kiss.

Still, at a loss for words, I reached for my drink, avoiding eye contact with Denise and her judgment. "You not gone say nothing? I just saw that, what's up?" I was baffled, but I laughed, at yet another unexplainable moment.

"I mean…what?"

"See, always the dumb shit."

"You know I fuck with girls."

"And cousins, bitch?"

"She just drunk, or whatever, that shit ain't nothing."

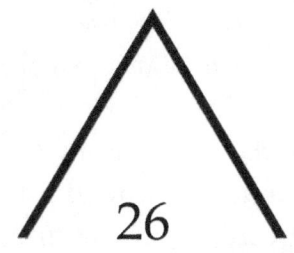

26

Communion

Tension lingered like an unanswered question, but Nooni was chill. To her, it was a show of appreciation. But the careless, incestuous vibe was too much. The ride home was awkward.

"Ah, you and you kissed in the mouth tonight…what the fuck was that?"

Laughter broke the tension temporarily.

"I'm sorry Risa, you went with it, so…" Nooni replied.

"How, though," Denise countered.

I smiled, pretending to be calm, driving with focus, fearful of another D.U.I. But it bothered the hell out of me, how good it felt, how careless my decision was, especially in front of Denise. I played unbothered.

"It took two to tango. Just don't tell nobody."

"I mean, what the fuck? I stopped looking at the girl on stage," Denise spoke.

Deep inside, I was scared to be alone with her again. However, by Sunday, Denise was off to De Soto, Gavin was out of town for a day, and nothing but space and opportunity remained. At first, I did all I could to stay busy, out of the house, running unnecessary errands, spending time alone, and ignoring all calls and texts. But I had to come home at some point. When I walked through the door, I heard the TV in the den, made a mad dash up the stairs, and ran to my room. *Why are you acting like this? You know you not gone fuck with her. It was a stupid, little kiss. Stop tripping.* I hopped in the shower, washing my sins away. Then I slipped into my favorite Bob Marley t-shirt and flannel pants and walked downstairs.

Nooni sprawled under a throw on the couch with a bowl of kettle flavored popcorn, watching *'Insecure.'* I climbed onto the chaise.

"Is this a new episode?"

"Yeah, with the dude from Houston," she answered.

Silence followed, but I wanted to talk about the kiss, but not be a vibe killer. Everything was mutual, but still. "Girl, we should talk…" Nooni sat up a bit, looking back, ready. I took a deep breath, gathered myself, and said, "I don't know where to start."

"Is this about the kiss?"

"Yeah…"

"Please don't trip."

"For real, Kim? Nah, that was uncomfortable."

"I mean…my bad for making you feel uncomfortable. I just thought I don't know. I was happy y'all showed up and shit. You was drinking; I popped a molly in the back, and things happen. But for real, I'm sorry."

"I'm not blaming you at all. But…"

"Did you not like the kiss, though?"

I shut down, looking at my clasped hands, before answering, "It's not about that." Nooni sat completely up, turned her body in my direction, and waited for more. We stared at each other, neither knowing what to say. "You're my family, my baby cousin, I can't be playing like that, we gotta have boundaries." Nooni's facial expression read confused. The kiss was a problem because I liked it, but my words sounded like a reprimand.

"No, I feel you, but is it a problem cause' you liked it?"

Again, she cornered me.

"I mean, it was cool, unexpected as fuck, but cool…it just can't happen again."

Nooni changed her position, now with her body language intent on asking a question.

"So, are you saying you kissed me cause' you was drunk, and not cause' you wanted to?"

"I'm saying, yeah, I was tipsy, I went with the flow, yeah."

"So, if I came over there and kissed you again..."

I burst out in nervous laughter, a cry for help, physically cornered on the chaise, with no wiggle room. One-touch could crumble my world.

"Look," I answered through a chuckle, "We just gotta chill..."

"All right, but let me kiss you one last time, Imma chill for good after that."

"Nooni, you're my cousin, stop, for real."

"We cousins by marriage."

I sat there, stunned at the checkmate Nooni pulled out her ass and placed in my lap. Of course, we were cousins by marriage, that was clear, but still, I knew little Kimberly, pigtails and all. She rose from her position, slowly walking towards me, while I shook my head 'no,' waving my finger, with a smirk. Her sexy, panther ass walk continued gaining ground. Nooni plopped down by me while I covered my face in protest. She patiently pulled at my arms and hands. "Don't do this...please." Nooni continued until I gave. I dropped my hands like Celie with Suge Avery.

As I slowly closed my eyes, I submitted to her will, with my lips dearly departed, with tongues, joined together, that no man put them asunder. Raunchy at times, but gentle mostly, an agreement took place. I pulled back, dropped my head, wiped my mouth, and nearly cried.

"You okay?"

"I'm good."

"We ain't gone never do this again, okay cuz?"

"Girl..."

Nooni went in for a hug, got up for the kitchen for some fruit juice, but I decided to go to bed.

"I'm going to bed…"

"Night Risa, love you," Nooni hollered back.

"Love you too."

When I got upstairs, I went to the bathroom mirror, looking at the woman who just French kissed her cousin again. I checked my panties, my wet panties. I looked back at myself and shook my head. "You're so fucking weak." I went back to the room, changed, and hopped in bed. For hours, I tossed and turned, falling in and out of sleep, in frustration. Out of desperation, I turned on the TV, to the classic movie channel, hoping to doze off for good, but still nothing. Randomly, I wondered what Nooni was up to if she were even awake. The curiosity to walk down the hall made me feel creepy, so I pulled my panties down, instead. Like a thief in the night, devious thoughts played in my mind.

Yeah, right there, I imagined, as I rang my bell. In another world, Nooni was scissored with me, gyrating in opposite directions, meat on meat, grinding for a breakthrough. Within minutes, I came so hard I stopped breathing, with my legs fully stretched like a good yawn. I laid there, panting for air, hoping for more. Quietly, I awaited the slow transition to glory, but curiosity killed the cat. I rose from my bed of iniquity, with an urge to creep down the hall and spy. Nooni's door appeared cracked, and inch by inch, I walked barefoot against the chill of wooden floors until getting a better view. I saw a glimpse of cell phone light, dimly over her back. I peeked through the crack, wanting to invite myself in for more. But my nerves were paralyzed. Slowly, I backed away from the door, stepping on the one creek in the damn hallway. "Clarissa?"

I was caught off guard, thinking of something to say, something believable at 2:42AM. "Hey girl, just coming from the kitchen… can't sleep." I kept walking, right into bed. But minutes later, I heard a knock at the door.

"Nooni?" I sat up, waiting to see her in full. "I can't sleep either…" We let time and space continue between us, one waiting for the other to say or do something. "Can I sleep with you?"

With the TV still playing an episode of *Gun Smoke*, I answered, "Come." Scooting over, taking Gavin's side of the bed, Nooni got in, with no other intention but to sleep. But instinctively, she got up behind me, put her arm around me, and said, "Goodnight." No other words, just the sounds from a TV show played. "This is funny, 'member how I used to rock you to sleep; we switched places, huh?" Nooni laughed, remembering those nights when all she had was the comfort of my singing, with my arms wrapped around her.

"What's the song you used to sing when I couldn't sleep, 'member that?"

"What was it, oh…twinkle, twinkle, little star."

"How I wonder where you are…"

It was sweet and innocent, and within thirty minutes or more, we eventually fell asleep, changing positions, with Nooni's back to me this time. My arm was now around baby cousin, who snored loudly enough to wake me back up.

In the stillness of the night, naughtiness reared its ugly head. I got the bright idea to explore Nooni's body while she laid sound asleep. First, I pulled back the cover to look at her ass, admiring the cuteness of her sheer turquoise panty. I noticed a tattoo that read *'Boo Thang'* with red lips underneath the words. I got back close to her, while Nooni continued snoring. I put my arm back around, but this time, I gently squeezed her right breast, hoping not to wake her.

Further, I reached under her t-shirt, patiently inching towards a full bosom, graciously cupping the right breast with ease. I snickered, imagining a more advantageous risk. Next, I put my hand by the waistline of her panty, slipping in a half-inch, mindful of my touch. Still nothing; slowly, I crept towards the bell, until discovery.

In the wake of all that was happening, I felt alive, like a little girl sneaking into her mother's purse or dresser drawers, hoping to make a great find, and I did. Nooni was clean-shaven, with her bell surrounded by full, fat lips. With the slightest touch, I began ringing the bell, for a reaction. A twitch here, a moan there, but nothing really happened, and then suddenly, Nooni changed positions, lying flat on her back. I stopped immediately, retreating to my side for safety. A full minute passed, until my next devious move, this time, pulling the comforter back completely, exposing Nooni in her t-shirt and panty. I tried pulling up her t-shirt unsuccessfully, so instead, I began kissing her nipple through the shirt, then teasing the nipple with a nibble, watching it get firm.

I kissed down to her navel, even further, until stopping to perform a sniff test; *water*. I puckered up, kissed it, and laid back down to the sounds of *I Dream of Jeannie*. But just as I thought my little field trip had gone unsuspected, I heard a whisper, "Keep going." My heart stopped as the world turned a thousand miles per hour. "Hmm," I answered, pretending to be half-sleep. Nooni pushed the envelope even further when she reached down and slowly removed her panties.

Left with no choice, I turned around, looked Nooni in the eyes, against the glare of a TV, and sighed. Acting hesitant, Nooni was accommodating, lifting her left leg to make space for me. I opted to pull the covers back over my head, but Nooni protested. "Hmm, hmm, I wanna watch." I smacked my lips. It was the first time in a long time, that a command was given to me, but I loved it. First, I looked up at Nooni, seductive, and coy, "You sure?" Nooni said nothing, laying back, ready for worship.

I had seconds to back out, even with my face, now cornered. The embellishment of cherry blossom flavored thighs, and the sweeter, more potent juicy fruit, welcomed my senses. And still hesitant, I wondered what Jesus would think. But in my mind, I answered, *You here now*.

With only the dimness of TV light, I stuck my tongue out on faith, tasting the tang of stimulation. Innocence was forever lost. Eyes closed, I went deeper and more undiscovered, while Nooni curled her toes in agreement. I began to *'blackout'* on pussy. Rarely did I serve but got served. I was the one grabbing the back of a bitch's head, the spoils of fame. Besides Charlotte, there was maybe one other woman I'd gone down on, but for many reasons, Nooni was different.

Under less than two minutes, Nooni's back was arched, as I cupped her left breast, and she, grabbing a nearby pillow with her right hand. "Ooh," she answered, succumbing to my frequent tongues, free in a confined space. I could feel Nooni's energy, ascending to the heavens. Occasionally, I'd look up, seeking more praise.

"You like that?" Nooni's responses were either moans or one-word answers like "yes" or "shit." The awkwardness was no longer an issue. I pushed her legs wider, losing myself in the darkness.

At one point, I rang the bell so good and consistent that Nooni looked up to watch, saying, "Ooh, yes…fuck," her first three-word sentence. She was now grabbing the back of my head.

After an easy ten-minute run, I rose with a greasy face, confident of a good first showing, and ready for reciprocation. "Get on top," Nooni commanded. Not sure of what she meant, I remained frozen until Nooni gave further instructions. Instead, Nooni motioned for me to climb up, with my entire body over her head, only supported by two goose-down pillows. Nooni was entirely under the pussy, ready to go off. In a matter of seconds, Nooni's version of oral sex was redefined by smacking and slurping noises that tried my soul. The very same woman, once a little girl, getting her hair braided between my legs, was now causing a pleasurable mess. My mouth remained open, as my eyes rolled several times; *she's gifted*.

Nooni, being sexually free, since a teenager, thought it reasonable to receive me this way, with both hands gripping my waistline, slow bobbing. Jokingly, Nooni stopped to say, "You looking down at me."

We laughed a second but went back into praise and worship. Nooni, ever so generous, continued her slow and seductive ice cream lick and bite. I refused to come fast, thinking of things to distract nature, but nothing worked. Nooni was that good. Out of courtesy, I announced, "I'm coming."

Nooni's eyes grew big, her grip firmer, and my motion, more fluid. I leaned back, doing all I could to hold on, but boom, I let my body go. All the muscles in my back, my thighs, and stomach tensed up. I looked down, fearing the aftermath of a wild orgasm, and the force in which it came. I came so hard that I nearly pulled a track from Nooni's sew-in. I fell forward against the headboard and said, "Oh my God… I'm sorry." Nooni smiled, got from under me, came back around to my ass, spread my cheeks, and rimmed away. Caught off guard, struggling with a proper reaction, I'd never expected my ass eaten by Nooni. And again, Nooni knew what to do. I laid against the headboard, eyes closed, toes curled, as Nooni tickled my fancy. Nooni's lollipop lick turned vicious, going from the back, all the way up front, thanks to my new bent over position. Again, the river flowed, deep in ecstasy, in the twilight. I looked down, thoroughly exhausted, with beads of sweat at my forehead and small of my back, and said, "The devil is a lie."

The very next night, while in bed with Gavin, watching 'Let's Make a Deal,' on TV Land, he asked, "Where are we on this arrangement?" I was already dozing off, giving no fucks of an arrangement after last night. "Huh?" He smacked his teeth.

"What?"

"What we talked about with the counselor."

"What about it?"

"What have we done about it?"

When we met Nooni that night at the strip club, it stomped the flame of a sexual hunt, in my mind.

"What must we do about it?"

"All right," he answered, turning the volume up slightly, in passive-aggressive protest.

"Okay, wait, why are you tripping? I'm asking you a question."

"All I know is, we had an agreement. Period."

"Yeah, but wasn't it because we weren't having sex, and now we are, so…"

"We had a decent sex life before you did what you did, so…"

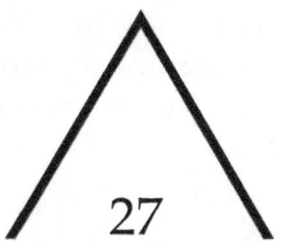

27

Sacrificial Lamb

"Uhm...let me get the five-wing special, with fries and a coke," Nooni ordered, at the Frenchy's drive-thru. It was an easy-breezy Wednesday afternoon in August, perfect for bad eating habits and good times. Three months since the rendezvous, neither of us spoke a word to a soul. But for Gavin, I was beginning to think he suspected something. He noticed cousins who'd become more affectionate, spending countless hours together, just girls being girls.

"It took thirty damn minutes to place our order; remind me to never waste half an hour of my life on chicken."

"You so bougie..." Nooni answered.

We pulled our phones out, waiting in a long ass line, checking likes on posts, and random timeline feeds. By now, Nooni finally stopped stripping, becoming a full-time student, with a different air about herself. Gavin and I even plopped down eight grand for a cash car, a used, 2008 Honda Accord. Nooni, not being one to take handouts, got a part-time job in the Galleria Mall, at a boutique clothing store. But most importantly, our sexual antics hadn't stopped. Even in the drive-thru line, Nooni was random, reaching over to caress my arm, while she looked at a video.

Along with the affectionate gesture, she proposed a friendly wager. "I bet I can make you cum before we get our food."

Clearly a joke about the wait, I laughed it off. "You stupid." Nooni then put her phone down and leaned over, placing her left hand on my right thigh. My truck's tint and the sundress I was wearing made it fair game.

"You stay on freak shit, don't you?"

"On God. And please...you right there wit' it."

Without waiting for an answer, Nooni inched my dress up, little by little, with a slight smirk, while my head remained at a tilt in silent protest. But with three cars ahead of us, it was possible. Nooni continued until reaching my black lace panty, and with my help, she slid them down just enough.

Gently, Nooni eased her middle finger into the valley, watching every reaction. Although mindful of our surroundings, I instinctively put my Saint Laurent shades on, for privacy. Nooni stopped in mid finger fuck, confused, and asked, "What the fuck is that gone do?" The very first car received its order, driving off, and now, we were two cars behind. Conscious of time, Nooni revved up the motion, nibbling on my ear, switching between ringing the bell and diving deep. Suddenly, it got right to me, grabbing Nooni's working arm, holding on for dear life. Those familiar rivers of joy flowed over Nooni's finger, down my thighs, and onto the expensive leather seat.

Unexpectedly, the next car drove off in under two minutes, and now, we were just one car behind. "Ooh, girl, hurry," I pled.

The muscles in Nooni's forearm burned, as adrenaline pushed a mission, *'operation make-her-cum-now.'* The cashier seemed to catch a glimpse of us, looking past the patron up front, and at Nooni's animated behavior. She squinted to make sure but resumed to the order. "You better come on...come on, Imma..." I spoke, stuck between possible onlookers and a nut. The white Toyota Camry in front received its order, and just as the brake lights changed from park to drive, I came. Again, with heavy panting, I nor the car moved for five seconds.

"Girl, pull up, 'for they honk at us," Nooni pled. I recalibrated, drove up, and rolled down my window, still wearing shades.

Although unorthodox, these were the moments I wanted with Gavin.

This thing with Nooni was becoming something therapeutic. We shared present fears, past regrets, and hopes for the future, especially about motherhood. Nooni still grieved for Jelani. The depression that went on during that time nearly destroyed her. Even without Bobby, I couldn't relate but felt a more profound empathy for Nooni's loss. She was more than an Instagram millennial, but a woman with layers.

Aside from the sexual shit, our revived relationship was indeed a sisterhood. Big sister looked out for little sister, giving her couture game, poise, and, most of all, reasons to love. I found a disciple in Nooni, someone to mold and uplift, sharing the pitfalls and successes that gave me character. We'd grown so close, the idea of Nooni eventually leaving hadn't crossed my mind. But Nooni knew the road would eventually end, just not when. She wanted a home of her own, a love life, and, most importantly, the chance to be a mother. But for now, this was a second chance.

Later in the evening, when we returned home, Gavin was in the den watching the news, slightly pissed at the time that passed; he was hungry. "Dang, where y'all been all day!" I walked over to boo and planted a 'shut the fuck up' kiss on his forehead.

"Hey, love."

"Why you ain't call?"

"My bad babe…" I answered, walking off.

His feelings seemed quietly hurt and the brush off, slick. But the house had become more peaceful, and his need for third-party ass simmered down. "What up G-Money," Nooni followed, walking in behind me. It was her new nickname for Gavin, something he hated.

"What up…" He dryly answered, still bruised from a simple kiss. "I got some O.G. Kush if you wanna burn." Gavin immediately stopped his pouting.

"Yeah, okay…right now?"

"Imma change first, ten minutes."

Gavin, now with a better mood, rationalized that he'd be much hungrier, a good reason for eating so late. Meanwhile, Nooni and I paused for a short kiss, out of his view, initiated by me, in response to Nooni's earlier bet. I grabbed her by the ass and said in a whisper, "I can make you cum before he gets off that couch." We laughed like schoolgirls, with Nooni running up the stairs to change. However, I didn't know that our little affair was starting to bother her.

One rainy afternoon, I joined her downstairs after waking from a mid-day nap with Gavin, who was still sleeping. She was watching a marathon of *'A Different World,'* comfortably lounging under the throw, with the lights off. I slid next to her, sitting Indian style, still tired, and laid my head on her shoulder. For minutes, it was silence against TV dialogue, until Nooni slid her hand down my pajama pants and played. From then on, sounds of pleasure began to build as I stuck my hand down her panty, in reciprocity. It was conflicted praise; her moans against my many choice words made for a special type of devotion. But just as it got right, we could hear the stride of house shoes on tile, from the kitchen. Boldly, we remained, even as Gavin came in total view of us, sitting on the couch, side by side, under the throw. "Y'all cold," he asked while yawning and stretching.

"It feels perfect to me."

"For real, though," Nooni chimed.

However, the very next day, she gathered the nerve to address the situation. "Do you think what we do is cool?" We sat outside on the patio of a *Starbucks*, at Post Oak and Westheimer, trying to have a conversation against Galleria traffic.

"What do you mean, though?" A genuine reply, my perception of things was different. To me, we were fucking around, but to Nooni, it felt like a thing.

"The stuff we do, sneaking around, fucking and shit." I took a drink of my macchiato, listening intently to something new.

"Sometimes…I feel like you cheating on him with me." It was a revelation, whether I agreed or not. I underestimated her intelligence, but still.

"Honestly, I never looked at it like that. Does it make you uncomfortable? Should we stop?" I took another sip, placing the ball back in her court, for manipulation sake.

"If it's gonna be a problem between y'all, yeah."

"How could it ever become a problem?"

Nooni hadn't thought that far out, but the more we fucked around, it did feel wrong. She sat there, shaking her head, without a reply.

"Do you want me to tell him?"

"You know you ain't gone do that."

I thought of our initial plan and how perfect Nooni was, but how imperfect the optics looked. I was fearful that Gavin would drown in lust as I had. And yet, the home fires could continue burning, without anyone feeling jaded or deceitful. *What if Nooni is our missing piece?*

"I caught him looking at you one day."

"What?"

Nooni blushed, but respected the boundaries, somewhat. However crazy our sexual shit, Nooni never thought of coming at Gavin, until I presented an allusion. "Would you fuck, cause I think he would." She leaned back in her chair, covered her mouth, and began laughing like a stunned teenaged girl. I noticed the movement in her body language. Perhaps she wanted to. "You are tripping, girl." I shook my head, looking deeper past the surface. *What if this love thang could be a triangle?* Then and there, an idea was born. If Gavin could be truthful about an advance from Nooni, I could trust the idea of us being something.

"Would you do a threesome?"

"With y'all?"

"Ah…yeah?"

"Stop it, you tripping," Nooni mocked, through laughter.

It was an informal invitation on the spot, straight with no chaser. I put it all on the line, only to hear her ask, "Is this a trick or something?"

I laughed at her innocence, wholesome at times, and answered, "Bitch, ain't we been fucking three months? Would you fuck or not?" Nooni got caught off guard.

"That's hella weird as fuck, Risa. You still family, regardless of what we do."

"Okay, that's weird as fuck too. Just think of it as…in-house, community dick."

She shook her head, even though I knew she thought Gavin was fine. She prided herself on never being a side piece…until me.

"Flirt with him, see what he does."

"You really for real?"

"Yes, pinch his ass, or some dumb shit. Don't overdo it, though."

She sat back in her chair, with a look that fell between, *are you serious*, and *I really could do that shit*. A pause remained. Maybe she thought, if she didn't comply, it could mean eviction or even the end of our marriage. Her new lifestyle, the plush living conditions, occasional spins in the Range, or random shopping sprees on my dime, could all be gone.

"Why you wanna do this," Nooni asked.

"All right, I'm just fucking with you…"

"No, you wasn't," Nooni countered.

Cornered yet again, I smirked and shook my head. I took another sip from my cup and asked, "So…what's up?" Nooni looked to the side, stuck between a rock and a hard place.

"This some weird shit."

"Haven't we already crossed that line?"

"I mean, kinda…"

"Really, bitch?"

Another pause for clarification, we remained silent in the cool breeze of Fall, washed in sun rays of uncertainty. A take it or leave it proposition sat in Nooni's lap. She looked up at me and said, "I don't wanna be the blame for some shit going bad." Perhaps I hadn't thought that far. What if neither Gavin nor Nooni told of what they did? What if they played shit like I did with Nooni?

"I like what we got going on; it's fun... I feel alive. It's like, I don't know how to explain it." It was more game for the youngster. "But as I said, you ain't gotta do it. I was just putting something out there." I took another sip from my cup and remained silent.

"So, if I do this, what's supposed to happen?"

"If he has eyes and a dick, he'll do what any man does."

"You still not telling me everything..."

"Nooni...this is not our first rodeo, baby."

"Threesomes?"

"Yes."

By Monday, I prearranged to disappear for most of the day. Nooni was off from work but had class at 6PM that evening. Gavin was lounging in his office, listening to A Tribe Called Quest, *Midnight Marauders* album, mulling over his next novel, and other business matters. Nothing much was to come of it until Nooni decided to initiate the play.

First, she considered her attire. Being quite aware of her physique, she decided on something tight and skimpy, the end. The weather was still reasonable, and coochie cutter jean shorts with a low-cut tank top, and no bra, made good sense. Then she sprayed on her trusty cherry blossom, *Bath & Body Works* mist. Lastly, she brushed a faint layer of foundation over her complexion and pulled her caramel-colored hair up in a bun. Looking in the mirror, she had one last chance to back out, to do 'right,' but a part of her wanted to see his reaction.

Confidently, she walked the hallway and stairs, excited and terrified. She'd never been tested, except that one time some guys dared her to kiss Keisha Johnson at a house party back in 2011. Her first instinct was to look in the kitchen, and then the den, but nothing. Next, she walked towards his office, where she could hear the linger of *'Award Tour.'* When she arrived, he sat behind his desk, looking perplexed at his iMac screen, about something. "You good," she asked, standing at the door, dripping in sex. When he looked up, he nearly died. Nooni, who was slightly pigeon-toed, stood at the door, leaning to her right of the entry, with the faint outline of her areolas behind a yellow tank top. Her shorts were cut high, with the pockets hanging over her upper thighs.

"You look like Summertime," he answered. He usually reserved his compliments, but today, he was feeling froggy.

"Oh, thank you...just trying to keep this weight off."

"Weight?"

"I was about fifteen pounds heavier when I moved in. That yoga be working."

"Oh, that's right, you go to class with Risa."

"For 'bout a couple of months now."

"How does yoga help you lose weight?" he asked, with a growing erection under his desk.

Nooni, being receptive to signals, followed his lead, and went right to it.

"Well, when I started, I couldn't even bend over and touch my toes, but now..."

She could bend over and touch her toes, and with ease. Her first stance was facing him. She was mindful of her words, avoiding an obvious booty play. But she did show some hang time, with cleavage fiercely protruding her top. Gavin stole every look he could with the five or so seconds of show and tell. When she stood up, she put her hands to her hips like a proud Sunnyside superhero. Gavin began clapping like an amazing douche.

"I can't do that shit," he proclaimed in praise.

"It just takes practice. I could show you."

Gavin, now completely rock-solid, couldn't afford to move in sweatpants. His dignity mattered.

"Nah, I'm good," he answered.

"You scared, professor?"

Gavin gave one of those laughs of indifference to mask the pain of an unusable erection. Yet, she remained, waiting for an answer.

"Maybe later. I hurt my back yesterday, lifting some shit in the garage."

"Dang, where it hurt?"

Nooni walked around to investigate the problem, while Gavin crossed his legs. He pointed to his lower back, and Nooni began to probe without invitation. The boner that maintained had gained new life, hidden by manly thighs.

"You're a masseuse, too, huh?"

"Strippers get cramps all the time. We massaged each other."

The thought alone made his penis throb even more, but he continued playing it cool until she slipped her hands under his t-shirt and rubbed his bare skin. "Oh..." he answered. He hadn't expected her rush to care, but he obliged. "I just need to lay on my back for a few minutes; it'll go away." His body heat began to rise, as he could feel her breathing on his neck. There was no barrier between them.

"I can feel a knot. You sure you don't want me to do my thang on that knot?" The way those words rolled off her tongue made him even more uncomfortable.

"Nah, for real, I need to lay down. Thanks, though."

"All right. Just let me know when you ready."

She walked out of the room, with the glory of God behind her. His unabashed ogling caused him to touch himself. It was just Monday. *What the fuck was that?* In the five or so months that they'd been living together, she'd never touched him in any way, unless a high five watching the Rockets play, or some other meaningless moment of agreement. But it didn't dawn on him that he passed a thorough exam.

Later that day, when I returned, I went up to Nooni's room for the tea.

"Oh, Kimberly."

"Hey, girl."

"Getting ready for class, huh?"

"Yeah, I'm running late too."

"Oh, well, let me get out your way. Good day though?"

The translation read, *did anything happen?* I raised my eyebrows to help her decipher semantics. Nooni, in mid shoe tie, looked up and said, "No deal. I tried to give him a massage, and he turned it down."

I was impressed, gave a nod of approval, and answered, "All right, hmm."

I was happy, but it wasn't enough. Shit needed to turn up before I allowed his initiation. But what else could be done, short of sucking and fucking? What would make him jump? And then it hit me. What if I bet Nooni $500 to get him to slip? I wouldn't be mad. The way I saw it, we could keep our thing going, and as punishment, he'd be out. I sent a text, 'I got another idea.' Nooni read it and shook her head as she rushed out. Low key, I was proud of Gavin. I was proud of both. However, the irony in my pride, being that I was the one with the infidelity, made me chuckle. Fifteen minutes later, I toweled off after a quick shower, put on my favorite flannel jammies, and walked back down to the kitchen, where Gavin was preparing his favorite array of assorted cheeses and salami, with watercress crackers.

"Gavy, baby," I called, followed by a soft kiss to his lips.

"How was your day?"

"Nothing much. That new yogurt spot on Gray is awesome," I followed.

I was waiting for him to spill about Nooni's yoga lesson but deferred.

"Did Nooni get on your nerves?"

Unbeknownst to me, the guilt of being aroused bothered him.

"Nah. She mentioned losing fifteen pounds since taking yoga," he nervously blabbed.

"You know she's so vain. Millennials."

For a second, I wondered if Gavin thought about bringing up the massage shit.

"We were talking the other day...I think she's lonely," I spoke.

"She's thirsty for a man, huh?"

"Yeah, but she got trust issues with guys her age."

"Well..." he answered.

"She's gonna confuse horniness for love."

A revelation came to Gavin; *oh...she ain't getting no dick?*

"We had a crazy conversation about her strip club days. Girls massaging girls, cramps from dancing on the pole and shit."

My eyes grew large as if an interesting factoid.

"Oh? How did y'all get on massages?"

Immediately, Gavin gave me that fuck boy face he makes when he's about to lie.

"I don't know. Shit was crazy."

"What?"

"Nah, it's nothing. Nooni is random sometimes, that's all."

I grabbed my phone to text Nooni, 'before I forget, wear your hair in a bang, he loves bangs.' All of it was covert, fueled by selfish intentions. Nooni sat near the front of the class, took a sneak at her phone, and smirked at the message. She became captivated by this game of cat & mouse. For a moment, she daydreamed about her next play. His loyalty had intrigued her. Surely any straight nigga would act on an urge, but why didn't he? *Am I not his type?*

Thursday, 1:25 in the afternoon, Nooni cooked seared salmon with sautéed spinach from a frozen bag, for her cousin-in-law. She even took the time to make lemonade from scratch. And all of it was done with a bang. Gavin was on the patio with his laptop, fleshing out ideas, between watching YouTube videos to kill time. He noticed Nooni in the kitchen, prepping to cook, but when he asked, she answered, "I'm making us lunch, it's a surprise." He appreciated her pulling her weight around the house, cleaning, cooking, and giving him something to look at. But today was going to be different. Nooni had an objective, with Gavin in mind. When the cooking was complete, she fixed their plates, went outside, and sat across from him.

"Want company," she asked as she placed the serving platter on the table.

"This looks good, thank you."

"You're welcomed. Something light, that's all."

"Just felt like cooking, huh?"

Nooni smirked and shrugged her shoulders. She remained quiet, bowing her head to say a prayer, before picking up her fork. Gavin said a prayer too, then nibbled on a piece of salmon, before resuming to his laptop. There was silence between them, nothing awkward, but slightly uncomfortable.

"How is it?"

"It's good…"

That was the extent of their dialogue. Gavin, being engrossed with research, was not in the mood for small talk until she asked, "Cousin, why can't I find a good man like you." He looked up, flattered, with a smile.

"What makes me a good man?"

"I mean, you and my cousin, y'all living good, y'all living the American dream and shit, so like, I don't know, I feel like, you a real man, you don't seem like a jealous nigga, you got your shit."

Gavin was now listening, with his hands completely away from the laptop.

"Well, specifically, what do you want in a man?"

"To be fucking honest, that's it. Stop lying for no reason."

She could see Gavin being sucked into her bullshit and decided to turn it up.

"I mean, the last dude I was with, I did everything for that bitch-ass. I cooked and cleaned, kept a day job, went to night school, sucked his dick, let him come in my mouth…" Gavin gave in to lust and the flow of blood rushing to his dick. "We had sex pretty much everyday…I did whatever he wanted, anal, all that, and he still lied." Gavin shook his head in support with a full hard-on.

"That's fucked up, for real."

"If I could just find a good dude, a faithful dude, with a decent job and no drama, I'll suck his dick every day."

Gavin's right hand went from the bench to his crouch, with more throbbing.

"Ah, man, you crazy," he nervously responded.

"I'm just saying, I know I give good head, and I got some good pussy."

Gavin's body language was uncomfortable, and his dick conflicted. "Just relax, you know, that's the best option. You're young, don't rush to be in a relationship. Just date, for now." Nooni was instantly ashamed of herself. This motherfucker was encouraging her with words of wisdom, not the expected reaction for her ego. With only seconds in the fourth quarter, she decided to lay it all on the line when she asked, "You mind if I give you a hug, I appreciate you."

Gavin shrugged his shoulders, "Okay," standing in faith, secured by his sturdier pair of *Levi's Jeans*. They got up together, taking steps towards each other. Nooni standing at 5'11, was under his frame, which made it easy for her to kiss his neck, before giving a full-bodied hug. The kiss to the neck crumbled him. But when their bodies collided, she felt the bulge. She buried her head in his chest and quietly celebrated with a smile. Gavin wanted to leave his body. He knew she could feel his erection, moving from his inner thigh. When they separated, he went back to his laptop, and she, to her senses.

Later in the day, when I returned, Nooni was ecstatic to share a praise report. She was busting at the seams, about Gavin's faithfulness. I looked forward to hearing the results of her mastermind attempt at breaking my husband. Our bond grew, over playing with him, and yet he persevered, which cemented my trust, and even deeper, my greed.

"You got you a good dude," Nooni softly spoke, as she followed me upstairs, into our master bathroom, where we shared a quaint hello kiss. I unbraided her ponytail in front of the mirror, waiting for more intel. "Girl, I threw it all at him, I was talking 'bout how much I like sucking dick, having sex, he ain't budge on none of that. You blessed."

Damn, I have to share the bitch. It was only fair; I made the rules, and he passed. "Wow, good Gavy baby," I reluctantly praised. A new task had come. It was the proposition of a threesome, his reward, and my way of maintaining variety.

"I guess I gotta reward this nigga, huh?"

"Like what," Nooni asked.

"Like, let him have a threesome with us."

"Huh? He just denied me twice. How he gone go from that to fucking me?"

"Niggas lie, okay? Gavin was a good boy, yes, but he wants that ass, please."

"I don't get it. He denied me, and now you want a threesome?"

"Gavin knows I'll fuck his shit up if he tries anything with you."

"So, you used me to test him?"

"What?"

"You was testing him to see if he was gone be honest, huh bitch," Nooni smiled.

I put the comb down, looked at Nooni through the reflection of the mirror, and answered, "Yes."

Nooni stared three seconds and then replied, "I get to fuck first," and walked out.

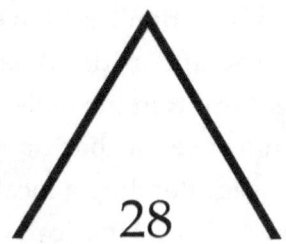

28

Chicana Glory and the Upper Room

"Nah, you should wear the black one I got you, and I'll wear my red one...that way," Nooni suggested. The ladies planned a surprise slumber party for Gavin, as a reward for being such a good man, but mostly, to justify a threesome. Clarissa was curious about their chemistry, but her sexual drive, in her forties, made sense enough.

We pre-gamed on the backyard patio with a bottle of apple-flavored Cîroc and Sprite, two grams of *gorilla glue*, and a deck of cards. "I was thinking, why don't we...nah. No...what if we was in the bed already when he got back?" Nooni's idea was freaky enough to pique my interest. I was sure he'd act appalled, out of respect for me. So, rather than having him pretend to have a moral compass, he could just walk in on the pussy.

"You want us to already be in bed when he gets home?"

It was unimaginative but to the point.

"We ain't gotta act no more."

"Okay, fuck it, Imma find out when he plans to be home, we can be ready, fuck it."

Nooni's eyes were thrilled, to the point that it alarmed me; *this bitch too motherfucking ready to fuck.* And now, in just hours, my man would have his way.

"He might play dumb, so don't get too excited."

Nooni shook her head and said, "When he sees us…oh, it's going down." Nooni got up from the table, dancing and walking up behind me, then leaning over my back, and cupping my breasts.

Meanwhile, Gavin was attending a local symposium at Texas Southern University on African-American writers, as the keynote speaker. His celebrity had afforded him engagements like this, where the money was easy for two-hour appearances. But more importantly, women were everywhere. He made strides to be faithful, but his adoring female fan base would not let a happy home, be. From single moms, pastor's wives, to presidents of book clubs, his DM's were crazy, ungodly advances, from women seeking a savior. Even during the symposium, he could see the wanderlust in the eyes of a few attendees. In the midst of it all, he received a text from Clarissa that read, 'What time do you think you'll get in?' He read it but chose to delay his response until plans with Miguel were confirmed. He immediately sent Miguel a text, 'We still on for 4?' He wanted to entertain fans over drinks, with Miguel as an alibi.

Back home, the girls got tipsy in their lingerie, in preparation. So, between Clarissa's full 'B' cups and Nooni's ample ass, Gavin would have a smorgasbord of flesh. And yet, he had no clue. The text he'd been waiting on had finally come. 'Let's do Davenport's.' Gavin responded to Clarissa's text, saying that he'd be home around 6, which meant 9.

When the symposium was over, he and Miguel, along with three professional women they met, agreed to drinks. The women ranged from a professor, a literary agent, and a tax attorney, all in their forties, two being African-American, and one Latina. They were aware that both men were married, and they, all single. It was the tide in social Americana; unavailable men with all the options.

On the car ride over, the men strategized. "That Camilla chick, that's you, man," Miguel suggested. Gavin, who'd been feeling the itch of infidelity, remained quiet and unfulfilled at home. He confided in Miguel of the arrangement, and the absence of it. A 'side piece' discussion had come up months ago, which led to this bar date and his inability to resist temptation. Clarissa was taking too long.

"Camilla's sexy, but that Teresa chick was nice too," Gavin spoke of the forty-two-year-old, Teresa James, a literary agent from Los Angeles. She was in town supporting a client at the symposium, with her sights set on Gavin. Besides his best-selling novels and good looks, rumor had it that he planned to jump from his publisher and agent, according to press. "Yeah, man, and what about the Mexican chick, Isabella?" Isabella Ruiz was a straight-up H-town, South Park, Milby High, girl. But by day, she was a tax attorney for *Bledsoe & Gaines*, a prominent downtown firm. The ladies jumped in her silver convertible 650i and followed the guys over.

When they arrived at Davenport's, a table to their immediate right, was available. The guys took the ladies' drink requests and stood at the bar. Gavin thought it to be a harmless afternoon; he wanted to get buzzed to pass the time. "So, who'd you choose?"

Gavin smiled, dropping his head at the annoyance of Miguel's constant digging. "I'm just having a good time."

Meanwhile, Clarissa and Nooni were prepping, doing each other's make-up to pass the time. They thought about fooling around but chose to drink, with kisses in-between strokes of lip gloss and brushes of Fenty foundation. "Girl, this nigga better eat all the pussy, waiting on his ass this long."

Gavin thought of his decision. He could entertain these women, but it would be like all the other times he was a hoe. Married man guilt stung worst. It was a conscious alarm clock that rang loudly before the act, and even louder, afterward. As thin as his patience had been, at least Clarissa was different than most. Surely, he was grateful and not wanting to fuck up a good thing, but damn.

"I'm not gonna stay long. I'm a little tired."

"Dude, you wanted this…"

"I know, man. I'll hang, not long."

"Are you okay, I mean…"

"No, it's cool."

They paused, waiting to be acknowledged by the bartender. The awkwardness of Gavin's change of heart bothered him. Miguel had been a reliable friend, lending an ear to the woes of his suspicions and truths. He held off on giving egotistical advice, solely for the fact that Clarissa was a babe. Perhaps, if she were an arrogant, selfish starfish with no soul, Gavin would've acted much sooner. Nonetheless, after receiving their drinks, the fellas returned to the table, ready to play.

"So, Gavin, a little birdie tells me you wanna take your talents elsewhere," Teresa spoke. For a second, he wondered if Miguel spilled about his personal life.

"What do you mean?" he asked, before realizing it was business. It was cute, but the wrong time, Gavin shook his head, responding, "Nothing's changed."

"You were so awesome today," Camilla said. Her compliment seemed genuine, but he wouldn't budge for fan love. "You working on anything new?" Isabella asked. Humorous and cute, she was sexy too. But the attention was enough. Right at that moment, he knew he didn't need to be there. After a second drink, he would hang it up and get home. But a funny thing happened on the way to civility. Thirty minutes of adult elixirs led to a conversation that went from cordial to skank.

"Guys just need to do more oral, that's really how y'all keep us happy…that and the rent," Isabella joked.

"And not just any head, you gotta make my back arch and toes curl, kind of head," Camilla offered, thanks to a second dirty martini.

Miguel was in pornographic heaven. Even with all the attention solely on Gavin, being in the orb of his influence, was enough. For a decade, he'd lived vicariously through him, with instances like these, sitting amongst beautiful women, with no chance in hell.

"Ladies, ladies, such potty mouths," he chimed. Gavin continued playing along, placating time for cheap thrills. But oddly, he thought of home. He went to the bar for his second and final drink, thinking of an exit plan. *Just drink 'til it's time to go.* When he got back to the group, he walked in on another interesting topic. "I've never let a guy come in my mouth; I just won't do it," Teresa proclaimed. Now he knew why he didn't like her.

"I don't mind it. It means I'm the shit," Isabella offered, while everyone laughed.

"I heard if a guy drinks pineapple juice, his cum will taste like it," said Camilla.

Gavin and Miguel remained quiet, enjoying the shenanigans. They weren't sure where things would go until Teresa added, "Any more of these dirty martinis, and I'm doing research," as she turned, looking straight at Gavin.

The girls jeered, Miguel bucked his eyes, with his fist over his mouth, and poor Gavin hung his head, embarrassed by the riches of being him. *Head from a conniving bitch, wouldn't be so bad.* Things got interesting, quick.

He decided to play along when he asked, "Anyone ever done a threesome?" The ladies all looked at each other, shaking their heads in unison, possibly out of denial for image sake. Gavin smacked his lips with an eye roll to tease the situation.

"I'm not opposed to it, but I don't eat pussy, so..." Teresa answered. There was no room for a bitch who wouldn't worship the queen, Clarissa Renee Adams.

"Back in college, I let a girl eat me out, once," Camilla offered.

"You weren't supposed to say anything," Isabella joked.

"No, seriously, I was super drunk, but she was good."

"But did you eat back," Isabella interrupted.

"I think I kissed it. Maybe I licked it a little...not like, all in and shit."

"Well, I've eaten pussy, and it tastes just like chicken," Isabella answered.

Isabella was checking off on all the freak boxes. He'd never been with a Latin chick.

"Ever been in a threesome, you and your wife," Isabella continued.

"Yes."

"Renee," Teresa gasped in shock.

"I'd eat Renee," Isabella answered, bluntly.

Everybody's mouth dropped, while Gavin raised his glass to a real 'G.' Isabella seemed qualified, through the jokes. *She could work. Shouldn't be a problem with Risa, she likes Mexican chicks.*

What initiated as an innocent, happy hour, turned, burdensome commitment, had pleasantly shifted to a play for new pussy. Isabella painted a perfect picture; an attractive, grown-ass woman, with hips and jet-black hair, professional, no drama type, and true to the game. He had an audience of two potential cock blockers, with Miguel, left in the cold. If they went outside to exchange numbers, all discretion would be lost.

Patiently, he carried on nearly an hour, and by now, Teresa and Camilla, were more relaxed, with every drink, drunk, and with every sexually tinged remark, welcomed. By this point, Gavin was anxious for the head. "Anybody on Instagram?" All the ladies answered yes, spitting out their tag names, as he looked the part of an interested man. But he only cared about hers, *@abogadobabe76*. He followed, and she followed back, followed by a DM that read his number.

Isabella smiled and immediately sent a text that read, 'What up?' He smiled, looking at the screen and replied, 'You and that potty mouth.'

When she read it, she laughed. The other women looked over curiously. He followed that text with a dare, 'What's next?' She looked at him bashfully. The time and space between them gently burned, out of time.

"Hey guys, I gotta go. Nice meeting y'all. Ladies, can you give my friend a ride home?" Miguel's hands went up in disgust, while Isabella felt salty.

Right when he reached the driver seat, a text from Isabella came through that read, 'What happened, Papi?' He looked at it and smiled; *I still got it.* As he turned the ignition, he was sure of getting what he deserved, regardless of Clarissa's feelings. So, as he drove, he decided that Isabella was worthy of the queen. When he arrived home, he thought of this new find, but he noticed most of the first-floor lights were off, except for the light over the stove. It was unusually quiet, especially with Nooni in the house.

The Range was still in the driveway. "Risa…Nooni," he called out, with no reply. Odd. He went to the den, then to his office, but no one. He turned his attention upstairs, wondering why they'd turn in so early, with it being only 6:15. *I know they ain't sleep.* Eagerly, he made his way up, buzzed on liquor and lust, ready for love and primed for disappointment. He walked towards the master bedroom door, slow and quietly; what he'd see next was a game-changer. He stood there, silent, quietly stunned, and immobilized. Cautiously, he stepped back out of the room, confused, and made a call to Miguel.

"Why did you fucking leave?"

"Man, you are not going to believe what I'm looking at…"

"You okay, what's up?"

Gavin sighed, his breathing, much heavier, a flush of heat washed over his body. Clarissa was in black lingerie, and Nooni, in a red one, lying in bed together, both sleep with a bottle of apple Cîroc on the floor. More specifically, Nooni was lying on her chest, with their legs intertwined.

"My wife and her cousin are lying in my bed, sleep…with lingerie on."

"What the fuck? Your night keeps getting better and better, huh motherfucker?"

"I don't know what the fuck they're doing in bed together…"

"Go fucking find out, fucker, get in there!"

Gavin pulled away from the phone for a quiet laugh, standing in the hallway, still confused, with a half boner.

"Maybe it's a family slumber party and shit. I don't wanna wake…"

Suddenly, Gavin heard a click; Miguel hung up on his bullshit. Bravely, he walked back in, guided by the bathroom light. He stood there, wondering what one does in a situation like this. Nooni, who was never an option, was in their bed, on his side. Slowly, he began taking off his blazer and unbuttoning his shirt, mindful of the noise he could make. He walked over to Clarissa's favorite burgundy suede chaise, took off his brown, monk strap, suede shoes, and stared. Then, he walked up to the edge of the bed and nudged her. "Risa…Risa," he whispered, but Nooni cracked her eyes. She was initially startled by his blurry frame but soon smiled. "G-Money," she called, in a tired voice. He stood there, waiting for an explanation. *What the fuck is this?* Nooni remained smiling, shaking her head; "You finsta get it."

"Get what?"

"Just watch…"

Their subtle conversation woke Clarissa, who turned and saw Gavin, standing there, with a shit-faced grin.

"Hey, baby…"

"Hey? What y'all doing?"

"We were waiting for you, daddy."

"Waiting for me?"

Clarissa looked over at Nooni, who got out the bed, walked up to Gavin, and began unbuckling his belt, with no protest. He looked at Clarissa, witnessing the beginnings of a revolution. He no longer chose to play dumb, accepting that this was the day that the Lord had made. His pants dropped to the ground; Nooni took the liberty of cupping his balls through his white cotton boxer briefs. She felt his erection growing and smiled; *he's in.* Gavin kept his eyes on Clarissa, reading her face for clues, wondering if condemnation would soon follow. But she smiled, with her hands behind her head, as Nooni lowered his briefs to give him some head. When she got on her knees, his facial expression read gratitude.

"You cool, babe?"

"Let me show you how cool it is."

She rose to join Nooni in fellatio, opting to jingle bells all the way. It felt like a lifetime since he'd gotten his way. He took the liberty of palming the backs of their heads, looking down at their diligent worship, watching a breakthrough unfold. The rhythm of their mouths caused him to close his eyes and curl his toes in praise. *What the fuck is this...thank you, God.* Nooni got the bright idea to commandeer his left nut, giving him a handjob in the process, while Clarissa worked the right.

Feeling ambitious, he opted that they transition to another plain. He stepped back, motioned to the bed, and in cadence, they rose from their knees, walking in the spirit, and then, laying before him. He smiled, nearly tripping on his pants before kicking them off, removing his shirt, and plopped on the bed, rolling between them. It was then that he orchestrated this rendezvous, boldly.

"You come up here, Nooni can ride," he spoke matter-of-factly. Clarissa straddled his torso until making her way to his face, where she looked down and asked, "Like this?" He smacked his lips, *c'mon.*

Meanwhile, Nooni took hold of him, guiding him to paradise. Finally, in the pussy, he slightly rolled his eyes before closing them completely. Clarissa, however, awaited worship.

He stuck his tongue out to the immediate scent of a grown woman, and the savory tang of love. All with eyes closed, theirs was a devotion of repentance, for past transgressions and unspoken apologies. At that moment, they would transcend time, to a new version of matrimony, while Nooni continued to ride.

Gavin, being mindful, gripped Nooni's cheeks, holding on for dear life. Her silky, milky way could make him blow any minute, ruining the evening, prematurely. He prayed for grace, focusing as hard as he could.

"Ooh shit, this dick good," Nooni called.

Clarissa was in her world but could hear her baby cousin complimenting her husband's dick. Gavin cracked his eyes to see her reaction. Forgoing that speed bump, all was well and divine, with all inhibitions removed. The synchronization of their bodies was tribal. It was their version of a ceremony.

"Let's switch," Gavin asked, after ten minutes, in mid eat and fuck.

"My turn to ride the pony, huh?"

"Dang, I wasn't finished," Nooni acquiesced.

"There's more where that came from."

They switched locations in this beautifully awkward dance. It was grown folks doing whatever the fuck their free will desired. Nooni walked up, climbed over his head, "You need to make me cum; I was close." He smiled at the welcomed challenge and replied, "Bet."

From the back, Clarissa watched Nooni riding his face, with a twinge of hate. Baby cuz got some dick and was about to get some head from her man. *Times have changed.* From her view, she studied the tattoos on Nooni's back, a beautiful arrangement of self-expression and tackiness. Her most massive tat was a set of rainbow-colored wings with a crown in the middle, in memory of Jelani. She had another tat representing her zodiac sign, Aquarius, just above her left shoulder and a pair of high heels on her right. The contour and flexibility of her back rolled with every lick and suck from Gavin's mouth.

"Ooh, right there, right there," Nooni called. Clarissa couldn't be left out; she began vigorously twerking for his attention. "Be easy baby," he pled. But there was no rest for the weary. A steady beat of slick love took hold of his soul, and before he knew it, he could hear the angels calling, and the rapture of his body slowly beginning to ascend. "Shit," he called, with all his might, tortured by pleasure. In an instant, raw and uncut, he let go, any and everywhere. The force of his release put a smile on Clarissa's face. Nooni turned around, noticing the commotion, and felt the gumption to follow up with a blow job.

"Girl, you so nasty."

"Oh my God, you nasty," he chimed.

"Y'all tripping, I'm ready for round two."

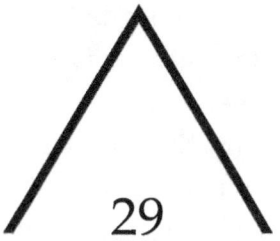

29

In the Fullness of Time

"Okay, …so, wait. You…y'all had a threesome with Nooni?" It took a minute to tell Denise, but I broke it to her Thanksgiving Day. By then, Gavin basked in the freeness of new pussy, taking liberties like smacking Nooni's ass or mannishly squeezing her breast, usually when I wasn't around. But a week ago, I came home after a long afternoon of nothingness and planted a long and drawn out, French kiss on her, by the kitchen sink. "Oh, okay," he answered. We laughed and frolicked in front of his ass. But still, I owed Denise an explanation.

"She ain't my cousin, cousin."

"But you used to braid the bitch hair…"

"Does this really bother you?"

"You really believe this is okay, like this is just who you are, don't worry about it, huh?"

"It was a freak accident, literally."

"Girl, stop."

It sounded reasonable, but it didn't matter, Nooni was mine.

"It was a snack for Gavin…"

"You got all the answers, huh? All right, play with fire, you know the rest."

"Ain't nobody getting burned, it's fun. Heard of spice?"

"Spice?"

Denise thought it was a phase, but when Charlotte happened, she knew it was real. But this was far too gone. Her sons called me 'auntie' for God's sake.

"Niecy, I'm having fun. She's moving out anyway..."

"You should chill, you do too much."

"I'm doing what I please; I'm grown. And you...where's Waldo? I ain't heard nothing about a nigga, in six months. Don't let it go dry."

"Okay, see, what we not gone do is play tit for tat. I'm not worried about Dallas, Frisco, De Soto, or Oak Cliff; I got a friend in the top drawer of my nightstand. How 'bout that?"

"Hmm, so a vibrator and good dick go hand in hand?"

"I'm not pressed."

The tone of the conversation was agitated. She was used to my antics, but it didn't change a thing. We loved each other like sisters with differences of opinion, and the occasional catfight.

"Well, good for you."

"Do you always take shit so lightly," Denise countered.

"What's with the judgment?"

"Now I'm judgmental? You fucked a woman you helped raise, and with your husband, y'all living together, and you can't see anything wrong?"

"What's supposed to be wrong? We have an open marriage, with a chick I happen to trust. That's safe for me, Niecy, and it works for both of us."

"What do you mean? It works for us; he wanted this? Since when you been that bitch?"

I paused, wishing to *unhear* everything. Denise didn't know about my fling, mainly out of embarrassment, but mostly, cause' she could turn it up a notch.

"I compromised, for the bigger picture."

"A compromise? Oh my God, you're such a liar."

"Now, I'm a liar?"

"I was there, Risa; you kissed Nooni back."

"She fucking initiated it, you know that."

Denise was right, but I had my truth.

"Whatever, girl, do you."

"Thanks. And since you know everything, why it take three times for Trenton to cheat on yo' ass?"

Harsh words lashed out from a hurt place. This time, sisters remained quiet, cautious. A slow-burn hit Denise in the base of her gut, enough for a tear that wouldn't fall. It was at this moment that I knew I fucked up with barely a breath to breathe.

"Imma talk to you later," click.

I held the phone to my ear, nearly ten seconds long after Denise hung up. Twenty - plus years of friendship flashed before my eyes. I hoped she'd forgive me later for my slick ass mouth. *I fucked up.*

I needed redemption, so I looked for Nooni down the hall, with tears welling in my eyes. I thought of Gavin and the petty madness we subjected him to. It wasn't fair, but it felt good. I knocked on her door.

"Come in."

"What's wrong?"

"Just some bullshit."

I plopped down on her bed, into her lap, as she instinctively began stroking my head. We remained quiet while tears rolled down the sides of my face. The truth still burned in my gut, down through to my soul.

"Are you okay with everything…how we been rocking with Gavin?"

"Why you asking," she responded with a confused look.

"I'm just making sure. I mean, it's not weird to you, what we doing?"

"We passed weird a long time ago…we grown, right?"

"Yeah, but don't you want a husband and kids, eventually?"

"Right now, this my family."

Nooni leaned over to kiss my forehead. I was moved by her clarity, wishing that at forty-four, I could be just as poised. But Denise was right; this had gone too far. It was selfish, manipulative, and downright trifling. Three days after that night with Gavin, we started sleeping together, wishing each other goodnight, with lustful lullabies in a bed of iniquity. Gavin even mustered the nerve to kiss Nooni in front of me, after coming home from a meeting, but not before kissing me first. It was the most liberated any of us had been in a while.

But over time, trust was replaced by overthinking and, eventually, the beginnings of jealousy. What was once a funny game of hide and seek, turned to finders, keepers. Every possible moment away from the tribe, the Adams wanted extra helpings of Nooni. As much as possible, Nooni and Gavin had multiple quickies throughout the day, on the backyard patio, anywhere that piqued their fancy. On Wednesday afternoon, Gavin, being adventurous, decided that they'd go to the movies, for a matinee.

"You want some popcorn," I asked, walking into *Greenway Marquee Theaters*.

"I want a hotdog."

When we went to the concession stand, she said, "Later, not now." I went about the business of buying a box of *Goobers*, *Raisinets,* and a large cherry *Icee*. When we walked into the theater, slightly cold, dim-lit, with previews playing, we were the only ones there. "We got this bitch to ourselves," Nooni cheered. I smiled, walking up the incline. "Where you wanna sit?"

"All the way up, nothing can stop us, we all the way up," she mocked. We continued until settling for two middle seats at the very top. We sat down, removing the armrest between us, waiting for the film to begin. As I cracked open my Goobers, she looked over at me, feeling horny and spontaneous, and said, "I want my hotdog now."

"Dang, why you ain't..." Then I paused.

"What was that?"

I stayed quiet with a smirk on my face while she politely unbuckled me, unzipped my pants, and removed me from my briefs.

"Oh…"

"You almost missed your blessing."

Most seductively, she looked at me, while the reflection of the movie screen lights flickered on my face. My anticipation was heightened by her drawn-out way, bending over to kiss my stomach or upper thighs. She was killing me softly, to the base of the shaft, up to the head. And then, she completely devoured all joy, just as a couple walked in.

"Nooni…Nooni," I whispered.

"What," she answered in mid suck.

"People coming up…"

"If I stop, I'm done."

I looked at her like, *'if you don't get your ass up,'* but she remained, waiting for me to choose, while I looked on at the other couple. When I saw that they settled on seats ten rows down, I palmed the back of her head, connecting with her eyes through movie lights. Her grace and care to please made my toes curl, with disregard for trailers. Flashes of my marriage popped in my head, but I ignored it like Clarissa's call the other day, while I was fucking Nooni. The only other distraction was the sound of sticky floors when I moved my feet in anxiousness.

Over time, we grew closer, sharing personal stories, like the time she told me, "If I would've found a nigga like you, I wouldn't be with y'all." I took it as a compliment, even if it sounded like game. I was feeling a way about her, beyond the freedom of squeezing her ass, groping her breast, and having sex whenever possible. She ignited something new in me, like when I first pursued *Renee.*

So, for months, things went on this way; we loved each other, and separately, a married couple was jealous, each wanting Nooni more and more, only sharing as a part of the deal. Emotions ran high, with public displays of affection. I could be reading my timeline, and Nooni would plop down beside me, laying her head on my shoulder or laying her legs over my lap. At the same time, Clarissa nonchalantly watched *Real Housewives of Atlanta,* with her peripheral view still intact. But as much as we fought to be cool, cracks began to form.

One rainy night in H-town kept everyone home, all in the den, Netflix and chilling, as a blunt filled with sour diesel made its rounds. We were watching *Black Mirror*, when suddenly, Nooni got the urge to do a cannonball. Nooni and I were a little too friendly on the couch, while Clarissa was trying to surf the net.

"Y'all noisy as fuck..." She spoke in frustration. Nooni and I looked at her, and then in unison, mocked her very words. She looked back, with her prescription Ray-Bans on, and stared with a look that could kill.

"Damn, baby," Nooni chimed.

"Somebody feeling left out?" I joked.

"Y'all, I'm trying to do some work."

"Sorry, babe," Nooni offered.

But I decided it was a fun moment to fuck with the queen. I stared at her a moment longer, looking at the shape of her body as she laid on the love seat. "You need to bring that ass over here and stop being anti-social." Clarissa looked up again, pausing to read my face before reading me. "Should I leave? You don't understand that I am asking y'all to keep it down; you know what, never mind." Clarissa abruptly got up to leave, and instantly it was uncomfortable. I shook my head in silent protest as she stormed out.

She went to the office down the hall. Nooni jumped to follow while I sat there, pissed at a changed mood; *bitches.* Clarissa sat behind the desk, as tears flowed, just as Nooni entered the room. "Babe?" Clarissa looked up before speaking, thinking carefully of her words. "I'm tripping...tired, hungry, all that shit wrapped up in one. I need some space." Nooni walked up behind her, offering a consoling rub to her back.

"You sure that's all it is?" Clarissa stopped looking at the computer screen, with a tear rolling down her face. She looked up into Nooni's eyes and said, "I love you. I don't wanna share anymore." Nooni, stunned at the admission, remained silent. At that moment, neither had any words to say, only feeling a vibe that meant everything.

"I love you too, but I thought this was cool for everybody."

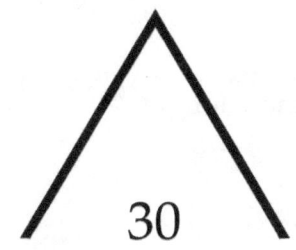

30

Benediction

'This just in; beloved film and television actor, Jacob Finch, known for his network series Desperate Measures, and most recently, the summer blockbuster, Kingdom Reign, suffered a stroke at his Malibu home, Wednesday evening. He's in critical condition...'

Bobby called around 11:52 that night, despite the ongoing cold war in my own home. For all the anguish caused by an ex, the last thing on my mind was death. Death was final, and somewhere underneath it all, I loved him. Bobby bird was now a seventeen-year-old manchild without his father and a mother, 1,392 miles away.

"I need to go to L.A."

"I know, when?"

"Tomorrow."

"How bad is it?"

"Slight paralysis, Bobby said."

The once athletic, graying stud of a man, who ran 5 miles a day, after having green machine smoothies and morning swims, was sidelined, in his Cedar-Sinai hospital bed.

"When you wanna leave?"

"No, it's okay, stay here."

"I don't mind..."

"It's cool, Nooni's here."

He looked at me, slighted.

"Okay?"

"What?"

"I'm trying to be there for you."

"Okay."

"What's that?"

"Please, it's okay."

"The semantics, though…"

"Really? Okay, all right."

"What's wrong," he asked, with an honest look.

I sighed and looked to the heavens in frustration. He was always, conveniently, dumb.

"Are you falling in love?"

"What…with Nooni?"

I stayed quiet, for the truth, all or nothing.

"Y'all real chummy."

"As are you, with her. Where is this coming from?"

The audacity; for six or more weeks, Nooni and I parlayed, while Gavin was in the dark. Now the tide had turned. Gavin could be openly gay with Nooni. And the expressions on their faces made me sick. Lovingly gazes and shit, with silly laughter for nothingness. It was how we use to be.

"This was supposed to be a trinity. No shady shit."

"And why isn't it?"

It was a fucking fair question that I cared not to entertain. *Are you falling in love, though?*

"Do you tell me every time y'all fuck, in advance…or after?"

He was on mute, all because of greed. Yes, he was falling in love.

"This is stupid. Are you jealous? Just say that."

"I'm jealous?"

"You ain't jealous? Maybe you're the one in love."

I smiled to mask something real, or maybe he saw through it, and it hurt. *How did this shit happen?*

"We can end all this shit, right now, just remember who started it. But Nooni has to go. She can't stay like nothing happened."

It was the honorable thing to do, and yet, I rebuked it.

"Why my family gotta leave, that's unfair."

"You picking this shit over our marriage?"

"I'm not picking anything, that's my cousin…"

"Fuck that family shit! We fucking her!"

Silence…we grappled with the truth. His facial expression and body language marked the ending of an arrangement. I stared a moment more, then walked out of the room.

"So, we gone leave it like this?"

The sudden coolness that swirled in our bedroom was more than the air conditioner, but a frigidness from the belief that a lie could be true. Gavin checked out, and behind something meant to bring us closer. He walked to the window, pulling the blind, as specks of dust flew like the memories of our best years. Peering out the window, the dusk of an evening sky gave him momentary peace, but still.

I went down to the office, started looking for flights to L.A., stubborn to make a point. I knew the potential for danger, but regret got the best of me. However, I must give credit to Nooni; she was always empathetic, from the beginning.

By two that morning, I had begun packing for a 10AM flight. I spoke with Nooni about L.A., wishing she could go under different circumstances.

"I'm gonna check on Jacob and Bobby."

"I'm praying for him."

"Thank you…Bobby wants to meet you. You'll love him."

"Are you bringing him back?"

It made good motherly sense, but not legally.

"In a perfect world, yes. But nah, it ain't happening. He'll come down for Christmas."

"Awe, I can't wait to meet him."

We held a moment of silence for motherhood and embraced.

10AM, I was in my seat, bound for LAX in four hours. With my iPad in hand, I scrolled through pictures of Bobby, reminiscing on memories we shared. A bittersweet reunion, this was the break I needed from the trinity.

Meanwhile, Gavin had time to think about the state of things. He figured a conversation with Nooni would nip shit in the bud. But not before another romp. So, later that evening, he called her into the den while the local news played.

"What up babe," she called.

"All good..."

She walked over in a tank top, no bra, and panties, and sat in his lap in a house all to themselves.

"What's your plan," I asked.

"What you mean?"

"What's your end game? You gotta plan?"

My tone was fatherly, but she was clueless.

"I been focused on my certification shit. I gotta year to go."

"What if you could own a salon?"

"Eventually, yeah, but I need experience."

I listened while thinking of a way to steer the conversation towards an exit interview.

"What if you had an investor and hired someone to run the salon?"

"Are you offering? I'm mean, what's up?"

It would kill two birds with one proverbial stone. I had a sufficient rainy-day fund of over $215,750, skillfully hidden off the books, over three years. I could be a sponsor with access.

"When you graduate, we can talk business."

She looked at me with joyous eyes, making it easier for me to sell what would come next.

"Are you for real, for real?!"

"I'm serious, but you gotta finish. And don't bring this up to Clarissa until I talk to her first, promise me that."

"Bet that! Ooh, I need a name."

"I got one."

"What?"

"Thanks-a-Thot!"

Nooni bucked her eyes and covered her mouth in shock.

"Fuck you, nigga!"

We continued laughing while I was framing the part 'b' of the deal.

"All right, my bad, but look, Imma help you with something else."

"Damn, its Christmas already, shit."

"I know, right, but seriously...we could help you get an apartment."

I paused for her reaction to what I considered a helluva deal.

"Awe, that's crazy, you serious?"

"Yeah. We figured you wanted your privacy."

"Honestly, it's lit here."

"Lit like how?"

"The situation...we cool, right?"

"Yeah, but...never mind."

"What?"

"I think Clarissa is jealous."

"For real?"

"We ain't gotta stop anything. Maybe just do it at your crib."

Nooni looked uneasy, assessing the sincerity of my offer.

"So, like, she knows about this new arrangement? 'Cause it sounds like you wanna fuck without her. But I wanna fuck both y'all."

"Nah, it's not like that. We can all fuck, just not here."

"Is it that bad? I think you want me to yourself."

"Yes, and yes."

When Clarissa landed Thursday afternoon, luscious California sun rays and the fresh sea breeze of the Pacific, welcomed her. With no intentions of hanging out or shooting the shit with old friends, every second, minute, hour, and day of that week was for Bobby and Jacob. And despite how things ended, underneath it all, she could reminisce on the days when he sincerely loved her, before fame and money became the drug of choice.

When I reached my hotel room, I made another call to Bobby.

"I'm here; take an Uber to the hotel, we'll ride over to the hospital." Nearly an hour later, Bobby was outside. When I came down to the car, I was emotional, seeing my son for the first time in six months. He was taller, slender, and had the nerve to have peach fuzz on his top lip and chin.

But most importantly, I could see the pain in his eyes. We embraced for an eternity, bonding through fear of the unknown. Tears rolled down both our faces, as either waited for the other to speak.

"Bobby bird, I missed you, baby."

"Missed you too, mom."

We hugged once more before getting in the car, off to Cedars-Sinai Hospital.

"Did you eat?"

"Pop-tart."

I smiled at his adolescence, vowing to fix home-cooked meals while I was there.

"We'll get lunch after we see your dad."

"Cool."

"How's what's her name, doing...his newest model girlfriend."

"You dislike Ivanka, don't you?"

"I forgot her name, really, I did."

"She left a month ago. I called to tell her about dad, and she hasn't responded."

"Well, she's a bitch, then, see?"

Bobby remained silent, opting not to play along; he was mature beyond his years.

"Mom, focus. Dad."

"You're right."

For the remainder of the ride, I tried conducting myself in a way, asking him random questions of his young life, but curious about Jacob's appearance. I wondered if his face was deformed or if he were hooked up to a breathing tube, non-responsive.

"How did everything go with getting him admitted?"

"It was cool. He's still on an IV. How long can you stay?"

"As long as you want."

"Cool," he answered in relief.

"How's Gavin?"

"Perfectly fine."

"Why didn't he come?"

"He's looking after my cousin Nooni."

"Isn't she like, twenty-five, six?"

I laughed at his dig.

"Anyway, where's your girlfriend? I know you got one."

"I'm chilling."

"Oh, you chilling, huh? Mr. Swag."

I was proud of my son's temperament. He was laid back and unbothered, a little like his mom. But now, I could see the little boy in him, the one afraid of the dark.

"You should stay here."

"Why?"

"Who knows how long it'll be before he's back to normal."

"What did the doctors say?"

"His speech may be slurred."

The rest of the ride turned depressing. The idea of uprooting my life was not in the cards, but my son was always the end game. I could rent a place in Calabasas, temporarily, and Nooni could stay. But of course, it had to make sense to Gavin, Mr. Logical.

When we reached the hospital lobby, I wondered how I'd be received. It was nearly a year since our last conversation. It was pleasant, and I even laughed at his jokes. Over time, we'd grown to be adults for Bobby. And now, I wondered what I needed to be for him.

After Bobby checked with the receptionist, a portly Hispanic man, appearing to be in his 30's, was the hospital representative that would escort us to the room. There were limitations on who could see Jacob, especially with paparazzi swirling for fresh blood.

But my status still held some weight, thanks to older staff members who remembered *'Renee.'*

As we walked the pristine halls and radiant floors of a celebrity hospital, bustling with medical professionals, my nerves got the best of me. The last time I'd been in a facility was a rehab stint ordered by the judge for the drunk driving case. And before that, the birth of my son. I hated hospitals.

"Right this way," the gentleman spoke. We continued walking into room 1702, unsure of what we'd see. Bobby was first around the corner while I watched his facial expression turn to tears. When I turned the corner, my former love and son's father, was on an oxygen tube. His hair was disheveled and grayer than before, with the stubble of a five o'clock shadow. But oddly, his eyes danced for me. Bobby immediately walked up to him, leaned over and hugged him. But when he saw me, his gratitude was more pronounced. I slowly made my way closer, with a look of sympathy, as a single tear rolled down his right cheek. "Clarissa," he called in a whisper. I was startled but grateful he could speak. Jacob stared, searching for the words.

"Rest," I offered.

"I'm fucked up," he slurred in a whisper.

Jacob motioned for me to come closer. I approached, leaned over, and hugged him, feeling his feeble strength, as he tried embracing me with his right arm. He held on much longer than his usual, laid-back self. In an instant, this was 1999, when the love was real. "Hi, kiddo," he whispered. We held a gaze reserved for the past, filled with hope and forgiveness.

"I don't know why you insist on talking,"

"I'm not dead," he groggily answered.

Still the smart ass, the truth was he looked like death.

"You and Bobby…all I have."

"I'll stay a few days…I'm still married."

"Married, smarried," Jacob joked.

"She stays with us this time, no hotels," Bobby commanded.

"I agree."

I was shocked.

"I'll have to talk to Gavin, seriously, guys."

"Mom, Gavin is cool, he'll understand."

"Yeah, Mom," Jacob chimed.

The opportunity to be with Bobby, full time, reignited something that died years ago.

"Seriously…stay," he continued, in a soft tone.

"Maybe, cause this guy on his own, in your house…a goddamn mess," I followed.

We laughed, but I wondered about the other women.

"What about all your little friends, are they gonna be coming around, if I'm here?"

"No more hoes…"

"Dad!"

It was a cloudy hour of my life, back in L.A., under the circumstance. Everything about moving back made sense and convincing Gavin would be the last hurdle. Surely, he'd flash a streak of jealousy, but Nooni, maybe she'd go for a California lifestyle. Either way, I'd be with my boy.

The Thursday afternoon of my arrival, I checked out of the Beverly Hills Hotel and made camp in Jacob's Malibu digs. The serenity of crashing waves and beautiful sunsets made the thought of eventually leaving, difficult. But every day of my stay, I cooked breakfast by request, drove him to school, and even cleaned up around the place during the day. When I would sit in the backyard, overlooking the Pacific Ocean, I thought of the rest of my life. The possible rekindling of motherhood made it clear. On a whim, I called Nooni to check on things.

"Hey, boo," Nooni answered.

"Hey, what y'all doing?"

"Gavin been gone all day. I'm cooking right now."

"Cooking? What you cooking?"

"Don't do me, you know I can burn."

"No, for real, though, I was calling to check on y'all."

"You ain't call Gavin?"

"Not yet."

"How's Jacob doing?"

During the time of my stay, Jacob's recovery was steady, with the possibility of him being released Saturday of next week. Bobby and I had to endure rumors of him being on his death bed. It was one of the things that made celebrity, burdensome.

"They're releasing him in a week."

"When you coming home?"

"Maybe a day after. I wanna make sure he's good before I go."

"How's Bobby?"

"He's good, holding it together."

"That's cool; I really miss you," Nooni offered.

"Awe, that's sweet babe, I miss you too. I might need to come right back."

"Dang, for real?"

"Yeah, he's not gonna be a hundred percent, for a while. So, you might be coming too."

It was a random decision I made on the fly, without her consent.

"For real? All of us?"

"I didn't say that."

Nooni fell silent, feeling speechless to a clear divide. *What was happening to the trinity*? What made sense months ago, had turned to a game of possession with Nooni being the coveted prize. It was not God's plan.

"Like, permanently?"

"Not right away. Maybe, eventually? I don't know."

"Hmm."

"You cool with the possibility…I thought you wanted to see Cali?"

Nooni held the phone, searching for an answer. Undoubtedly, California would be amazing, but this was different. I was breaking a promise to never letting Nooni come between our marriage.

"Yeah, I'm cool."

"All right, well, think about it some more, I gotta go, talk to you later."

"Bye."

We hung up, with one of us confused and the other determined, but both, curious of what was next. I still needed dialogue with Gavin, not for permission, but clarity. But using sound judgment, I decided to fly back much earlier than planned. I'd return when Jacob got home, just until Bobby finished his Senior year, in a few months. Nooni could fly out after her finals. It would be a nice summer vacation.

I arrived back in Houston Tuesday night, with a new resolve. Motherhood was my calling, again. My affairs needed to be in order, mama and daddy needed to know, but of all people, I wanted counseling from Denise. Nevertheless, as soon as we got home from the airport, I rushed upstairs, undressed, hopped in the shower for 10 minutes, and came back down in my favorite oversized Michael Jackson t-shirt. Sounds from the den TV made me feel at home on my loveseat, while he lounged on the chaise.

"You wanna order something, Chinese or pizza?"

"Chinese is cool with me."

He picked up his phone and placed an order to Butterfly Chop Stix, a hip spot in The Village. He ordered the same four dishes as always, much like the same four sex positions we had, before Nooni came along. He started flipping through channels after placing the order, which prompted me to break the ice.

"I need to go back again."

"When?"

"This Saturday; they're supposed to be releasing him."

"Why are you going back so soon? Doesn't he have assistants?"

His jealousy was heartbreaking. Why didn't he see this as being more about Bobby than anything?

"Jacob is not out of the woods. He's healing now, and he only has one assistant. I'm more concerned with Bobby anyway. I don't want someone else doing the things I could do for him, while his father gets better."

"Bobby is practically grown."

"Understandable."

"I was thinking of staying there until he flies back with me for Christmas."

"So, basically three weeks."

"Basically."

The burden of disclosure lifted from my shoulders, but my intent remained guarded.

"I get it," he answered.

"Yeah, plus, I thought Nooni could come too."

Gavin sat up, repositioning himself, seeming bothered by the idea.

"Now, I don't get that. She's still in school and has a job."

"After her finals, and I'm sure she can get vacation time."

"Yeah, but...I thought this was about Bobby?"

"It is, I want him to meet his family," I answered with a straight face.

"If you don't stop with that family shit..."

"Hey, you see it how you want, that's my cousin, bottom line!"

"She don't need to go."

"Who's jealous now?"

We were facing the truth that neither of us wanted to be without Nooni. The tension in the room was thick enough that when Nooni returned home from work, she sensed the end an argument had.

"Hey, y'all..."

"Hey, girl."

"What up," Gavin spoke.

"All good; how was L.A.?"

"Jacob's gonna be home soon; I'm flying back Saturday. You coming for the weekend?"

Gavin smacked his lips while Nooni hesitated to answer. It was a blindsided chess play.

"I gotta see about work. I ain't talked to them..."

"Girl, I know you ain't tripping over $8.25 an hour."

It was an asshole thing to say as if Nooni hadn't taken pride in a job that took her from a stripper pole and back to life.

"Ah, I like my little job, so, not too much on that. I'll talk to my supervisor tomorrow. I'm tired, goodnight."

Nooni walked upstairs to her room, removing herself from the hostility of a broken marriage. It was clear that she'd become a pawn in our game. She sat on the edge of her bed, shaking her head, thinking of tomorrow and the will of God. Meanwhile, the battle of egos and untethered words put a chokehold on reconciliation. Gavin was no longer interested in my company, nor anything on TV.

"I'm going to bed." But before walking pass Nooni's door, he knocked, peeked in, and offered, "I'm sorry about that. Have fun in L.A. Goodnight."

I remained downstairs, replaying things the way I saw it, hoping to trace the moment when all things went to shit. I regretted my dig at Nooni's job, but it was hard relating to a working girl. I thought about apologizing, but in a moment of pride, I figured she'd get over it. I walked over to the couch, laid down, and pulled the throw over my body. I was over them.

Within the three days since Tuesday night's spat, I apologized the following day. I knew I was saying some slick shit when I said it. It was crass and uncalled for, but my offer was more about my insecurities and less about the sex they'd have while I was gone. Within the days leading up to my second trip, we laughed, had drinks, and smoked more on the patio, but it was never enough.

On Saturday morning, at 7AM, to be exact, I woke to take my shower. My suitcases were packed and by the door. I moved about, while Gavin snored in bed. When I finally got dressed, I went down the hall to check on Nooni, knocking on her door.

"Nooni...Nooni. You up," I asked, but heard no response. I took the liberty of opening the door, only to discover a neatly made bed, missing luggage, a cell phone, and a note on the nightstand. I immediately rushed back to the room to alert Gavin.

"She's gone…she left!"

Gavin, barely coherent, tried making sense of the commotion, but couldn't care less; "What?"

Kimberly "Nooni" Ralston, being cognitive of overstaying her welcome, turned proactive, and decided to rewrite history.

Monday afternoon, she went apartment hunting and lucked up on a one-bedroom, one-bath second-floor walkup, in the medical center, off Almeda Road.

By Wednesday, her affairs were in order, signing on with electric and cable services. She went to furniture stores, getting store credit at *Havenworth Furniture* on the Southwest side. She had access to her new apartment, Thursday afternoon. She went *Fabuloso* crazy in the bathroom and kitchen thoroughly before going back 'home' to pack.

By 2:15AM, Saturday morning, she dipped out, cautious of every peep and ping she made, walking up and down, carrying one piece of luggage at a time. With everything packed, she sat and wrote a note to Gavin and Clarissa, and left it on the nightstand, next to the phone they'd given her. She quietly got in her car, put it in neutral, and rolled out to the street, before starting her departure to a new promised land.

Clarissa had no words and was stunned by this selfish act of indecision. Maybe they stretched Nooni to the extreme, but it was her father's voice that gave her guidance. *'Always make a way for yourself.'*

"She's probably hanging at a homegirls' for the weekend," Gavin offered. But Clarissa read her note and shook her head, disappointed by it.

"Read this, my Uber's downstairs."

Gavin got up to help, while reading the note, and was no longer delusional.

"Let her be."

I love both y'all, but I can't do this no more. I am clearly the problem. Thank you for showing me love. I will pay you back for the car. I had to go. I don't want to be the cause of your divorce. I will call y'all when I'm settled. Bye for now.

Nooni

As we walked down, I looked over at him, looking for a read. I saw the heartbreak. Nooni could've told us better than this. I asked that bitch a million times if she was okay; it wasn't like I was gone kick her out or something. And now, back at square one, this was a thorn in my side, piercing perfectly good intentions. Some people just can't take help. But it's cool, though. At least I knew where I stood with Gavin.

"I'll call when I land."

"You okay," he asked.

"I should be asking you."

"I'm good…shit. We ain't running no sex slave operation."

"So what you gone do for pussy while I'm gone?"

"You tripping."

"Be careful…"

We kissed goodbye, and it was off to the airport, to L.A., and Bobby's last few months of adolescence. And still, the joys of this trip would be overshadowed by the pain of this love. I loved Nooni, fell in love, and in lust with her. I'm not sure if blood relations would've stopped us, we were too deep. So now, without my other soulmate, and without my best friend, my son was my only redemption.

Epilogue

In '92, at *Jamaica Jamaica Nite Club*, Johnson "Baby D" Jones, a has-been music producer from the late seventies, early cocaine eighties, put on a two-bit talent show and thought I was a diamond in the rough. He promised fame and fortune, reciprocated by some eighteen-year-old pussy, and soon, I was singing background vocals for B-list recording artists on tour.

But my big break came from a writing session with Boogie Larelle, a music producer out of New York City. It was my first number one hit as a songwriter on the R&B Billboard charts. I once got a publishing check for $110,673, and I was barely twenty-one.

I purchased a house in Sugar Creek for my parents, out in the suburbs of Houston, and later moved to L.A. in '96 when I was 22. I worked my ass off, writing and schmoozing, until getting a record deal in '97, and creating "Renee," the alter-ego to Clarissa Renee Gentry.

Give you more, my debut album, went gold, selling over 569,843 copies within five weeks; my hit song, *"Love is real,"* went to number one on the R&B charts, and #5 on the top 100 *Billboard* charts. I was the shit for a hot second, all the way from Houston's Third Ward. Then came the parties in the Hollywood Hills that went on until the wee hours of a dream, fueled by cocaine escapades and sexual romps with celebrity boys. This is how my son came to be against the wishes of my management. The acceleration of my life was uncontrolled by anyone or anything. It was a hell of a ride, until one day, the bottom fell out.

My second album in 2001, *Forever Love,* was a flop, barely selling one hundred thousand copies; and like that, the mojo, and the attention of the industry, was gone. Depressed and embarrassed, I cried through it with Jack and cocaine, still writing songs for myself and other artists, with a hit song for a pop duo out of France, in 2002. But nothing compared to the summer of '99, singing in front of ten thousand screaming fans at Soul Fest in New Orleans. But by 2003, I was burnt; the record label dropped me, appearances dried up, and the royalty checks fell off.

When my management created the "Renee" brand, I hated it, but eventually, the fame and money kept my mouth shut. But most of all, I'd fallen in love with Jacob Finch, a fresh-faced Toronto bred actor. We met at a party in '99, but I never had a "White boy." He shot at me with a Jamaican accent, for the love of chocolate girls. Our management teams hated the situation. But in pure rebellious form, our biggest middle finger to them was the birth of our son, Robert Finch, a.k.a. "Bobby," named in honor of Bob Marley.

Years later, when our relationship fizzled, my second beau, and most exotic, came at a time when I'd grown frustrated with God and life. Daily baptisms in whiskey with the aid of a burning bush, led to an eventual lover from my management team. I'd never known that type of compassion from a woman. Charlotte Price penetrated the barrier of a Baptist upbringing and replaced Jacob's side of the bed.

My paranoia ruined Jacob and me; the tabloids and paparazzi flashes fucked everything. It got bad enough for me to question his intentions. Being the hot girl at the time, he only had two commercials, and a guest spot on a sitcom that was canceled after seven episodes.

When I started fooling around with Charlotte, it was after she reached out to me when Jacob and I broke up. She was never a possibility, strictly management, but she knew how to trigger me. She knew how to pour the right drinks to spark the proper conversation. We were a couple, on the low, way before America accepted same-sex couples, much less Black ones.

As for Charlotte, I gave her too much access. We kept it lowkey and distinct from public life, with private moments in my bedroom, praying to maintain my relevance. The façade had gotten to be too much, so she dipped. It was then that I completely hit rock bottom. Charlotte was my personal Jesus, but she disoriented everything I believed. Within the year, I packed my things, with a promise to little Bobby that it was a short visit to grandma.

In 2005, with less than $400,000, a stint in rehab a year prior, and a failed custody battle with my son's father, I chose to go back to Houston. Ezra and Hazel Gentry, my parents, saved me from the "life" and a crazy eight years.

Moving in with my parents, in the house, I bought them, embarrassed me. I put all my shit in storage and took a room upstairs. I cried for a week straight, feeling sorry for myself, thousands of miles from the love of my life, and the hopes and dreams that once were. Jacob didn't give a fuck at this point. He landed on a hit network series, becoming the new darling star boy in L.A. It's funny how life works; I was his ex.

I collected myself, humbled by irrelevance, assembled a band, and did gigs around town, on the road, for love and money. And still, the hourglass of fame gradually faded, but an appreciation grew for the simple things; life away from the lights.

Fast forward, years later, when I met Gavin, I was already prepared to be single for a very long time. I wasn't giving up sex, just bullshit. And to be honest, he was a little corny, handsome, but corny.

That day in Whole Foods, when he walked up to me, I wasn't in the mood, to begin with, but his persistence made the difference. I mistook genuine interest for thirst, but the kiss in the garage changed everything. Being in a relationship with the right "one" was always the goal, but given my bilingual way, I never had the balls to man up. In my heart, the conflict of a label came from the conviction of my father's words. Bottom line, I made a promise at a very young age that I couldn't keep, and for that, I blamed Hazel and Ezra, but most of all, myself. Charlotte had my heart, but not my soul, only because I wouldn't surrender.

So, when I landed, I called my son to let him know. Then, I called Denise, but it went to voicemail; she called back later, and we hashed things out. And when I reached Jacob's place, unpacked, took a shower, fixed a glass of chardonnay, and sat in the lounge chair overlooking the Pacific Ocean, I called her.

"Clarissa?"

"Yes…"

www.ingramcontent.com/pod-product-compliance
Lightning Source LLC
Chambersburg PA
CBHW021218250626
47155CB00008B/2857